ELLE HARTFORD

Beauty and the Alchemist

The Alchemical Tales, Book One

Phoenix
&
Kelpie

In fairy tales, goodness to animals is almost always rewarded.

So it only seems fitting to start this series by recognizing the fluffy dog and the grumpy tortoise who came together to inspire Red's most constant companion.

Thank you. My story wouldn't be the same without you.

Contents

Preface

Long, long ago, a coven of witches created a world just beyond ours—a realm of fairy tales.

In Beyond, humans rub shoulders with mythical creatures, and magic mixes with science.

There are only three rules:

Happily
accept that we share the same home

Ever
remember that what you take, you must also give

After
struggle will always lead to new beginnings

So, if you are ready . . . you are welcome here.

* * *

Belville & nearby forest

1

Life in the Hood

Once upon a time, a beauty fell in love with a beast, and she cured him—that's the story everyone tells. But what if, instead, he betrayed her and she murdered him?

I'm sure such a thing has happened, at least once. If there's one thing that living in a fairy tale world has taught me, it's that any story, no matter how familiar, can be written with a new ending.

I come from a family of Seers, and when my mothers gave me the nickname Red—yes, like Little Red Riding Hood—they knew what they were doing. They told me it was a reminder to keep my eyes open. To always look closely to find the truth. I used to think that maybe they were making fun of me by giving me that name, because I never seemed to see the world the way the people around me did. When at last I left my home behind to become a traveling alchemist, no one was surprised.

No one *else* was surprised, that is. I ended up being quite surprised, not least when I chose to settle in the rural town of Belville and instead of peacefully making potions, I began running into crime at every turn.

I suppose I set myself up for it.

But there's nothing I hate more than feeling out of control of my own life. That's why I snuck out the front door of my shop while the earliest of the sun's rays stretched over Belville's cobblestone streets. An autumn chill tugged at the edges of my cloak. Giant oaks and maples standing sentinel in Market Square seemed to watch with interest. Luckily for me, I didn't see any witnesses who might talk.

Red's Alchemy and Potions. The wooden sign swinging in the autumn breeze above my door was nice enough, but I'd come to accept that it was inaccurate. I'd thought Belville was the perfect place to focus on alchemy: the local mountains and forests provided plenty of minerals and plants, and constant trade and travelers would be good for business. I'd intended to solve mysteries in my lab, not out in the woods. But since my arrival only two seasons earlier, I'd earned a reputation in town.

With a sigh, I set up my rickety old ladder. Steadying a brush and a small pail of everlasting gold paint—my own recipe—in one hand, I made the climb. Today was the day that I would really *own* my new role in town. No more hiding or protesting.

Or so I thought.

My mother would tell me it was cosmic justice that as soon as I figured I'd get a jump on fate, fate—in the form of an absent-minded bookseller—got the paint-splattered jump on me.

"Oh Red, I'm glad I caught you," a friendly voice said as I finished the final *s* on my sign's new subscript, *and object finding services*. I wobbled atop my perch as I glanced down at my visitor: Luca, Belville's local scholar. To be a "scholar" was almost like being a witch or a Seer—it was more a way of life

2

than a job, complete with its own training (via correspondence course) and wardrobe (black robes, *always*). Many towns across Pastoria had a scholar, or even a handful of them. Luca served Belville as historian and bookstore manager. "Listen, I have to run but I thought I should warn you because—well, it's really bad, but try not to tell anyone, okay? Not yet. It's *really* bad. Owl escaped from jail. I think he must have murdered his g-guard and—Red! Are you okay?"

Would anyone be "okay" after tumbling down from atop a ladder that may as well have been two old brooms held together with twine?

Or, moreover, upon hearing that a deadly criminal was, rather than awaiting judgment, roaming the countryside free as a bird?

Three weeks before, I'd helped the police catch Owl and retrieve a number of magic artifacts he'd stolen from all over town. A strange accomplishment for an alchemist, I'll admit, and the truth is I wouldn't have been so involved if Owl hadn't been so *beastly* toward Luca. For all his quirks, Luca was one of my best friends, and Owl had been his boss at the bookstore—his cold-hearted, antagonistic, sometimes violent boss.

On top of struggling to make sense of this danger, I now had to deal with gold paint flecked all over my goggles and throughout my long black ponytail. It's a very minor point, but my hair already had tiny glittery threads interwoven in it, courtesy of my Seer heritage—something I usually tried not to advertise.

"Red?" Luca leaned over me as I lay on the sidewalk. When we both were standing he only had a couple inches on my five-foot-nine, so to see him looming against a purple morning sky

3

felt comically out of proportion. I had to bite back a laugh.

Come on, Red, I thought to myself. I stared at the mess around me, trying to focus. Against the deep brown of my skin, traces of the paint looked like the veins in polished jasper.

Luca, however, had apparently lost patience with my marveling. His normally bubbly voice sounded harsh. "Red!"

"Urgh." I'd landed right on my back. Even if I'd tried, I couldn't say much more. As I rolled to my side and began to stand shakily, my mind raced. *How could Owl have escaped? And why does Luca know all about this if no one's supposed to tell anyone about it?*

"I, um, I like your sign." Seeing that at least I hadn't lost any brain function, Luca fell back on a habit of his—that is, continuing to talk to fill a reeling silence. He shuffled around me, the hem of his dark scholars' robes drifting through my sparkly just-like-gold-plating paint.

"Good, because you're going to have bits of it on that outfit forever," I mumbled.

"Oh, it's fine. I've got a bunch more at home just like this one." Luca's brightness faded as he helped me up. He repeated, "Are you okay, Red?"

"Wonderful." I shook my head, trying to get a grip on my morning. "Luca, what *happened*?"

For a moment, Luca's green eyes met mine, and he sobered. The shadows cast from his robe's hood across his dark skin heightened the worry in his face. "I don't really know. I think—I think he might have murdered the guard they brought over from Pine. Did I say that already? I—I just can't imagine how he did it. I think Thorn's organizing a search for him. But I don't think you should—I mean, you should stay here, okay? I only told you about it because I had to tell *someone,*

4

and, well, you need to stay safe. While he's around, the last thing you should do is go out into the woods alone."

* * *

After delivering this somewhat baffling warning, Luca bustled off to the bookstore. My own shop presided over the square's northeastern corner, diagonal from Lavender's tavern—a local landmark—and down the street from Officer Thorn's police station. Apparently this location made my shop the perfect place for gathering information. So my magical, highly independent "pet," William, had informed me. He used that as his excuse for spending most of his days in the bay window, watching passersby, until I insisted at least three times that he *ought* to be helping in the shop.

William had once been a sorcerer's familiar. Despite looking like a big black sheepdog, he could do a few protection spells and, mostly, offer unasked for sarcastic commentary on any given situation. At that point, so early in the day, I knew William would still be asleep. That meant I'd have to clean up the mess on my own, but more annoyingly, it meant I had no one to share Luca's monumental news with. I couldn't very well stop people in the street to talk it over. Everyone in town knew Owl as a criminal, but a *murderer on the loose* was something else.

Quickly I glanced over my shoulders, wondering if any early shoppers had been near enough to hear Luca talk. The streets were bare except for a few farmers straggling in to the grocer's across the square. But just as I breathed my sigh of relief, I noticed that there *was* someone watching me.

Two someones.

5

"Better and better," I whispered to myself.

Two pointed, pale fairy faces peered out from the darkened window next door to mine. I knew them: a pair of sisters as tall as my elbow, who worked at the salon, Hair and Beauty by Gloria. Gloria herself seemed to exist on another planet and had said about three words to me since I'd moved in. The fairy sisters, on the other hand, were known for saying as many words as possible to as many people as would listen. Putting my head down, I scuttled into my shop for some cleaning tools.

Red's Alchemy and Potions comfortably filled the old brick building I'd purchased almost a year ago. The second floor housed a snug studio apartment which William and I shared, and behind the building, we had access to a tiny, scruffy yard. But the shop floor and the workroom behind it were my true pride and joy. The main room held exactly what I advertised: all manner of potions, mineral samples, inventive powders and goops, some dried herbs, and a few odd books and scientific tools. Behind the sales counter a smaller room served as my workshop, where I could make more stock or work on custom orders—anything from lightsticks to false gold to solidifying goo.

I bustled through the chest-high shelves and island displays, grabbing a mop from its hiding place. On my return trip out, I swiped half a dozen cleaning potions out of a bookcase built into the wall. Bright blue liquid swirled as the glass jars clinked against each other. Because I'd risen so early—a habit leftover from years of traveling—I had time to wash away, scrape up, or dissolve most of the paint on my doorstep before most folks in Belville had finished breakfast. Warm scents of cheese omelettes and wild-raspberry scones floated across the Square from Lavender's as I finally headed inside to make some strong black tea.

This "keep your head down and do your work" approach worked for me throughout a busy—but luckily, criminal- and rumor-free—morning. I'd already sold a dozen growth potions, a handful of vials of quicksilver, one made-to-order solution and a suspicious amount of powdered amethyst when lunch time hit. With it came a change in my luck: another visitor, this one about as opposite to Luca as could be. She swept into my empty shop like she owned the place.

"I'm organizing a search of town in half an hour. *You* are not invited." Officer Thorn helped herself to a mug of the tea I keep on hand for customers. Today's blend was calendula and chamomile and I must say, it seemed to work wonders on my friend the police officer. She seemed remarkably calm, if a little tactless.

"If I'm not invited, then why did you have to come by my shop to tell me about it?" I asked, my hands on my hips. Ever since I'd arrived in Belville, no amount of lab coats or shop ownership had been enough to prove to Thorn that I am a scientist and a merchant, *not* a wannabe-police assistant. It's common in rural areas of Beyond for police officers to recruit unofficial help, but Thorn—with her usual style—often took this to an extreme.

"I had to come to tell you to keep out of it." Half-orc Officer Thorn sat primly in the armchair I kept for folks waiting for orders. Though the plush chair was large, it was barely big enough for her. She was probably twice my weight and a good foot taller than me, light green skin and serious muscles peeking out from the collar and cuffs of her military-style uniform. As usual, she was perfectly made up. "I'm trying to

7

keep this one quiet. Or I *was* trying. I'd hoped I could track him down myself this morning, and leave no one the wiser. But none of the usual tracking spells did the trick."

I ran a hand over my forehead and shook loose yet *more* flakes of paint. "Well, Luca seemed pretty worked up about it, and I think he has reason to be. We *are* talking about Owl, right?"

"He escaped sometime late last night." Thorn's brown eyes narrowed as she downed her tea. "Luca told you? How did *he* know about it?"

"I assumed he was on his way from talking to you." Thorn made her way through another cup of tea as I settled my hip against a nearby shelf. "He didn't come to you this morning?"

"No, and what's more, he didn't say anything about it when I was over at the bookstore just now." Thorn rubbed one hand over her long chin before shrugging the matter off. "That's scholars for you, always knowing things they shouldn't. Not unlike alchemists, eh, Red?"

"So you don't know where Owl's gone?" I ignored her question with one of my own.

"That's what the search is for. My bet is he's holed up in that ruined castle out in the woods. There's enough ancient magic hanging around that place to make any tracing spell go haywire, if you ask me. But this is one I don't want you getting mixed up in, Red. No running off into the forest or confronting the criminal on your own, you hear?"

"That's exactly what Luca said, no running off." I nodded along. "Exactly who do you people think I am, the avenging spirit of Robin Hood?"

"We all know how you felt about him at the end," Thorn insisted, setting down her cup and leaning forward over her knees. "Goddess knows some of us sympathize with you. Belville hasn't seen a criminal like that in decades."

I eyed her skeptically. *"You're* the one who wants to run off."

"But you have to be more careful this time around, Red," Thorn continued, louder. Without giving me a chance to ask *more careful than what?,* she added, "He's got an accomplice this time, a real flesh-and-blood one. I know you and Luca had some story about a ghost lurking around that old castle, but that wasn't it. I'm talking about a real person strong enough to carry out murder."

"Wait. Someone really has been murdered?" I bolted up, glass vials and jars tinkling in my wake.

"Right in the station." Thorn pulled back self-consciously. "I'm making the official statement this afternoon, so you'll know soon enough. The victim was Vic—terrible cosmic irony there—you know, the extra guard that came in to help me? Nice guy. Merfolk. He'd taken the night shifts for me, and when I went in this morning I found him on the floor, dead by a blow to the head.

"It could even be more than one murder," she added before I could comment. "Before the Guild sent Vic, I had the Witch make up some animated helpers for me."

I grimaced. Witches and their helpful spells were respected members of rural towns all across the county Pastoria, and I happened to like the one who lived in Belville, but still, in my opinion magic wasn't something to trust around criminals.

Thorn must have thought my reaction was about enlisting the Witch's help. She went on, "It's an allowable procedure. In the Guild guidebook and everything. He just magicked a couple broomsticks and a flowerpot, but they had powerful protection spells on 'em. This morning they were all in pieces.

Plus, all the wards around the place had been busted through, and Owl's chains were broken. When I finally got the mess cleaned up, I realized they took the keys I used for that old castle. It's good luck I carry spares." Officer Thorn tugged at one pointy ear. "Do you think it *is* murder if the animated object also had a live object inside? That little geranium must count for something, right?"

I pressed my own fingertips over the bridge of my nose. "I am *not* going to debate the morality of animated objects with you. Who in Beyond would help Owl?"

"If I knew, I'd have them in custody." Thorn shrugged her massive shoulders and added, "I got the Witch involved, first thing. He says it was probably the work of a sorcerer's gimmick, the kind that might have been sold during the summer festival. A high price, mind you, but still freely available." Thorn glanced at the back staircase. "Where was that assistant of yours early this morning?"

"Asleep in the upstairs window, as usual."

"Are you sure? Could be one of the gnomes made him a recording device and—"

Abruptly the snoring above us ceased and William's gruff voice came radiating through the ceiling. "I can hear you, you know. And familiars can't use 'gimmicks.'"

"Good," Thorn shouted. Then she looked back at me. "How about Gloria? She's the one shop owner I haven't been able to get in touch with."

I shrugged. "I haven't seen her. But then, I usually don't."

"She's been out," William's voice informed us through the rafters.

Thorn looked intrigued. Before I could comment on the manners of conducting an interview on two floors, she called back, "How do you know?"

"Everyone coming out of the salon's been covered in fairy dust and smiling."

The officer and I exchanged a glance. William's observation was glib, but he *did* have a point. Gloria wasn't the sort who stood for stray sparkles or cheery grins.

"I'll keep poking around after the search," Thorn decided, levering herself out of the chair. "The way I see it, we're sure to find him out there. No need for dramatics. If you want to do something, come to Vic's vigil this evening. We're holding it out by the lake."

"We'll be there," I promised for William and myself.

Little did we know then that the story wasn't as simple as Officer Thorn wished.

2

Lights Over the Lake

That evening, the nearly-full moon shone brightly over an unusually quiet town. Many cultures all across Beyond considered the full moon to be a time of power. In Pastoria the full moon was a time for trials; Owl had been due to face justice in Pine, the county seat, in just two days. I could only imagine what kind of reminder that waxing moon was for Officer Thorn.

Across Beyond in small towns where people mixed, like Belville, there was often a police presence. But the police were part of a guild, just like any artisan or skilled worker. Large decisions like retribution were out of an officer's hands, though it was customary for a town to hold onto their criminals until the last minute. That's when a local court would mete out punishment (usually some sort of magically-bound indentured service at the nearest police guild). No one in Belville had seemed too sad about the idea of Owl being shipped off to become someone else's problem. No one had thought we might be marking the occasion by mourning a murder.

As soon as William and I closed up the shop, we headed out to the lake for Vic's vigil. Neither of us had known him very well—he'd only been in town a week at most, and he'd kept to the police station—but still, his unfortunate end deserved sympathy and respect.

"Not to mention," said William, when I pointed this out, "the whole town will probably be there."

"What, are you worried about fitting in?" I teased him as we ambled through the darkened streets.

William snorted, his breath misty in the cold air. "More like I need to catch up on my gossip."

I rolled my eyes but said nothing, opting only to pull my cloak tighter around my shoulders. The sun had not yet fully set, but the tall forest and mountains surrounding Belville on three sides meant that shadows started early. Even down by the lake, which formed the southwestern edge of town, it was sure to be chilly.

We had to cross through the entire town to get there, passing by Luca's bookshop as well as clusters of homes. Belville was a quaint mishmash of peaked roofs, wood-burning chimneys, and crooked lanes. Walking through town always made me pensive, even when there wasn't an unfortunate death to contemplate. In my days as a traveling alchemist, I'd been all over Beyond: through smoky, gleaming magitech cities, across dangerous swamps, even over the deserts of the Shifting Sands. Belville was nothing like anywhere else I'd been. It was straight out of an old storybook.

And thinking of Vic, wondering about his poor family, made me think of my own roots. If Belville, and indeed all of Pastoria, was a stronghold of traditional ways and magic, so was my home island. I'd left because I'd thought a more

13

scientifically-minded community might be more comfortable for an alchemist. *And yet I ended up here!* I sighed. My mother always told me that fairy tales and magic have purpose, but I preferred my purposes to be clear and direct.

"Remind me," I said, speaking to William without preamble (he was used to it), "to write a letter to the island when we get home."

"What do you think I am, an alarm clock?" William shook his fluffy ears. "I still don't see why you don't get a magitech communicator or a speech spell. You're probably the only alchemist in the world without some kind of telephone."

"I am not," I retorted. "Most of the old masters chose to be more reclusive. It helps them focus."

"So you say. But I remember you drooling all over all the gadgets they had in Brass!"

I grinned briefly. William and I had been together for years; I'd first met him on the road outside a big university. He'd chosen to come along with me and he liked to think he was keeping me safe from my "cursed optimism," but I knew better.

"You've seen for yourself how little magitech they use in Belville," I told him. "Even if I *had* bought one of those 'gadgets'—which, may I remind you, cost about as much as we used to make in a month—there'd be no one here to help me fix it when it inevitably broke."

William sneezed, startling a family of elves who walked along the street across from us. This argument was a familiar one between us, a pleasant distraction from the sadness of the evening. And for once it looked like I'd talked him into a corner, instead of the other way round.

After a moment, he said, "If we're going to be staying here, and you're going to be branching out into new businesses, you might at least help this teeny town modernize."

He gave me a beady-eyed look through the evening shadow, a look which clearly said that he'd seen my addition to the shop sign and did not approve. I suppressed a laugh. I hadn't expected him to like it: for a traveling companion, William was extremely resistant to change.

Much like the residents of Belville. "Please. No one's going to convince anyone here of anything they didn't come up with themselves," I said. "They're quite happy with their magic lights and elemental ice boxes. Bringing in magitech and steam would only be a headache for everyone."

By this point we'd neared the beach, and any comment William wanted to make was silenced as a figure straddling the line where the dirt road met the sand waved to us. It was Cairn, owner of the antiquities store catty-corner to my potions shop and resident "little grandmother." Her pale wrinkles, wispy white hair, gingham dress, and tendency to refer to everyone as "dear" were something of a fixture in Belville. I wasn't surprised to find that she'd taken over organizing the vigil.

"We're gathering down by the water," Cairn said as William and I drew closer. "Take a candle from the basket, here, and would you mind signing the scroll there on the table? We're sending it back to the Guild, and they're sending it on to Vic's relatives."

"No problem. Thanks for doing this, Cairn." I glanced around while William rooted through the candle basket as though some of the little white tealights might be better than others. Behind Cairn a line of carts and wagons ran parallel to the shore: parking for people who'd chosen not to walk, or fly, if they were capable. The sun burned brightly at the edge of the mountain across the lake, casting red and yellow streaks over the water. All along the curved beach, people milled beside calm waves. The atmosphere was quiet and thoughtful, but I could smell cinnamon in the air. Someone had stopped at the bakery before leaving town.

"Not at all, dear. Thank you both for coming," Cairn said. She watched benevolently as I leaned over William to sign the scroll set out on a temporary table.

"Did they find Owl earlier?" A normal dog would have had to carry the candles in his mouth, but William's voice was unmuffled. The tips of his black fur glowed starry blue, the color of his magic. Tendrils of the stuff curled around the candles he'd chosen, hovering just beside his shoulder.

I looked up just as a grimace flickered across Cairn's face. She reached up to give my shoulder a reassuring pat as she said, "No, the search was inconclusive. But they will, don't you worry."

We left Cairn to welcome other newcomers and headed down to the beach. Even though it was lighter here than in town, the temperature dropped several degrees as we neared the water. I tightened my cloak again, surreptitiously checking out what other people had worn. Many had shown up in somber tunics and coats as a sign of respect for the dead, as I'd expected. However, my people believed that nothing's worth wearing if it isn't bright as a gem under the tropical sun, and in that regard I remained true to my heritage. My lightweight autumn cloak swirled in vibrant orange with a green leaf motif.

Deciding that it wasn't worth worrying about my wardrobe, I began scanning the crowd for Officer Thorn or Luca, or any other friendly face. Amid the dark mourners, it was hard to distinguish Luca's scholarly robes. But Thorn couldn't do anything *but* stand out in a crowd, I reasoned, and furthermore I expected her to be officiating the event. I'd just caught a glimpse of her presiding over a cluster of people of all shapes and sizes when I heard William groan beside me.

I turned back toward him. "What is it?"

Even before the words left my lips, I knew the answer. And that was fortunate, because William had no time to respond.

"Red! William! We're so glad you could come! Isn't it just such a *nice* night for an event? Aren't you so excited to see the candles all lit up? We're going to float them over the lake!"

We'd been cornered by the fairy sisters, Ari and Stella. Despite giving the impression of being joined at the hip—complete with speaking in unison—they'd ensured our participation in the conversation by flanking us. Ari stood in the sand to my left; Stella, held aloft by a pair of magic iridescent wings sprouting from her back, hovered beside William.

"It's a pity it has to be for such a sad event," Ari continued.

"Yes, I think we should do this sort of thing more often, but for *fun!*" said Stella. The two were almost identical, small-boned and elf-like, with big shimmering eyes and expressive hands. The main distinguishing factor was that Ari glittered head to foot in gold, while Stella was pink from the toes of her slippers to the fringe of her short hair.

"Hey Ari, hey Stella," I said politely. "Did Gloria come with you?"

"Gloria? Why would you be looking for *her*?" said Stella.

"Pfft. She's been out *all day*," said Ari.

"Not that we mind, because we handled the shop!" Stella reminded her sister.

Ari brightened. "It was nice. And she always brings fun flowers from the castle when she comes back from her walks!

She's good with them, you know. Sometimes she even finds roses. It's because she's part-elf and has plant magic!"

"Well, from what William said, it sounds like you two did great watching the shop," I said, trying to stay on one topic at a time. This prompted them both to look curiously at William, and—knowing his feelings about creatures who spoke in unison or wanted to do things purely for fun—I hastened to add, "Hey, do you think you'd ever go and open your own salon?"

"*Us* go? Away from Belville?"

Both sisters looked shocked, and I couldn't help but smile. The reaction was typical of most residents. The fairies quickly dismissed the idea, instead asking if we'd known Vic. When I admitted we hadn't, and asked what they knew of him, they faltered again.

Stella's nose wrinkled. "He didn't smile very much."

"And he only ever wore his uniform," Ari added. "Like he was *always* on business."

"Well, the police do take their job seriously," I said, struggling to be the voice of reason. "Especially in cases like—"

"He never came into the salon," they said together.

This seemed to be the final note on Vic, as far as the fairies were concerned. Again I hid a smile. Fairies in general were known for glamour magic—that is, making things appear different than they really are. It was clear that appearance was very important to Ari and Stella. But I could also understand why Vic might feel he had more important matters on his plate.

"Speaking of police," I said, "I want to go talk to Officer Thorn. Do—"

"Oh, we'll catch up with you later!" said Ari.

"Byeee, tell her we say hello," Stella waved.

William grumbled as we turned and walked across the beach. "You should have said that at the beginning."

"I didn't want to be rude. And besides, they—" I paused, thinking back over Ari and Stella's conversation. "Wait. Did they say Gloria's been out at the castle all day?"

"Something like that." William sniffed at the lake breeze as we ambled past strings of groups along the shore. "Why, what's it to you?"

"William." I stopped in place as the realization hit me. "Officer Thorn said Owl was probably at the castle. But if they didn't find anyone in the search, then Gloria could be in danger!"

3

Into the Forest

"Hey! Where do you think you are going?!"

Oops. For the second time that evening, I stopped dead in my tracks. I'd made it about three-quarters of the way back up the beach, with William trailing behind me, before Officer Thorn's voice rang out.

I turned to face the officer, whose skin seemed to glow strangely in the light from the torch she carried. She fixed me with a disapproving look. "You're going out to investigate on your own."

"I am not!" I protested.

"She thinks Gloria's lost at the castle," William said. "Though if you ask me, Gloria's probably in cahoots with Owl. At the castle."

"We checked the castle during the search. Empty and as overgrown as ever," Officer Thorn said. Nonetheless, she lowered her torch a little, thinking. "You say Gloria still hasn't shown up?"

"Nope." Speaking quickly, I filled her in on what Ari and Stella had said. I didn't tell her the rest of my plan, namely, that I *had* been headed to the castle to look for Gloria. My plan wasn't as reckless as William made it sound: everyone in my clan was born swift-footed, so I could be there and back quickly if all went well. But the Officer wouldn't realize that.

Instead, she insisted on coming along for another search.

"Wait," I sputtered, "don't you have to run this ceremony?"

"Me? No, Lavender will, along with the Mayor. She always does. It's an old town tradition," said Thorn. "Vic would understand. Three of us makes a good stealth party. But there's not much daylight left. Onward! March!"

* * *

And that's how I found myself striding into the forest at night.

Exactly what I'd been warned not to do.

Under my cloak I shivered, but nothing would make me turn back if Gloria really did need help. And besides, Officer Thorn and William *did* make an excellent search party. William would be able to sense spells performed nearby. And on the physical side, what creature could we possibly meet in the forest that would give the hulking officer and her gnome-sized club a run for their money? Belville was a gentle, pastoral place. Before Owl went rampant, the most dangerous thing around town was William's attitude.

And though Officer Thorn had made note of Luca's stories about a ghost in the castle, she clearly had no fear of any paranormal traps herself. If a ghost tried to haunt her, she'd probably laugh in its face.

As we followed the dirt road out of town, disappearing under the tall fir trees, I decided to test my theory.

"Hey, Officer," I asked, looking up at Thorn. "Have you met

Jade yet?"

Officer Thorn didn't pause. In fact she hardly stopped whistling to ask, "Jade? Is that the new server over at the diner?"

William, who trotted along beside us, snorted.

I sighed. "No, no. Jade's a—a spirit, I guess. He—I *think* 'he' is right—he's the being we thought was working with Owl?"

"Right, the ghost." Thorn squinted into the darkness around us, then at me. "Owl never said anything during interrogations about a ghost minion, Red."

"Well, like I said, I don't know if Jade's a spirit or a ghost or what." *Or if Jade was being controlled by Owl, or maybe controlling him.* I bit my lip. "Are you sure you never met anyone like that? Mostly invisible except for bright eyes and pointy elfish ears?"

"Can't recall," Thorn said.

No surprise there, then. Maybe it was for the best, I mused. In silence, the three of us crossed over the small bridge that marked the end of "town" territory and the beginning of "creepy castle" territory.

"You don't really think there's a ghost at the castle," Thorn pressed. To our left, just off the road, vine-covered walls loomed into view.

"We'll find out if there is or not," growled William. The tips of his black tufts of fur glowed blue in the dark. Most likely, he was using magic to try to sense anyone hiding nearby.

"And we're not letting it escape," Officer Thorn agreed, looking down at him. "You stay here and stop anyone trying to leave. Red and I will go and have a look."

* * *

22

No matter whether they believe in ghosts or not, all of Belville's residents can agree that the castle—it's the only one for miles, so it's known simply as "the castle"—is creepy. On a particularly stormy day during the summer it had simply appeared, without any living creatures on the premises (but *with* a few suspicious bones). Set back from the dirt road, nestled on the mountainside behind high walls, full of pointy spires and old rotting wood, it wasn't a particularly hospitable place. Its isolation about a half hour's walk outside of town probably made it a great criminal haunt, though.

Together, the officer and I entered the castle grounds the usual way: clambering through a hole in the old walls caused by a fallen tree. The night, which had been still and cloudy outside the castle walls, changed the moment we entered. It became brisk and filled with distant howling, like a strong wind had surrounded us but not yet made itself felt. Thorn frowned and shook her head when I started on a beeline for the vine-covered side door.

"Perimeter check first," she said firmly, holding her club at the ready.

"Fine. Lead on." I fell into step behind her once more. Though from the outside the castle was barely visible, inside the grounds it dominated the landscape. Unlike most old castles, this one was made of wood, which gave it a "spooky haunted stump" feel. It cast deep shadows over a rugged, wild yard; even its rounded corners felt eerie in the night. The shadows cast by the twirling towers seemed to shift and follow our path.

Thorn paced along the side of the castle and circled the first corner, every movement alert. I, too, was wary. What had felt like a chilly, mournful night by the lake now felt like the winter solstice, and I hadn't had time to grab any lightsticks from my shop on the way here. As we walked, I tugged my goggles down from my forehead so that they covered my eyes. Along with my gloves, my goggles are my most useful tool, and I'm never without them. The specially-made lenses adjusted magically to the dark, helping me see.

Thorn paused in the deep shadow at the base of the tower and looked across the back of the castle. In the broken starlight, the panes of an old glass greenhouse gleamed.

"You hear that wind, right?" I asked, glancing around from behind the safety of my goggles.

"Course I do." She shouldered her club and continued on.

But she didn't make it very far. About two-thirds down the length of the greenhouse, she pulled up short.

"Did Luca ever figure out where this castle came from?"

"No," I said, feeling a tug of sympathy for my friend. As the town's resident scholar, he was called upon to know an awful lot. "Why? Having second thoughts about investigating it at night?"

"Doesn't matter what time it is."

I looked around us, wondering what had made Thorn stop. At last I shrugged and agreed. "Crimes can happen at any time, I suppose."

Thorn's response to this bit of philosophy was to trudge away again. I hurried to keep up.

The wind rose as we rounded the second corner, but there was nothing to be seen—only the same towering bushes on one side, and the unfeeling wooden castle on the other. Thorn prowled down the narrow path in between, batting away vines with her club.

When we hit the third corner, I stopped dead. It felt as

though a bucket of ice-water raced down my back. The darkness was so thick that even with my goggles, I could barely see beyond my own hand. The front of the castle stretched away into inkiness.

Thorn, already a pace ahead and nearly disappearing, looked over her shoulder. "What's wrong?"

"Something here," I mumbled incoherently. "There's some-thing wrong with being here. Don't you feel it?"

"To tell you the truth, I've never been haunted, so I wouldn't know what it feels like," Thorn replied blithely.

"Can you—can you actually see? I can't see hardly anything."

"Maybe your glasses failed." Thorn waited while I cautiously rose one side of my goggles, ignoring her jab at my equipment. To my naked eye, the castle grounds were swarming with shadows. Struck by vertigo, I hastily put my goggles back in place.

"I don't think that's it." I sucked air into my lungs. *The fastest way out of here is forward,* I reminded myself. Gritting my teeth, I took a step toward Officer Thorn. "Just stay close, okay? No bounding off after evidence or what have you."

She grinned, her long teeth flashing. "We want whoever's out there to come bounding to us, Red. That way we can ask them about Gloria. Or Owl."

"Once again, your unique style has me out in danger," I muttered as we began to walk. Focusing on my ire made the trip through the darkness less interminable. "If I'd have run into this alone, I'd've had the sense to stay away."

"Ha!" Thorn laughed—too loudly for my taste—and refused to explain the reason for her amusement, instead saying simply, "The sooner we catch Owl, the better."

"I don't think Owl is what's making these shadows," I said.

25

Thorn was impervious. "Then it could be Gloria alone, and that's worse. Stop complaining, Red. I didn't want to get you involved in this, but it's better to be here with company."

"Let me think." Again I focused to distract my nerves. I wasn't scared of hauntings, exactly. Ghosts didn't bother me; surprises did. My people were a desert island people, a wide-open-spaces-where-you-can-see-for-leagues people. Not a close-quarters-come-and-fight-me people, as apparently Thorn's were. "The fairies said Gloria comes here for flowers—"

"Which means either they are lying, or she lied to them," Thorn interrupted.

"—and some flowers are best picked under the moonlight," I continued, ignoring both her and my feet, which were itching to flee.

"*No* flowers take all day to pick," Thorn pointed out.

I had to agree with her there. "Not to mention the fact that somehow the moonlight around here is incredibly weak."

"Exactly. Forget flowers. See, Red, your problem is—"

I never got to hear what my problem was, unfortunately. The grass we'd been edging along gave way to a stone patio set a few inches below the surrounding ground, and I stumbled. With that jarring step came recognition of the fact that we were right in front of the castle's main entrance, and another bone-penetrating chill.

"Wh-wh-whatever it is y-you want to s-see, it must be h-here," I said, my teeth chattering.

"It's just a little cold, Red. Are all islanders such wimps?"

"Hush, and look around!" I insisted. I was starting to think that maybe Thorn hadn't ever been haunted simply because she refused to see anything other than what she wanted to.

"It's the front of the castle," she informed me matter-of-factly. She began stalking about the patio, with me close on her heels. "I was on the inside team during the search earlier, so I missed this. Nice carvings on the doorway. Old and worn down, but they've held up well considering. Good sturdy door. See that ironwork across the front? Guess we're not dealing with the fey, eh? And what's this—gems inlaid in the doors, too. Surprised those haven't walked off over time. Maybe they're locked down—get it? Ha ha. What's this?"

I'd only been paying half-attention to Thorn's monologue, but the repetition of the phrase in a new tone of surprise caught my ear. I turned from looking over my shoulder to see that Thorn held something small and rectangular in one large hand.

"Did you just find a book?" I asked, startled.

"Did I?" She handed the object to me for inspection. As I took it, though, the air around us thickened. I had to hold the slim volume very close to my face to see the bark binding. My gaze drifted over the title and the gold leaf to notice that, rather than blackness, a silver fluidity filled my vision.

"Why is it foggy?" I tucked the book into a pocket in my cloak for safe-keeping and frowned as I looked up. Officer Thorn looked just as surprised as me. I could see her face well, despite the cloudiness, because the moonlight had reappeared. It bounced off the water in the air. The world was brighter now, but it was also much closer.

Officer Thorn's club rose, sending swirls ricocheting through the air. "Never mind the fog, Red. Look here, at the corner of the doorway. Doesn't that look like—"

Again, I was destined not to hear the officer's thoughts. Only fair, really, considering how often she interrupted mine.

But I wasn't thinking that at the time. At the time, I was screaming like a banshee, because something had grabbed me from behind.

4

What Lurks in the Night

My middle was pinned in place and something icy covered my mouth.

From behind my left ear, someone said, "Rrred. Didn't you bring any lights?"

I knew that rolled "r" could only mean Jade.

The familiar voice jolted me right out of panic and into searing indignation. "Let go of me right this instant, you traitorous creep! I'm not giving you anything—you'd probably just take it to Owl!"

"I'm not holding you," Officer Thorn said, bewildered. She looked back over her shoulder at me, pausing just for a moment in her quest for the other side of the arched doorway.

"Not you. *Jade,*" I told her, shaking my head free but unable to liberate my body. "Didn't you hear anything?"

"The Officer can't hear me. To her, I am only a shadow."

"Well that's just great and entirely unhelpful, as usual," I spat back. "Are you not listening either? I told you to let me go!"

"Red, I think we have more company," said Thorn. Her club hovered beside her head as she squatted beside the second of

29

the double doors. "And not the live kind."

My first thought was *wait, so you* can *see Jade?* But then it hit me. Thorn was talking about something she was looking at, something her broad shoulders blocked from my view. A body.

The wafting fog became ten degrees colder.

"Rrred. You mustn't go near him. He was left for—"

"Red, would you come here and look at this?" Thorn swore quietly. "There's no pulse. Looks like someone put something all over the body. This on the head—is it *hair?*"

"This really is not the time for puns, Officer," I said. I didn't move—in part because I couldn't. But also because my hackles were up, warning me that something other than Jade lurked just over my shoulder.

"—them," Jade was still murmuring. "Do not go close to him, or they will catch your scent too. Tell her to come away from him. You both must leave."

"Who is it, Jade?" I asked, uncertain if I meant the body or whatever else I could feel in the castle garden. Whoever 'they' were.

"They're here already. I cannot keep them back for long."

"Not a pun, Red," Officer Thorn said, oblivious. Her investigation made her slow to respond. "This wasn't here during the search earlier. Someone's really made them up. Saints of law preserve us, it's *Owl.*"

Thorn stood abruptly, swearing again as she turned to me. When she looked behind me, she stopped still.

"What was it you were saying about ghosts?" she asked.

Carefully, cautiously, I turned and looked over my shoulder, out into the fog. Just at the edges, where it lost its silvery light, shapes shimmered in darkness.

"They are the cold," Jade whispered in my ear, as though talking too loudly would draw their attention. "They are drawn here, and to the body. Lights are the only thing to keep them away."

Lights. I cursed inwardly. The one thing I didn't keep in my many pockets or on my trusty tool belt as a matter of course. *That* would definitely have to change. If I made it through the night.

Briefly, my enmity vanished. In that moment I trusted Jade without thinking about it. I turned to Officer Thorn. "Do you have anything on you that'll make a light?"

"Is that all we need?" The officer looked incredulous and yet also a little pleased, like a child about to show off a new toy. "Well, we can try it."

In one swift, self-assured movement, she swung her club down through the mist. The shadows beyond leapt and twisted. The club scraped as it hit the ground, and there was a strange sizzle—and then the fog around us glowed iridescently orange. Thorn had struck her club against the stone patio and, like a giant match, it came back up alight.

"Nice, isn't it?" Her toothy grin loomed in the firelight. "The Witch did it for me as a gift at the last harvest festival. Won't burn forever, but it'll go a good while, and at the end my club'll be as good as new."

"Then let's get out of here," I said, feeling myself free to move again. I thought I heard Jade sigh somewhere behind me, but it was impossible to be sure over the airy growls of the shadows as they retreated from the light.

"Not without that body," Officer Thorn said. "By rights, I ought to be working through the crime scene checklist—"

"But Jade said—"

"Never mind Jade," Thorn declared. "I'm not leaving a body to the likes of these—whatever they are!"

The 'whatever they are' were not leaving, either. They were still there, just beyond the light. This was a standoff. And it seemed to be taking all of Jade's concentration.

"I think Jade's helping hold them off," I informed her. "But they want the body. So if you want it too, I think we're going to have to take it and run. You can come back tomorrow in the daylight to investigate properly."

"'Take it and run,'" Officer Thorn repeated, handing me her club and turning back to Owl's body, hunched at the edge of the light. Moving slowly and precisely—she'd once shared with me that under her uniform, she always wore a back brace, due to an old injury—the officer squatted once more. After a moment of adjustment, she lifted the corpse as though it was no more than a pile of blankets and added, "All right, fine. Get set. Go!"

* * *

I was so keyed up I could have sprinted all the way back to town, and I nearly did. But as Thorn and I veered around the castle, picking up speed, a spine-tingling howl went up from the wall.

"Huh," Officer Thorn panted, shifting Owl's body to one massive shoulder as she looked around. "I didn't know he could do that."

"He" being William, the magical creature Thorn routinely referred to as a simple "dog." I might have rolled my eyes if I hadn't been hightailing it for the source of the noise.

"Red!" William heard me coming and called out across the

32

tangled, shadowy weeds. He didn't sound distressed—in fact, he sounded triumphant. "Look what I got!"

I slowed, my arms tangling painfully with thorny vines as I approached him. Here at the outer edge of the grounds, the fog thinned, and the night seemed almost normal. Except for the fact that William sat panting on the massive log splitting the wall, and at his feet lay another body.

"Oh, no," I said, pulling up short. "They aren't—"

"Urrrgh," said the body.

"Okay, not dead. Is it—is it—" I turned to Officer Thorn as she caught up with me. Her expression seemed shaky at first but then I realized the movement was because my own arm was shaking as I held her club-turned-torch aloft. The thing was *heavy,* and my shoulder ached already.

"Managed to catch someone, have you?" said Thorn to William.

"There wasn't any 'managed' about it." William huffed. "She came sneaking along the wall and tried to escape, and I stopped her. Expertly. I defy you to have done better."

"Listen," I broke in, because I'd found the best thing to do when Officer Thorn and William started talking to one another was to be so loud and distracting that they forgot whatever they meant to fight about. "We can sort out the details in town where it's safe. I don't want to be here when those creatures get away from Jade."

William's wrinkled nose was visible in the firelight. "So Jade *did* show up?"

"And so did a bunch of mist creatures," Thorn informed him.

My feet itched. My spine tingled. I leapt up on the log, urging Thorn to finish her preliminary inspection of William's catch. "Which we want to avoid, remember?"

"Are you sure they aren't just more of whatever Jade is?" William asked pointedly.

"I'm sure I don't want to meet one up close," I returned tartly. "Come *on*, let's get out of here."

"Hey," said Thorn. "This is Gloria."

I was already halfway out the hole in the wall when my head whipped around. "Excuse me?"

William's voice was smug. "Found her."

5

The Phoenix and the Owl

"Why are you here, again?" asked Gloria.

I ran my hand through my hair and counted to ten. When that didn't work, I started looking around for another out. To my left I could almost see the streetlamps of Market Square, and the sanctuary of my own shop. We'd made it back into Belville mist-creature-free, but I really could have used a refuge and a hot cup of tea. Instead, Thorn had disappeared into her squat, wooden police station to properly lay out Owl's body, leaving Gloria and me sitting on the bench out front.

William ignored us all and sat smack in the middle of the road looking up at the stars. Since the station guarded the edge of town nearest the forest, it was a good place for stargazing, I supposed.

"I mean, you can't tell me you were *worried*." Gloria's voice was distinctly snide, the kind of snide which clearly stated that the listener ranked in the world's top 100 airheads. The kind of snide that made me wonder why she bothered talking to me in the first place.

"Actually," said I, rallying, "I'd be worried about anyone out in the forest alone, given everything we've seen tonight."

"Please. You didn't even wonder who you had to trample over to get out of the castle grounds."

Technically, she was correct. But I had been the one to turn back and offer her a revival elixir, which had helped her walk back into town, so I should've earned some points for that.

I could have told her I'd been distracted at first, or in a hurry, or too shaken to think straight. But truthfully, I hadn't wanted to know who William had nearly knocked out because I'd been afraid. Afraid that it *was* Gloria.

The thing about Gloria was that if she wasn't so rude, she'd have been really cool. When I first moved to Belville and learned that she was a transplant like me—apparently each owner of the beauty salon inherited the name along with the store—I'd hoped that we could be friends, since everyone else seemed to have lived in the neighborhood for generations, if not centuries.

From within the police station, a bang and loud swearing broke the quiet.

"No wonder no one ever sees justice in this town." Gloria hunched, holding her head in her hands. Her words wafted pepper-scented smoke in my direction. She wasn't smoking—not a pipe or cigarettes, anyway; Gloria was what was commonly known as "featherkin." Phoenixkin, to be precise. There were all kinds of "kin" across Beyond: catkin, snakekin, even some new folks calling themselves robotkin in the cities. Usually "kin" meant a human or elf or other bipedal person who had characteristics of an animal (or machine). Sometimes it was a result of a magical pact, crossbreeding, religious devotion, or even a spell gone wrong. Gloria, with her burnt orange skin and crest of red feathers atop her head, had to be from an elf family devoted to the phoenix. She was curvy and bold and also incredibly beautiful, the kind of beauty that opened doors, whether consciously or not. I often wondered who she'd been before she came to Belville.

"Is that why you were there?" I asked her without thinking. "To get justice for—or against—Owl?"

Gloria shifted as little as possible to look at me out of the corner of one eye framed by pointed, deep black nails. "What do you know about me and Owl?"

"How about you and that other guy?" William startled us both by taking a sudden interest in our conversation. He trotted over, a faint blue sparkle left in his wake.

Gloria glared at him. She'd lifted her head, but still leaned heavily on her knees; a pang went through me as I thought of how sore she must feel. Sure, I'd given her a potion, but I wasn't a healer. My remedies were a metaphorical band-aid, and Gloria must have taken some hard hits.

"There wasn't any other guy," Gloria said icily.

"Wasn't any what?" Thorn stepped out from the station and slammed the door behind her, brushing her hands off on her uniform as if to say, *job well done.* Rural police stations often had devices that could be activated to preserve a body, and judging by the waves of chill and dusty scent rolling off her, Thorn had won her battle with hers.

"There was someone else on the road outside the castle," William told us. "I saw them after you left. But because *someone* didn't leave me with any backup, I couldn't chase them and find out who it was."

"Why are you all looking at me? Am *I* the keeper of the castle?" Gloria frowned.

Thorn began pacing slowly in front of our bench. "From

what your employees say, you're there quite a bit."

"I like to go walking. There's nothing else to see around here. So what?"

"There definitely was someone," William insisted.

My stomach growled. *What time is it?* I thought regretfully of the seven-spice chili I'd planned to eat after Vic's vigil.

Thorn continued questioning Gloria. "What were you doing there today?"

"Walking," Gloria retorted. Her hard stare fell on William. "Until *someone* prevented me from going home."

William growled. "You're the one who chose to have a meeting out there and not tell anyone about it."

"I wasn't meeting anyone. You could have seen anything."

"I saw a person walking down the road!"

"That doesn't mean anything," Gloria snapped, the crest of feathers atop her head shivering. "Everyone knows sorcerer's familiars can be fooled by sorcerer's illusions. You could have seen anything and not known it."

"If you want to bring magic into it, I could have seen *you* using a glamour." William rose to his feet, his tail in the air. "You could have been sneaking all over that castle."

"I was *walking*. Mind your own business, you overgrown spell-puppet."

"Hey!" I leapt to my feet, blocking William from Gloria's view. "You leave him alone. He's right. It's not his fault you were out there. And you could make this a lot easier for everyone by telling us what happened."

"If it was any more obvious than it is already, it'd be a children's book," Gloria said spitefully as she, too, rose. With the bench at her back, she was a lot closer to me than I'd expected, but I wasn't about to back down.

That word, *book,* rang in my mind but I ignored it.

"Is there a *reason* you want to pick a fight with us?" I shot back, my fists curling in frustration. "We haven't done anything to you."

"Except knock me over the head and impede my rights!"

"Again, you only have—"

"All right, that's enough." Officer Thorn, who had been watching the entire show with the air of a connoisseur, pressed her arm between us and knocked me back. "Gloria, you're coming in the station with me. Same to you, Mr. Roadside Witness. Red, I want you to go home. I told you earlier, no drama. You're too personal about this case."

"Fine by me," I said through gritted teeth, glaring at Gloria. She was smoking properly now, something phoenixkin were rumored to do whenever they got mad. It didn't scare me. But I knew that Officer Thorn had a point, so I told William to mind his manners and went home alone.

* * *

I let myself in through the shop's back door and collapsed on my workbench. The shop and lab were utterly still. My workbench took up one wall of the lab, and above it, I'd knocked an interior window into the wall so that I could work on experiments or stocking while keeping an eye on the sales floor. A large furnace used for alchemical processes stood in the corner, behind the door from the patio. To my right, cabinets full of ingredients and tools waited patiently above another, smaller stove. In the blissful silence, I grabbed a lightstick, dug a tin of salve out of my overflow storage, and hung up my cloak.

In my annoyance at Gloria, I'd forgotten all about my casualties from running through the overgrown castle garden. I rolled up my sleeves and, after washing up in the sink in the corner, began smearing the comfrey-scented goop on my forearms. My heartbeat slowed gradually, but still my ears remained pricked, waiting for the sound of William's plodding steps or a police siren or the shrieks of castle-haunting corpse-hungry ghosts or anything, in short, except for what I heard, which was a knock at the door.

I startled and the tin of salve rolled away over the tiles.

Pull yourself together, Cinnabar. I reprimanded myself the same way my mother had often done, using the same childhood name she'd use whenever she especially needed me to listen. *Nothing evil followed you all the way from the castle just to knock politely on the door.*

Of course, William's protection spells *were* very good; anything that had followed me wouldn't be able to get into the shop unless I invited it. When the knock sounded again, I sighed and rose to catch a glimpse of my late-night caller.

But when I peered out the window set into the door, no one was there.

Cautiously, I opened the door wide enough for one eye to peer out. "Yes?"

"Rrred." Jade's voice was laden with relief, and surprisingly breathless for the usually-suave enigma. "Forgive the intrusion, but I had to be sure you had made it home unharmed."

I hesitated. Gloria's unpleasantness faded into memory, but I recalled William's skepticism about Jade, not to mention my own misgivings. But it wouldn't do to be rude. "I'm fine—just some scratches. And you . . . you're okay?"

"I'm not. I have made a mistake, Rred. I should have

explained everything to you. If you would be good enough to listen, I will try to do so now."

I let go of the door to cross my arms as I considered this offer. Jade *had* just helped us out, but I still had a feeling I should keep my distance, otherwise—*otherwise what?* I wasn't sure. And it was difficult to stare skeptically at something invisible, so I quickly came to two conclusions. "I'll hear what you have to say. But first—you made yourself corporeal earlier, or at least, it sure felt like it. Is there some way you can make yourself visible?"

"I can." Jade's response was immediate. "That is, if you do not mind leaving the lights off, Rred. What I told you is true: I am a shadow. It is the darkness that gives me back my form."

Experimentally, I stowed my lightstick. As I did so I racked my brain, trying to remember if I'd ever heard William or Luca or even Owl talk about such a thing. And even as my brain turned up empty, Jade proved it true. My night vision was just good enough that I could see a tall, elf-like person take shape on my back stair—a masculine figure in cape and boots. Every detail about him was rendered in shades of gray except for his eyes, which were the faint green I had once named Jade for.

Eyes which were, I realized, a lot closer than I had expected. Jade leaned against the door frame, peering into my face.

"Well," I mumbled, trying to ignore the heat in my cheeks. "You could have done that a long time ago."

He smiled. "It wouldn't have been polite to ask you to turn off all your lights."

"And going around haunting people *is* polite?" This time I was gratified to have a target for my skeptical look. It didn't seem to have any effect, though. Jade, I saw, was not going anywhere.

41

Sighing, I stepped back and said, "Come on in to the workroom, and tell me exactly what is up with you and that castle. And Owl."

"There are things in my past I cannot speak of," he answered and, as though sensing my ire, quickly added, "But I had no part in Owl's demise. It is true I had some dealings with him when he was alive, and that he was a danger to you. Owl's presence in town was like a blight, bending everyone around him to his will. But I have *never* meant to harm you or your friends." When I was silent, Jade added, "I swear it, Rred."

Still uncertain, I crossed to my workbench and sat, my legs crossed and my foot tapping. Everything Jade said made sense. But was that only because I really, really wanted it to? All the great alchemists cautioned against carrying out an experiment when hoping for one result and not being open to others.

But then, I decided, all the great alchemists hadn't been above hope themselves. Otherwise they wouldn't have been alchemists to begin with. What was alchemy, if not the hope that everything in the world could be a little bit better?

"I'll believe you, Jade. For now, at least. So—do you have an actual name you'd rather I use?"

"My name is Jade," said the shadow firmly, nearing my bench with eyes alight. "Thank you."

"Don't mention it. So, I'm guessing the things you can't tell me are why you're a shadow and how you got this way, right? That still leaves the castle and Owl and whoever *did* that for us to talk about."

"Of course. But may I say something else first?"

I had been watching Jade move. He strode about like any normal person. And yet it seemed sudden that he was close, one gloved hand on the table beside me, head bent toward

42

mine.

I licked my dry lips and wondered where all the butterflies in my stomach had come from. "Is it why shadows seem to have no sense of personal space?"

Jade chuckled. Over that quiet sound I heard the gruff voice I'd been half-expecting since I'd opened the back door.

"That particular shadow is cursed," William announced from the back door. In the darkness, his edges glowed a bright blue. "For sky's sake, Red, do you always have to find the cursed ones?"

Next to me, Jade shifted and bowed. "You are right. But that, alas, is all I can say. William, I take it?"

"I'm surprised you have anything to say at all. You just look like a smudge to me," William continued without budging or acknowledging the pleasantries. "But you'd be a good accomplice even so, I bet."

"William, honestly," I protested.

"I am able to do very little," said Jade. I couldn't tell if he was amused or not.

"But you can move objects?" William circled around to a sharp-edged point, and everyone in the room realized what he meant. *The flowerpot and broom at the police station, and Officer Thorn's keys, which someone helped Owl steal . . . Not to mention Owl's body.*

Jade answered quickly. "I am able to move small things in the dark. I am not able to manipulate large objects or bodies, nor am I equipped to deal with enchantments."

William's only response was "Huh."

"Jade," I broke in, thinking of Owl's demise, "if you didn't set up the body like that, did you see who did? There must have been someone. I mean, he didn't wait until the search was over, then stick himself in that corner and cover himself up, did he?"

"I doubt it," said Jade, his dark face somber. "But I cannot say for sure. I did not see the act take place. I can often tell when living beings come into the castle, but after the Officer's search party, no one did. I came upon him outside, just as you did. But . . ."

"But what?" I prompted.

"The cloths covering his body," Jade said quietly. "They came from the castle kitchen. And yet, aside from the searchers, no one has been there."

"We're *not* going over this again," William huffed. "I *did* see someone. Someone besides Gloria. Although she's suspicious enough on her own."

As briefly as I could, I informed Jade about Gloria and our evening up to this point.

This time he was more definite. "I have often seen her—Glorria?—yes. She and Owl would often meet on the castle grounds. As to why—that is not my secret to share."

I sat back, crossing my arms. "Jade, two people have died, and the murderer clearly had access to the castle. That's more serious than secret-keeping."

Jade paused, watching me keenly, as though he really was thinking this over. Finally, he said, "Much as I might wish to, I can not speak freely about Owl. However, Rred, I believe you will figure everything out in time."

6

Lost Stories

William soon shooed Jade away and insisted I go to bed, with his classic style which left me wondering if he was worried about me or if I was under house arrest, or both. But when he slept late the next morning, I took my chance for escape. I figured that with Thorn preoccupied by Gloria and the castle, it fell to me to pay Luca a visit. After all, he'd been the one to first tell me about the whole business; it was only fair to keep him updated. And no matter what everyone kept telling me about not getting involved, I was obviously involved already—might as well make the best of it.

Tossing on a sky blue tunic and woolen purple leggings, then grabbing a sage scone smeared with butter, I hit the street just as the sun emerged from behind the hills. My plan was to catch Luca at the bookstore before business picked up. In addition to filling him in, I could show him the book Thorn had found hidden in the ironwork on the castle door. I'd taken a look at it myself before heading to bed, but nothing about it made sense to me. Even the title, *Beauty and Shadow; or, the downfall of the cursed prince of the Ring of the Moon, Part 1 of 6,* left me with more questions than answers. I hoped Luca had volumes two through six and that Thorn's discovery wouldn't set off a research fever.

And okay, maybe—just maybe—I wanted to make sure that Luca had an alibi for Owl's murder. There wasn't any part of me that really believed sweet, scatter-brained Luca was capable of hurting anyone. But I couldn't help thinking that maybe Gloria *wasn't* the shoo-in for "Belville Murderess" that she appeared to be, and crossing her off the list meant it was anyone's game. Half the town had been in the search party, after all.

The bookstore, which had no name I'd ever been able to discern, hunched at the corner one block south of Market Square. The three-story building seemed rounded not so much by design as by the passage of time. Nothing about it, not even the plethora of small windows, contained a straight line. I spotted Luca first through one of those windows, more ship's porthole than anything else.

Clearly, Luca hadn't got the hang of running a shop by himself. His head bobbed among stacks of books as he paced around the desk at one side of the sales floor. As a shopkeeper myself, I recognized the movements: checking the till, trying desperately to rearrange piles of merchandise, and continually coming back to the pre-opening cup of coffee. As soon as he saw me staring and making faces at him, Luca unlocked the front door and let me in.

"You could have come to the back, you know," he said. "It's almost always open."

I smiled at him. "Geez, Luca, why don't you say that a little louder so any thieves in the neighborhood can hear?"

"Listen, Red, we don't all have a magical ward-weaving ex-familiar like you do," Luca grinned back. He beckoned me inside and retreated to the stool behind his desk, his robe and hood drawn around his body like a blanket. "Besides, this edge of town is pretty quiet. No one would dare break in someplace within shouting distance of the Witch's Hut."

Just as each town in Pastoria had a Witch, each Witch had a Hut: inevitably holey, irregular, and in fact practically condemnable, nestled somewhere among the outskirts of town. The Witch and their Hut were the epitome of "appearances can be deceiving."

"Still, you might want to consider some locks, at least," I told him. Having little other option, I took a seat on the desk itself. Behind me, a scroll fell; I pretended not to hear the protesting rustles of old parchment.

Luca sipped steaming, fragrant coffee. "Trent did give me some charms of protection against Owl, if that's what you mean."

Right. "About that." I bit my lip. While I considered myself to have a few more social graces than, say, William or Officer Thorn, I hadn't ever had to break the news of death to someone like this before. *But Luca's never been one for ceremony,* I reminded myself. "Officer Thorn and I went out to the castle last night, and we found an old book. And—we also found Owl. Dead." I pulled the book out of my cloak and offered it to Luca.

"You did? *What?* Why'd you go?" Despite his obvious surprise, Luca reached out to take the book. As I explained what had happened, his fingers listlessly traced the pages, though his eyes were unseeing, fixed on my face.

Finally—several long moments after I'd stopped talking—Luca shook himself, as though waking up. "Cursed," he murmured, looking down at the bark-covered book like it had just teleported into his grip. He flipped it open and began to read.

"Maybe," I agreed, playing along. Luca's shock was painful to be close to, and it made me move carefully, as if I was holding an overflowing glass. "So, anything good in the book?"

"Hm? Oh." Luca snapped the book shut and handed it to me. "It's a social history, you might say, nothing too . . . too . . ."

Dangerous? I wondered if that was the word Luca wanted. The book *had* been awfully close to Owl's body. But Owl might never have known that.

I took the book mutely. *Beauty and Shadow* was a picture book of sorts. Each page contained a precise ink drawing: scenes of trees arching into the sky, dark skinny figures, and intricate interiors that remind me of the castle. Beneath each picture ran one single line of text written in old-fashioned cursive. Strung together, the captions read:

> *The Ring of the Moon was well hidden, a society within the other societies of the forest. The tree-elves who dwelt in this society knew themselves as Drus. The Drus were free to live in any tree they liked, but the Drus of the Ring of the Moon valued the sweet-cherry above all other trees, and made their great castle within it. Hidden in the spaces of the inner rings lay their world, a world full of intricate carvings and the magic of cherry pits and long dances in the moonlight, for the Ring of the Moon was a nocturnal society. They lived long, as long as the sweet-cherries they took care of and took guidance from: often each member would live to see two and a half*

centuries, and yet the society was small. Upon reaching adulthood at fifteen years, each Drus of the Ring of the Moon took a vow to live life by the moon and the trees' wisdom: steadily, peacefully, and independently. Each one knew their place within the rings of society, and went about it quietly. The Ring of the Moon was not a society of drama and war.

"I guess we know where that's going," I mused as I closed the book and handed it back to Luca.

He looked pensive. "Do we?"

"Well, you would know more about it than me. Have you ever heard about the Drus?"

"No. I'm not even sure we can say that the castle was theirs. Owl always says the castle is—he always *said* it is—" Luca went quiet abruptly, like his train of thought had bucked him off.

I said gently, "Hey, I know this is a lot all at once. I didn't mean to overwhelm you. I just thought you should know. Do you—would you like to talk about it, or would you rather be alone?"

"You don't have to leave just yet. I mean, not on my account." Luca shuffled, or maybe shrugged; between the darkness of his skin, the blackness of his hooded robe, and the dustiness of his shop, it was difficult to track exactly what he did. Some people said shop owners came to look like their shops over time; I certainly ended up *wearing* my shop, or at least my potions, pretty often. At that moment Luca looked like a veritable library's worth of uncertainties.

"Luca." When the faraway look didn't leave his eyes, I reached out and nudged his shoulder. If he didn't want me to leave, then I decided we might as well talk. "Do you think

49

there really was anything cursed about the way we found Owl, and all the things coming to get him? Think it has anything to do with the books?"

"Could be wendigos." Luca's hands rustled, clasped over the book. "William was there, right? What did he say?"

I rolled my eyes. "Something about the creatures and Jade probably being the same. That's about it. It might even be right, for all I know."

"Being magical himself, he would have a good sense for that stuff," Luca mused. "But even so . . . I don't know if that has anything to do with the books, or Jade either. Wendigos are generally recorded as being obsessed with consumption, be it environmental or people, but Jade hasn't shown any inclination to eat you."

"And that's the other thing," I said, seeing from the hesitation in Luca's face that another distraction might be in order. Remembering William's comment about Jade being a "smudge," I asked, "Why me? I mean, it isn't just me, is it? You've seen Jade too, right?"

Luca looked down, swirling the forgotten coffee in his brightly colored elf-made mug. "I always knew something was there, at the castle, but I never actually saw him, no. But I believe you, of course," he added hastily, glancing at me.

"I appreciate that. Still, it's bugging me that somehow in the past day, three or four mysteries have cropped up when we didn't want any of them to begin with."

"No, I mean, of course you're right." Luca looked down again, at the book on the desk. "It's kind of . . . I mean . . . Are you sure?" He met my gaze and held it this time. "Are you really sure Owl is dead?"

"Yes," I told him quietly. "If he wasn't, Thorn carrying him into town would certainly have gotten a reaction out of him. She'll want to talk to you at some point, you know."

Luca shrugged, listing on his stool. "I don't know what I could say about it. I haven't seen him, not since, you know. I've just been in the shop, except for when I stopped to talk to you yesterday."

"I figured. But you know how she is. Did anyone see you, maybe?"

"You mean like an alibi." Luca slipped and re-centered himself. "Um, I . . . I'm sure someone came in. I'd have to think about it."

"Maybe look through your sales records," I said, casting a doubtful eye over his hideous mess of a desk.

This produced an absent nod, and in the silence I heard the sound of voices and creaky wheels in the street. Mindful of the time, I offered once more to stay while the bookshop was open, but Luca waved the offer away.

"In that case, I better go make sure no one's champing at the bit for alchemical doodads." I smiled and added, "If you think of anything else about the book or the Drus, let me know."

"Yeah. I will," Luca said, a strange, rueful look on his face. His head tipped and he smiled faintly back. "I know it seems like a lot of mysteries, Red, but I'm sure everything will work out."

I wasn't too sure about that, but I took my leave and hurried out of the bookstore to give Luca some space. The cobbled streets of Belville had begun to fill with sunshine and shoppers; in the absence of errant police officers or angry neighbors, peace reigned. I made my way back to my own shop, thinking. *So Luca hasn't seen Jade either . . .*

Most people in Beyond didn't recognize this, but the

truth was, there were different types of Seers. Each clan was devoted to a different totem animal and had different strengths; some were good at seeing visions of possible futures, some exclusively dealt in romance. My mothers and their matriarchal clan practiced an ambitious variety of Seeing that focused on finding truth, in whatever form it might appear: life, energy, death, things I never fully understood. As a result, my people were known—among other Seers, at least—for often being "haunted."

My faraway home was full of ghost stories and fairy tales, but I'd never expected to find them in Belville. And yet it seemed I was in the middle of two, or even three, weaving in and out just like I dodged passersby in the street. Jade and the castle, Gloria and her flowers, Owl and his sordid past . . .

And whatever had been haunting Owl, be it alive or dead, had caught up with him.

7

Local Expertise

When I got to my shop, I was surprised to find the door unlocked. I hadn't expected William to open the store in my absence; to do so would be wishing for rain out of a clear blue sky. I also, therefore, had not expected to hear voices coming from inside.

For a moment I paused outside the door, feet rooted to the stone step nestled between my two display windows. The events of the night before had made me wary.

Wary, sure, but not weak-willed, I thought, reminding myself that it was *my* shop and that I wasn't about to lurk fearfully outside my own front door. I pushed my way in, setting off a cheerful jangle from the bell above the door frame.

"You aren't back *already,* are you?" William grumped from the back.

"Morning, Red!" This latter voice was much friendlier, a welcome sound.

"Hey Dusty," I called back, already grinning as I rounded a stand of shelves and came upon the little party in the reading nook. In a flash I could tell what had happened: Dusty had come by hoping for gossip, as he was wont to do at all hours, and William hadn't been able to say no. Dusty, tinkerer and plumber extraordinaire, a gnome about as high as my thigh and perpetually clad in baggy green overalls, was William's best friend. Aside from me, of course.

"I thought you'd be out meddling for hours," William complained. He was curled up in the overstuffed armchair, shedding by the second, no doubt. Dusty had perched atop the side table which usually held a teapot and mugs.

"I wasn't meddling, I was checking on Luca," I said. "How are you doing, Dusty?"

"Heard you got taken off the case," the gnome chuckled. Under his floppy cap, his blue eyes twinkled. "Folks around town are saying ghosts killed Owl. 'Sat so?"

"Honestly, one of you is just as bad as the other," I smiled back, admonishing the pair of gossip-mongers. "Do you want tea? I'm going to get some started. How about a spiced Assam, since it's such a lovely fall day?"

William snorted.

"Whatever you've got. We're speculating as to who Gloria might've been meeting," Dusty continued as though my reprimand had been nothing but chimes in the wind. "Cairn saw her six days back meeting with the real estate man. Rumor has it she's planning on selling the beauty parlor, and Owl might've been one to buy it. Now, what do you make of that?"

"I don't make anything of it," I called lightly from my workroom. "I'm not on the case, remember? Have you tried talking to Thorn about all your wild theories?"

"Wild theories, huh? Guess I showed up just in time," a new voice said from the front of the shop.

I poked my head out my lab window to look. I'd left the

front door unlocked since we were due to open soon anyway. Still, the bells should have announced a newcomer. *Why didn't they ring?*

This mystery was solved as I caught sight of the local Witch, grinning, his hand upstretched and the purple glow of his magic woven around my shop door. When he saw me looking, he gestured with both hands as if to say *look what I can do!* and whatever spell he'd been concentrating on broke. The bells clanged wildly against the door, and from his seat in the armchair, William sneezed.

"Hey, everyone." Belville's Witch, Trent, announced himself rather sheepishly. "Wasn't trying to sneak up on you, promise. I was practicing for sneaking around the castle later."

"No problem, there's nothing to overhear here but speculation anyway," I told him, waving him into the shop. Despite purple streaks in his shoulder-length black hair and bright purple eyes, Trent could have passed for an average human teenager. From my previous encounters with him I knew he had the appetite of one, at least. Tall, pale, and scraggly, he had just started out in his Witch career.

Witches had a lot of folklore built up around them. The position was a very respected one despite the fact that most of us layfolks never understood how Witches were trained, where they came from, or how they got assigned to the town they'd be making charms and spells for throughout their lives. Though so far Trent had struck me as a bit of a loner—or perhaps so busy with improvements to the Hut that he had little time for hanging around Belville's tavern or Market Square—Officer Thorn had wasted no time in conscripting him for her unofficial police force.

"You're in time for tea if you have a moment to wait," I added with a smile. "Officer Thorn has you on the case, huh? Good, you can be my replacement."

"Oh, I am. Something about you and Gloria going for each other's throats and getting in the way of collecting evidence," Trent informed me, tucking his hands into the pockets of a pair of jeans. Denim was a favorite fabric among gnomes, but I'd never seen anyone as big as Trent wear them. He was never without them, not even at the most serious of events. Beat-up sneakers and a t-shirt proclaiming "frogs are friends" completed the outfit today. "Just for the record," he added, leaning in, "I would totally have your back in that fight."

I laughed. "I think William is the one we have to be worried about getting into fights. But I don't mind sitting this one out. I've got a lot of new winter stock to get started on."

"Come on, Red," said Dusty as he and William crowded round the sales counter to be part of the new conversation. "Don't spend *all* day working. If you ask me, it's a day to celebrate!"

Trent looked down—very far down—at Dusty, amiable but confused. "Why's that?"

"Because Owl is gone," William answered in a rumble. He scrambled up onto the stool behind the counter and cocked his head over his shoulder at me, no doubt knowing what my reaction would be. Disapproval. It's not that I didn't agree with them, but I couldn't help but think both William and Dusty could use a *little* more decorum. I glanced between the two apprehensively.

Trent also hesitated before leaning his elbows on the counter and settling in. "Did people around here not like him or something? Like, even before the whole jail thing."

My tea kettle on the lab's Ever-Hot Burner whistled, and

I turned to my tea, keeping one ear on the conversation. *That's right, Trent showed up this summer,* I remembered. *He probably never met Owl.* This set the gears in my head turning, wondering who might have been in town long enough to have a personal grudge against Owl. *William and I are the newest residents aside from Trent, and before us the new person in town would have been Gloria, or actually, maybe Cairn, since she used to travel just like William and me . . .* hot water spilling over my work gloves reminded me to focus. *Not on the case,* I reminded myself firmly.

"—scum," Dusty was saying. This caught my attention; I'd never heard Dusty speak so harshly before. "You'd never believe the things I see when I'm on a job. People forget I'm there. The way he'd deal with his 'prentice ought to be outlawed."

"Luca?" I turned too fast, again sloshing hot water out of my teapot. At this rate, I'd have to make another batch. Technically scholars didn't have "apprentices," but Luca *had* been studying with Owl, and it made sense that Dusty—as a tradesperson, much like myself—would see Luca's role that way. "I *knew* there was something not right there, with him and Owl."

"Owl was a bully, and that's being *nice,*" said Dusty. "Luca wasn't the only one, but he had it worst. And it's a gods-cursed pity, when you think the poor lad was only—"

"Look sharp!" This time the voice at the door was recognizable immediately. Officer Thorn. She often introduced herself in this fashion. However, she didn't usually push a person in through the door ahead of her as she arrived, and this anomaly chilled my blood. "We've got a new suspect, and I've got a side job that needs *your* expertise, Red. Go on! Tell

57

them what you told me."

Those last two sentences were directed at the figure cringing in the center of the shop, caught between myself and my friends, and Officer Thorn and the small crowd gathered around the windows behind her.

Luca.

8

A Dark Glow

I stormed out of my lab. In fact, if William and Dusty and Trent hadn't been leaning all over the sales counter, blocking my way, I would have vaulted right out the lab window. Instead I went the normal route, slamming the lab door behind me.

"Officer Thorn, what in *Beyond* do you think you're doing?" I seethed, brushing right past Luca to yank the officer into the shop and shut the door behind her, flipping my sign to "closed." I yanked on the thin silver chains which let curtains down across the bay windows. The shop darkened at once, but at least we weren't putting on a show for the entire town. Once again I stomped past Thorn, this time to stand next to Luca, my hands on my hips. Even in my anger there was no chance I could intimidate the half-orc police officer, but that didn't stop me from showing how I felt. "This is ridiculous. You can't go dragging people all over town and giving them commands. Did you even *look* at Luca? You've scared him stiff! And what is everyone in Belville going to think, now that you've gone and yelled at him right on my front doorstep?"

For a moment the shop was still. Not even a dust mote

dared to swirl in the light filtering down from the upper, un-curtained windows.

Officer Thorn blinked at me, which was probably the closest to a shamed expression I'd ever seen on her perfect face. "He doesn't have an alibi, Red. You ought to know that, he says he told you himself."

"That's the other thing, I was *just* talking to Luca, so I don't see why—" I stopped short. Thorn had gone straight to talking about alibis, which meant that Luca wasn't meant to be offering information *about* a new suspect like I'd hoped. "Are you telling me that Luca *is* your new suspect?"

"You tell her," Officer Thorn insisted, looking over my shoulder at the hand-wringing scholar. Her big eyes slid back to mine as she said it, though, and she lowered her voice from "drill sergeant" to "enthusiastic lawyer" levels, which at least was an indoor volume. I ground my teeth but said nothing, instead turning to Luca.

"U-u-um," he said. He glanced all around the shop, but I wasn't sure he took anything in. He shifted so he was just facing me. "Um, hi, Red. Uh, long time no see. See, O-officer Thorn came by after you left, and she—she—um, I don't really remember how it happened, but the thing is, I should have told you while you were there, at the bookstore I mean, the thing is I think the books might be really important for Owl's d-death—"

"Not that," Officer Thorn interrupted, exasperated. "Listen, Red, I don't have to explain my investigation to you, but since you're about to help with it, I'll tell you how it came about. Now, we both know that the scholar here has known way too much from the very beginning. On top of that, we have a witness saying that Owl was concerned about retaliation—"

"'Retaliation'?" I interrupted, disbelieving. *As if Luca would even think of something like that. That sounds more like—* "You heard that from Gloria. Gloria's your witness, isn't she. Does that even count when she's clearly trying to save herself from suspicion?"

"Does the source matter if the information is true?" Officer Thorn shot back.

At the back of the room, Trent coughed and raised his hand like a kid in school. I'd forgotten all about our wide-eyed audience.

"Not you, too," said Thorn.

Trent took this as an invitation to wade in. "I gave him a charm for checking on the station. You know, since you're talking about him knowing too much? It's probably the status spell, right, Luca?" Luca's hood shook like the last leaf on a tree as he nodded, and Trent went on, "We talked about this, Officer. I ran it by you. When I gave him the protection charm for the bookshop, he was a little extra worried about Owl escaping, so I set up a status spell. You know, the quartz crystal I put on your desk at the station? It's linked to one at the bookshop. Clear white glow for 'everything's normal,' yellow glow for 'something's not so good,' red for 'things are bad.'"

"It went black," Luca muttered, glancing back at me. "That morning, it glowed black."

"That just makes the case against him even stronger," Thorn said. "He could have been waiting for Owl to escape so that he could murder him. Crystal clear case, if you ask me."

"Don't you dare make puns right now," I said, turning back to Officer Thorn. "What's the point of all this evidence? *How* do you think Luca murdered Owl?"

61

"He could've snuck off to the castle at any time," Thorn said. "A preliminary look at Owl points to death by a heavy object hitting the back of the head. I'm waiting on any word on Owl's relatives to get permission for taking a closer look, but for the moment, that's enough to start with. A heavy object—like a *book*."

I inhaled sharply, and let the breath go very, very slowly. Police guilds across Beyond—but particularly in Pastoria—were very respectful of the family's wishes regarding the deceased, which normally was a good thing, but this time the delay made my feet itch. I felt certain that when Thorn examined the body more closely, she'd find that there was no way Luca had committed a murder. *But we can't focus on that now,* I told myself. *Focus on the present.*

"I can see how there might be a case," I said at last. "I think it's wrong, but I'll play along for a minute. So why did you insist on bringing Luca *here*?"

"Because he started talking gibberish about the castle and hidden symbols," Thorn said. After a pause, she looked over my shoulder at Luca and added, "No offense."

Luca shuffled but didn't respond.

From somewhere in the shadowed recesses of the shop, William scoffed.

"Oh, you're here too, are you?" Officer Thorn squinted, probably more out of calculation than the strain of looking for a pitch-black magic dog in a darkened building. "I'm following up on *your* lead too, you'll be glad to know. Trent and I are headed out there now to see if we can find any traces of illusions or glamours. Or strangers on the road.

"And that means," she continued, looking round at all of us, "that I'm busy. This is big crime we're talking about, people.

Police business comes first at times like this. And that's why I want *you*, Red, to make sense of these hidden symbols. From the sound of it, you'll have to take Luca with you. William, you're in charge of watching her and the suspect while they collect evidence. In fact, why don't you go too, Dusty?"

I startled. I hadn't realized Dusty was still in the shop. Part of me was glad to have him there: gossip aside, I knew Dusty was honest and loyal.

The gnome in question cleared his throat. "Go where? To the castle?"

"That's right. Go in the daytime, stick together, and you should be perfectly safe."

"What about Gloria?" I blurted.

"I'll be checking up on her later, but for now she's at her shop. The fairies are watching her. Don't get any ideas," Thorn warned me.

I crossed my arms. "I still don't get—"

"You will," she said, waving at Trent that it was time to go. As they headed for the door, she said over her shoulder, "Like I told you, Luca, tell her what you told me. I'll be checking up on all of you later!"

The door snapped shut behind the officer and the Witch. Just before it did so, I caught a glimpse of the street outside: people still loitered in front of the shop.

With a sigh, I turned to Luca, William, and Dusty. "Is everyone okay with what Thorn proposed?" After each person had nodded, I added in a nod of my own. "Okay. How about this as a plan: William, you and Dusty grab some lunch stuff from upstairs, and anything out of the workroom that you think we might need. Luca and I will talk here for a minute, and when you're ready, we'll all head out the back door. Sound good?"

William eyed me for a moment, glowing, probably thinking about his newfound role as "watcher of the suspect" and wondering if I was planning to let Luca escape while everyone else made sandwiches. I held his gaze. At last he agreed, following Dusty up the stairs.

"Right." Again I sighed, this time in the silence as Luca and I were left alone.

Luca gulped. "It's kind of funny actually, when you think about it I mean, because if Thorn hadn't c-come by I was thinking I should come see you. I wanted to apologize. See, the truth is, I *did* know about that book. The one you brought me?"

"Why would knowing about the book mean that you need to apologize?" I asked, running my fingers over the top of my head, through hair pulled back in a ponytail. It was an annoying habit because it inevitably knocked strands loose from their confinement, but I couldn't seem to stop.

"I just didn't think at the time," said Luca. "That's my problem, I never can think of the right thing to say or do. Then Officer Thorn came by and she was asking all about Owl and why he might be out there and I didn't know, I have no idea about the things Owl did, but then I thought about the book you found. And I thought maybe that was *why* he was there. Maybe he was looking for them."

"'Them'?" I prompted. I knew from experience that once Luca got going, he didn't need much to keep going.

"The books. All six of them. They're all hidden, out there at the castle, Red. They're all there. It's kind of a—it's supposed to be some kind of secret," Luca said, covering his face with his hands.

"Okayyy," I said, thinking. "Who told you it's a secret? Owl?"
Luca nodded.

"And Thorn mentioned symbols. Is that how to find them?"

"I think so," said Luca, green eyes peeking out at me from between his dark fingers. Self-consciously he pulled his hands down to his sides and addressed my wall-mounted shelves of potions as he asked, "Did you notice how the book had a symbol on the first page?"

"Nope. I didn't really take the time to examine it, though."

"There's one on the back page too. I recognized that one." He dropped on to the edge of a potted lemon tree marking the end of a row, rustling the leaves and releasing its scent. "The one on the first page isn't a big deal. Just a tree. But the one at the end—it looked like pages. I've seen it before, at the castle. It's *special.* I wouldn't have done anything about it except I was looking at that book you found and thinking about that symbol and I realized, maybe it's part of an organizational system. Like a clue, you know? The first book ends with the pages symbol and that probably means—probably means that where I saw that symbol in the castle, that's where the second book is hidden."

"Okay. That makes sense. Come to think of it, I think the iron on the castle door *is* in the shape of a tree, so I can see how that supports your idea." I glanced carefully at Luca. "Where'd you see the pages?"

"Er. In the greenhouse. In the well." He shuddered.

I understood his reaction. After the original showdown with Owl, the one that had led to his arrest in the first place, William and I had found Luca imprisoned at the bottom of the castle's well. The well wasn't deep, but that didn't matter: it had been a horrible experience.

"So," I summarized, beginning to pace the central aisle, "we know where to look for the second book. Which Owl might have been looking for, along with the others, when he was murdered. But why, Luca?"

It took Luca a minute to answer. Finally he said, "The castle has actually always been there. That storm in the summer, when the tree came down across the wall—that's just when everyone realized it was there, hidden in the forest, like a protection spell keeping it hidden had been broken—does that make sense? But Owl always knew it was there. He—he had a picture of it. Once I asked him about it and he said it has a history, like anything else. He said that history is in a series of books but that I shouldn't ever go near them if I see them. He said they hold dark power. He said any scholar would know them by the symbols on the covers and that all together the books would bring freedom to people in shadow but to anyone else they'd be a terrible curse and then he said of course *I* am a light person and then he . . . he laughed."

I pushed the goggles on my forehead higher up over my hair, thinking.

"And by 'I,' I mean me, in that story," Luca added as an afterthought.

"I know. I wasn't about to see Owl as a 'light' person." More importantly, I asked, "So Thorn thinks you and Owl had a fight over whatever power the books hold?"

"*Someone* and Owl did." Under his hood, Luca's eyes were huge and solemn. "I think Officer Thorn thinks the books must be some kind of key for a hidden magic or treasure, since the castle's been protected for so long. Maybe it's something Owl could have used to escape, she thinks. But after looking at the book you found, I don't think they lead to *that* kind of power. I just think the books are a history, that's all. Probably left behind by whoever lived in the castle last."

My pacing slowed. "Did you tell Thorn all that?"

"I tried, but Red, she doesn't get it. You're my friend, and I know you understand. But everyone else—they just think I'm a scholar, even if I'm kind of funny sometimes. If I go on about books having power they just say, 'well of course you *would* think books are important on their own, but you ought to know that's silly,' and of course murder must have a bigger reason. And I'm sure it *does,* I just couldn't explain it right to Officer Thorn."

At this I stopped. *Luca sees the books as having value, but not enough value to commit murder over. In fact he seems scared of them. But Thorn would say he's lying, that all together the books have magic or some secret, which he and Owl fought over. So if I can find all the books and prove that there's nothing special there, that Luca is right about them being just a history, then that's a point in his favor. It means Owl could have been murdered for something he was doing in town, not because of some strange magical scheme.*

I turned back to Luca, smiling. "Don't worry, we'll figure it out. You know, alchemists deal with symbols all the time. A little scavenger hunt at the castle shouldn't be any problem."

9

Follies and Traps

William and Dusty rejoined us, carrying sacks full of provisions and tools. After distributing the load and grabbing my own cloak and tool belt, I led the little party in sneaking out the back door and hurrying out of town before anyone else caught on. Our trip down the forest road and over the little bridge would have been pleasant, if not for Thorn's accusations following us like a storm cloud. The weight of them made me quiet, and determined.

The castle, too, was quiet. The interior was eerily like the exterior—full of rounded edges, all made of wood; and all the paneling was intricately carved in vine and flower motifs reminiscent of the unruly garden.

"Did this place get an extra hundred years older since I was here last?" Dusty joked as the four of us poured inside. He glanced over the vaunted ceilings and musty walls with an expert eye as William glowed blue, checking for enchantments, and Luca helped me wrestle the door closed. We'd come in by the side door; no one had ever been able to get the castle's monstrous double front doors to budge. Officer Thorn usually kept the side door padlocked, but even that precaution was overkill: vines grew over the entrance in a matter of minutes. Normal people would have needed Thorn's spare keys and a hatchet to get inside, but being an alchemist with a utility belt full of strange substances and tiny tools was occasionally useful.

I smiled briefly at Dusty. I knew that his joke was a cover for his unease at being there—since the castle's discovery, he'd avoided venturing so far out of town. I decided to follow his lead, keeping things light. "Gloria did tell me once that the castle has its own time."

I wonder if Thorn knows Gloria believes that, I added silently, making a mental note to tell the officer later. *Although it might not be convincing, since most of town probably believes it too.* I brushed my long ponytail over my shoulder as I turned to assess the hall. It smelled as mossy as ever.

William snorted and shook his fur. "We need to worry about the present, not the past. I don't notice any spells, but someone could still be hiding somewhere."

Dusty, who had wandered down the entry hall toward the multi-story central room, turned back at this. "An' if they are, there's one of them and four of us."

"It's the creatures I'm really worried about, so let's make sure we're done before dark," I said. William rolled his eyes at me through the gloom but I ignored him, adding lightly, "That gives us six hours or so. Let's try *not* to get into any fights, shall we?"

"*You* certainly don't seem like you'll be fighting." William glared past me at Luca, who stood with his back against the door and his arms wrapped around himself. "Starting to have second thoughts about telling us to look for the books?"

"Comments like that aren't helping." I glared at my rude companion. Since Luca didn't seem like he was going to speak up for himself, I went on, "Unless you've suddenly turned into a book expert, Luca's knowledge will be very useful. Besides, he's the one who knows where to look. Apparently we're headed for some kind of secret room under the greenhouse, so get ready for some digging."

I was kidding—mostly—but William seemed to get my larger point: *play nice.* The four of us made our way through the castle, myself and Dusty carrying lights aloft. We passed by empty reading rooms on either side, moving across a floor tiled in dusty wood. Despite the bright sun outside, the castle was as dark as ever, and perhaps even more creepy. I wondered if Jade was present and almost resolved to try calling to him when a spine-tingling wind picked up and whistled through the central hall around us. Luca shivered behind me, and William grumbled.

"Sense anything now?" I asked him.

"No." The blue glow around William increased for a moment, then subsided. "There's no one else here as far as I can tell. I can't even sense your ghost boyfriend."

"I do *not* have a ghost boyfriend," I said, ignoring curious looks from our friends.

Followed by that chilly breeze, my companions and I traversed the main hall and turned down a corridor toward the back of the castle. There, pressed up against the wood exterior like a lover desperate for attention, was the overgrown greenhouse. We emerged from the back door into its jungle. The light there was teal and green, tainted by ancient glass and waving leaves. The air was tinted by the smell of leaves and wet dirt, and felt far more normal and alive than the air in

70

the castle had. Near the center of the room was the infamous well in which Luca had seen a picture of pages.

"No one's doing any digging here," Dusty remarked, casting a hand over potted plants and plant-ridden pots. "Flagstone floor. Good construction. Tight fit. Now, if we went down that folly, we might find a crack to use. Might be better off finding the door that goes where you want to get, though."

For a moment the rest of us were silent, as though struck by this entirely sensical deduction. I recovered first. "For the record, I was kidding about digging. And I'm very glad you agreed to come along, Dusty. One thing. What's a folly?"

"That's a folly," the gnome answered, walking over to the side of the well and giving it a solid kick before scrambling up the side and dropping his lightstick into the shadowy hole. I leapt after him, struck once more—this time by concern—but Dusty leaned back, oblivious. "See? Thing's barely a story deep. Not even wet any more. Probably they piped or spelled water in, once upon a time. A folly's something that looks like it ought to have a use but doesn't or was made to look old but ain't. Besides, this is all lined with bricks. Only a fool would think that's a real well."

"Guilty," said Luca with a cautious smile at me.

"Stop grinning," William growled, "unless you have an idea how we're supposed to find this lost book of yours and get out of here."

"That's why Red's here." Luca's voice wavered a little, and he held on to the edge of the folly as he paced around it. Its mouth was easily a yard wide—more pond-size than well-size, I realized. Once Luca was halfway around, his face lit by the faint yellow glow of the lightstick below, he pointed down. "There's a chink in the wall down there and a brick

71

loose. That's how I found it. One of the bricks must have fallen out and been put back the wrong way, because it had this symbol on it none of the others did, and when I pried it out, I could see something behind it—rotted stuff, I think—"

"—old shelf," Dusty suggested knowledgeably.

"—and something that looked kind of like leather, like the back of a book, only it wasn't," Luca concluded. "But I couldn't get any of the other bricks out of the wall."

"Wait, it was only *like* a book?" grumbled William.

"Mortar was prob'ly treated to be watertight," Dusty added helpfully.

"Still a stupid place for an actual book," said William.

"It could have been put there after the folly went dry," I pointed out. "Luca said earlier the books were probably left when the castle was abandoned."

This was all William needed to round on me, letting loose all his folly-related frustration. "Oh, so you *did* gather some facts before jumping into this 'investigation.' How reassuring. Here I thought you didn't want to be the local police assistant, and yet the moment Officer Thorn and some blasted scholar come calling—"

"Thorn gave you a job, too. It's not like any of us had much choice."

But William was undeterred. "Ha! If I were to give you a choice between selling potions and getting yourself in harebrained escapades without any plan whatsoever—"

"I have a plan," I interrupted, pausing for dramatic effect while racking my brain for something that sounded methodical. "We're going to do exactly what Dusty suggested. Look for a door."

* * *

We split into two groups. One would search the greenhouse for a trapdoor or hidden staircase; the other would search outside for cellar doors, tunnels, and whatever else could be excavated from the tangle of vines that made up the castle garden. I was eager to find out what kind of plants inhabited the greenhouse (and not too excited by the idea of tromping around in the mud), so I volunteered for inside duty. Dusty, with his construction knowledge, offered to join me. William hustled Luca out the greenhouse's exterior door, mumbling all the while.

"You take this side, I'll take that one. Let's see how quickly we can be done," Dusty said as soon as we were alone, immediately ruining our "stick together and no one gets lost or abducted by criminals" philosophy. Figuring that neither of us could get into too much trouble in one large greenhouse—and that Dusty wouldn't want to wait for me to take samples of every interesting plant—I agreed.

"Should I look for anything in particular?" I asked as I brushed a palm frond from my face and eyed the southern wall, which was all but swallowed up in ivy. I had assumed the wall would be entirely glass, as the western side was, but upon closer inspection I saw stonework reaching about seven feet high, supporting the glass ceiling. *Must've been growing shade plants,* I thought to myself, noting the lack of light.

"The usual," Dusty called, kicking his feet as he meandered north. This was not very helpful until he added, "Outlines of rectangles where there shouldn't be any, grooves in the floor, marks of critters or weather getting in. Things't look like you could press or pull them and something would happen."

73

I bit back a grin. "I suppose I'll know such a thing if I see it?"

"Or after you pull it and something happens," Dusty suggested.

"Dusty, that doesn't sound very careful. I don't think William would approve."

"That's why he's outside!"

Laughing, I turned to work in earnest. Dusty's approach was haphazard, but I had to be at least a little scientific. I started at one corner, right up against the wall, and decided I'd move on from there in orderly lines until I'd zigzagged back to the center of the room. The faster I worked, the sooner we could all get away from the castle and any thought of mist creatures.

Our intent search lengthened into an hour, if not an age. Two sample vials, one pricked finger, three near trippings, and innumerable vines of thorny ivy later, I heard Dusty shout.

"What is it?" I popped my head up from a veil of leaves. I was kneeling at the edge of the wall, trying to find any scour marks on the stones. All I'd gotten so far was a noseful of pollen.

"Tugged on this unmatched sconce," Dusty replied—or at least I thought he did; I struggled to hear him. I staggered to my feet, leaning on a nearby urn. Dusty was still talking. "And this mess of plants fell right on my head."

"So you didn't find the door?" My heart sank—and yet I remained confused. If Dusty hadn't set a mechanism in motion, why could I hear a low, mysterious rumbling?

"Red." Dusty appeared on the other side of the greenhouse from beneath a brown tangle of stems. "*You* just did!"

The moment he said it, I reached the same conclusion. While he was speaking, vines had snaked around my middle and

74

pulled me straight back into the wall, where I went tumbling through darkness.

10

The Forbidden Room

The thing people rarely realized about alchemy was that it was not all mad science and tinkering. The core premise of alchemy, good alchemy, was making things into better, truer versions of themselves. And to make things better, it helped to be prepared for wherever things might start.

That's why, when I found myself lurching backward through frigid air, I had an instant reflex to make things better.

Better how? Stopping myself from falling, for a start. From my hip I grabbed a flask and jammed it straight into the greenhouse floor as it sailed by. The glass shattered against the flagstones—good thing I had on my goggles and griffon talon-tipped gloves—and the potion inside, a thick, instant glue-like substance, solidified around my hand. For an unpleasant moment, I was stuck between the vines on my waist and the glue on my fingers. Fortunately the vines gave up first. I landed with one hand on the floor above my head and my boots scrabbling against a dirt wall, hanging down into a hole in the greenhouse floor.

"What kind of a plan was that?" William barked. I should

have known that even if he was in Luca's group, he'd be monitoring my status or whatever it was that familiars did. Even though he wasn't technically *my* familiar, we'd spent enough time together that no matter where we were, he could sense if I was in danger. He appeared at the edge of the hole above me, glowing fiercely.

"Wasn't . . . really a plan," I admitted, catching my breath. "I panicked."

"Red!" Luca said. "I thought we were being careful!"

"Ugh, not you, too," I grimaced as Luca's head hovered beside William, his eyes scrunched up in concern and censure. In part to avoid their judgmental stares, I focused on the wall in front of me.

"Yes, me too," Luca replied as I hauled myself up, my boots scraping against packed dirt. "What am I supposed to do if you get sucked into some vine dungeon?"

"Find your books a lot more slowly, that's what," I muttered, lurching awkwardly onto the flagstones and searching my pockets for the antidote to the glue.

"Might be a dungeon," Dusty observed from behind William. "But it might also be the cellar you wanted."

"Exactly!" I freed my hand and looked up to find William still glaring at me. "Shine a light down there and see," I challenged him.

Dusty and Luca obliged. William huffed as he peered down. Where I had fallen, the floor was easily a story below us; but the chasm which had opened up ran the length of the wall, and off to our left, a rough-cut staircase was evident.

"Told you," I informed William. "We can go down that way. I just discovered a shortcut."

He didn't look convinced. "You can go, but I'm standing

guard here in case anyone comes," he said. "Send in Prince Charming over there first."

* * *

Luca was indeed stricken over the whole affair, much like a romantic hero. But William's distrust of the scholar had left him ignorant of the real reason for Luca's distress. Remembering the waver in his voice as he recounted Owl's story about the books, it seemed to me that Luca really did believe that the castle was haunted, the books were cursed, or worse—that somehow the ghost of Owl would jump out and claim them.

That was nonsense, of course. Ghosts could only be created in specific circumstances, and I was pretty sure Owl's death didn't fit the bill. But still, I couldn't shake the notion that we had ventured into something off-limits.

Together Luca and I eased ourselves down into the cellar, clambering over stairs as deep as my thigh. The space we descended into was exactly what one would expect: dark, damp, and full of the heady fumes of fungus. In the yellow glow of my homemade lightsticks, the fluorescent mosses coating the earthen walls twinkled like sinister fairy lights. From the middle of the room rose a wide column—the outside of the folly we'd looked into above. A curved desk hugged its rounded edge, stacked high with cabinets. The wall beyond boasted its own array of shelves, all containing jars of all sizes, some still sealed and filled with delightfully oozy things.

With great restraint, I refrained from heading straight for the jars and instead helped Luca look for his book somewhere in the cabinets above the desk.

"Find it and let's get out of here," William rumbled above us.

Dusty remained in between, inspecting the stairwell.

I decided not to fight with William. Truthfully, I wanted to find the books and be gone as much as he did. I had a strange itch between my shoulder blades.

"Hey," I said quietly, leaning over Luca's shoulder as he searched the ponderous wooden furniture. "Find anything promising?"

"No. Not yet." Luca sounded frustrated. "I can't open any of the doors on the cabinets. Red, can you do something about that?"

"Didn't your mother teach you any manners?" I teased, but I was already reaching for a series of small vials sewn into my belt. "I've got a couple different oils. Here, let me look at each door first. I'll use this blade coated in oil to loosen the doors, and then you can open them. We'll go around the circle."

Quickly we fell into a rhythm, working our way around the huge desk. My part of the task was merely mechanical, so my mind wandered. *What in Beyond were the castle owners doing down here?* The desk and shelves would be lovely for experiments, and there were a number of great alchemical fertilizers they could have been making for the greenhouse upstairs. *But the room is so dark.* A lot of creatures in Beyond had night vision to varying degrees. My own wasn't too bad, certainly better than that of the average human, especially with the help of my goggles. But even with them on and my lightstick tucked over my ear, the oppressive gloom of the room hung over me while I worked.

"Red!" William's bark made me jump and nearly drop my knife. "I heard something move."

Luca and I both went deadly still. "Here?"

"No. Somewhere else in the castle," said William reluctantly.

His voice was muffled by the foot or so of earth and flagstone between us.

"I found the mechanism to close the stairs," Dusty called from the corner.

I still hadn't moved. Luca might have stopped breathing. "Okay, but do you know how to open them again?" I asked.

"Pretty sure," said Dusty.

Despite his cheerfulness, I wasn't entirely reassured.

"Just hurry up." William's suggestion was more growl than speech, and I could tell Luca hadn't recognized a word of it. His eyes were round and shiny in the dark.

"It's okay," I told him. "Come on. We're almost halfway round. Can you tell where your loose brick might have been?"

"I'm all turned around," Luca admitted. He began to move again, now yanking open cabinets and frantically running his hands through the interiors.

I resumed work too, asking as I went, "Do you need a light?"

"Yours is good. It's fine. It's fine, it's fine," Luca continued mumbling to himself. "I think it must be somewhere around here. Right around here. Let's see, it would have been the lower shelf. Like—here, Red!"

Luca's voice rose, so loud I almost shushed him. But as I leaned closer, I saw he held an old book in his hands. It was small and slender, but the cover was bulky, covered in the same bark as the first book. And in that familiar gold leaf, the embossed cover read, *Beauty and Shadow; or, the downfall of the cursed prince of the Ring of the Moon, Part 2 of 6.*

"It's only the second one," Luca whispered. "The rest will be somewhere else."

"Come on. Let's open the other cabinets, just in case."

The book disappeared into Luca's voluminous robes. I

moved around the rest of the desk as fast as possible, lurching awkwardly, with Luca practically plastered to my side. The instant I loosened a door, he was inside it. Faintly, I could hear William whine upstairs.

"That's it." Luca fell back a pace once we'd gone full circle. His voice wavered. "But we don't know where—"

"If that's all, then let's get out of here," William rumbled down the stairs. Sometimes his excellent sense of hearing was annoying. But in this case, he was probably right.

"We already figured they were hidden separately," I reminded Luca. "Let's just take this one for now and study it."

"You're right." Luca turned toward the stairs willingly, which was good, because if we'd delayed one minute longer William probably would have dragged us out by our shirt collars. "Okay, let's go."

* * *

Luca and I clambered out of the cellar, and the four of us ran silently through the chilly castle. Even after we'd made it safely out of the grounds, it took a lot of convincing to get William to stop in a glen so that the less athletic among us could catch their breaths.

Convince I did, however. Soon we all sat on a fallen log in the afternoon light, lined up like sun-hungry turtles. As Dusty snacked and rambled about the nutritional value of almonds compared to walnuts compared to dried apricots and the optimal ratios for a good trail mix, I got Luca to accept a cheese and cress sandwich in exchange for the book he'd found.

I took the book mutely. It was just like the first, filled with black and white ink drawings contextualized by simple sentences written in cursive. Altogether, it read:

Unbeknownst to the Drus, another society had taken notice of their revered sweet-cherry tree. The elves who made their home in the same woods where the Ring of the Moon thrived believed that the sweet-cherry was a symbol of honor, the pit at its core a reminder that at its heart, life is ever the same. The elves were led by a council, which was often divided into many warring opinions. The most solid, most powerful group on this council were known as the Stagers, and they used the sweet-cherry as a symbol on all of their pennants. But there came a time when a rebellious group rose up against the Stagers and made a statement of defiance by burning sweet-cherry trees. These elves earned for themselves the name Firebrands. As the two groups of elves fought, the Ring of the Moon suffered, for their most precious trees were dying awful deaths. And so it was that many of the Drus became angry and resolved to fight on behalf of the elven Stagers, to avenge the murdered trees. But there were some Drus who were traitors to this cause, who did not decry the Firebrands. One such Drus was the Prince himself.

"So?" asked Dusty, interrupting his own culinary lecture. "What is it, Red?"

"Something about the Ring of the Moon and a society of elves." I closed the book and handed it back to Luca before rooting around in my satchel for a sandwich of my own. "Was there an elf war around here at one time?"

"Ring of the Moon? Never heard of 'em." Dusty downed the last of his salted cashews and cranberries. "Might've been a bunch of wars back in the day. Belville was just an outpost in the wilderness then. Never heard an elf talk about it nowadays, though."

I looked at William, who shook his floppy ears and looked away. I took that as a "me neither."

"Erm. About that." Luca leaned from his perch so he could see both Dusty and me. I wondered how he didn't overheat, wearing all black out in direct sunlight as he did. "Owl never kept any elven records. He said they weren't worth anything, just stories."

Dusty's chewing paused. "Wasn't he an elf? Or part one, at least?"

"We both are, were, actually." Luca shrugged, then nodded, then held up his hands. "I—I never really asked him about it. It didn't seem like he wanted to talk about it. But there's supposed to be four more books, so maybe they'll tell us more—if we can find them."

"*You're* an elf." From his place at the end of the log, William looked down on Luca like a presiding judge. He was lucky that I'd just taken a huge bite of bread and cheddar, because I'd have given him an earful if I could have. Sure, Luca's scholar uniform made it hard to know much about his ethnicity, but what did that matter? It certainly didn't mean that he ought to be met with hostility when identifying his heritage.

"Um—yes?" said Luca, with the inflection of a child who could sense disapproval but hadn't yet figured out why.

"And as an elf," William continued, "how did you feel about your history being taken from you by your superior?"

Luca's head whipped round to me, his eyes as round and trembly as jelly rings. "I didn't—um—I never—I mean I *did* try to tell him that maybe we shouldn't, but he—"

"And how would you feel," William continued, "upon discovering that a complete set of history books relating to elves had been discovered, and that it might—like all the others—be yanked out of your grasp?"

I swallowed. "Get a grip, William. Thorn said Owl wanted all the books so he could control the castle, not so that he could destroy them."

"She doesn't know that for sure. But she *was* right when she said you're too close to this case." William stared me down, his panting breath ending in a whine. "Either way, I think it's pretty clear who would fight with a scholar over books." With his eyes narrowed at Luca, he clarified, "Another scholar."

I kept my gaze on William, but out of the corner of my eye I watched Luca. He'd buried his head in his hands again. My heart sank like it'd been chained to a free-falling anchor.

He has *had those thoughts.* I knew it at once: Luca, not particularly eloquent at the best of times, couldn't argue with William because William was right. In part. *And why shouldn't Luca feel that way? Owl was awful. But it doesn't mean Luca did anything equally as bad.*

I set my sandwich aside. *We really need to find some other suspects for William and Thorn to focus on.*

11

No Way Out

My resolve was only strengthened as we made it back to Market Square. William ran off to the station to wait for Thorn to get back from her investigations, and Luca slunk off to his shop like he'd already been placed under house arrest. I stood there in the grass of the Square, looking around at the families and couples finishing up their day's shopping or just beginning their afternoon out. My legs tingled, yearning to run. But Dusty was still there, lingering amiably at my side. In the shadow of the trees, he looked older than ever.

"You know it wasn't Luca, right?" I said finally.

Dusty shrugged. "If 't was, I wouldn't blame the boy."

This harkened back to the conversation we'd had that morning, before Thorn had shown up. I shifted, thinking of the things Dusty had told us. "You said Owl was cruel to a lot of people, though, right?"

"Whoever got him did us all a favor." The words stretched thin in his habitually pleasant voice. "Any who can do what Owl did deserves it back at 'em threefold."

The threefold return was a common belief across Beyond,

and I had to admit, I didn't disagree. "Was there anyone aside from Luca that Owl was especially cruel to? Anyone else who would have been mad about the history thing, maybe?"

Dusty snorted. "There's all sorts of elves in town, if you want to go asking every single one. I doubt many of them care much, though. Owl was doing worse than getting rid of some books."

"You keep saying that," I said, dropping down to sit in the cool grass so that I could see Dusty's face better. "But what do you actually mean?"

For a moment he simply shifted from foot to foot, looking off into the distance. The maple branches above us crackled in a light breeze. Birds trilled. Across the Square, children's voices rose sharply in an argument.

"You never met my youngest sister and her kids, did you," Dusty said at last, almost as though the thought had fallen out of the blue sky.

"No, but you've mentioned them quite a bit. They live across the lake, in Highridge, right?"

Dusty turned to look down at me. "D'you have any idea how big that lake is, to someone sized like me?"

"I—I guess I never thought about it," I admitted. Even to me, the lake which abutted Belville was pretty big.

"Why would you." Dusty shrugged. "'Sa thing among gnomes, you know. We don't move. Too much hassle. Too far to go. You stick around town. There's plenty of places there to go, if you know where to look." Just when I was beginning to wonder where all this was headed, Dusty added, "Two years ago my sister packed up her kids and moved 'em all *all the way* out there. Because that's how far she felt like she had to go. See?"

"I'm sorry, Dusty," I said as I started to understand. "She wanted to get away from Owl?"

"Blackmail." Dusty scuffed at the dirt among the tree's roots. "I would've told her even Highridge wasn't far enough to someone like Owl. She should've stayed."

"Does Thorn know?"

"She'd have to be senseless not to," Dusty said, tipping up his cap defiantly. "Blackmail was his game. In the end he never had to follow my sister. There was enough money for him to make here in Belville, bleedin' everybody else dry."

I hesitated. I wanted to ask if Dusty knew of anyone else Owl was blackmailing, but it seemed a little insensitive. The poor gnome seemed to be holding back tears as he thought of his lost family members.

"You'n Luca are good friends," Dusty observed suddenly. "You can ask him what it was like for him, back before you came to town. Ask him if Owl ever had any *real* friends, or if it was all just victims he was reeling in. That's what they do, people like him. They go for the people closest to them. Because they don't care."

"I can see what you mean." *But why would me coming to town have changed anything?* Frowning, I'd just thought to ask Dusty what he meant when I realized he was staring across the park, where a farmer was setting up a stand selling sausages and someone else stood on the corner with roasted hazelnuts. It was only mid afternoon, but my stomach rumbled, reminding me of a half-eaten lunch.

"You could join William and me for dinner, if you want to stick around," I offered to Dusty. "I was thinking of doing a fall pasta."

"Any other day," the gnome replied. The dark cloud surrounding him eased, and he smiled in a way that promised he'd take me up on the offer. "I have to go help Cairn at the antiques shop before closing."

"Oh, in that case, don't let me keep you," I told him. "But thank you, Dusty, for your help today. And for telling me about Owl."

"Don't mention it. Let me know if you go again," said Dusty, just before disappearing. Even though I knew which shop he was headed to, I had to squint through the falling autumn leaves to see him enter. Had he actually rung the bell? Or had he simply leapt down the chimney?

I shook my head and stood, ready to return to my shop. Dusty had given me a lot to think about. Nearly anyone in town could have been angry at Owl, so that left me to focus on other questions. *Who would have sprung him out of jail? And was it the same person who followed him to the castle to kill him?* That seemed like a lot of work, but it wasn't out of the question. *Who was free that afternoon to go kill Owl?* Not many people in Belville had that kind of mobility; most of us were tied to our shops. I thought again of Dusty's disappearing act, and smiled. *Maybe I should look into people who can travel quickly. Although, that could end up being a job and a half, and it'd be hard to say where to begin. I mean really, who'd have thought gnomes would get around so easily?*

As it turned out, it didn't matter how Dusty had left; all that mattered was that I was entirely alone on the street when, like a waft of putrid gas, a sickly-sweet voice washed over me.

"Well, well, well," Gloria said. "Look who decided to return to her shop."

"And a very nice afternoon to you, too," I said without looking. *Four more steps and I can just close my door in her face,* I thought.

"Strange how someone can think it's okay to leave so many dangerous potions all alone. I'd expect a shop owner to be more responsible, wouldn't you?"

"Gloria." I stopped and turned on the spot, already glaring. My eyes found her leaning in the doorway to the beauty salon, as though she was posing for a promotional picture. "The shop is warded, as you very well know. And for those of us who *aren't* withholding information from the police, it's not a crime to leave town."

"I bet it *is* a crime to break and enter a place that doesn't belong to you, though." Gloria examined her shiny nails.

"You couldn't possibly have any idea where I've been." Exasperated, I let my gaze slide past her, looking for any assistance. Ari and Stella were at least civil, unlike their employer. Weren't they supposed to be watching her?

"Couldn't I? I think your defensive attitude says enough, personally. The rest, I leave up to Officer Thorn."

"What do you—seriously?" The last drops of my good mood evaporated. I could have spat on the ground at her well-polished boots. "You went and told Thorn what, exactly? That I happened to not be home? She already knew all about it, thanks very much. It was her idea in the first place."

"Was it? Well, at least I wasn't fool enough to go prancing through the forest when there's criminals on the loose," said Gloria sweetly. "Oh, wait—I forgot, the main suspect is your friend, right?"

Of course she heard Officer Thorn talking to Luca this morning. I glowered. "You aren't so far from being the main suspect yourself, Gloria. If I were you, I'd watch my step."

"Threatening me now, are you?" Gloria's eyes narrowed.

"That's all you ever do. You think I don't notice the way you line up all your poisonous plants on *my* property?"

"Excuse me?" I broke off, running my hands through my hair. Of course I'd noticed how some of the potted plants on my back patio shifted sometimes, but I'd always assumed it was William, or even Gloria herself. Since the plants were unharmed, I didn't care. *And who even knows where the property line between our shops actually is?* A tiny alley divided our two storefronts, and even when I'd bought the building, there had been uncertainty about how much was mine. I'd figured the alley was communal property.

"Keep doing that," said Gloria approvingly as I tugged at loose strands behind my goggles. "Maybe you'll finally shake loose some of the dirt in there."

Now she's going after my hair *of all things? This from the woman who has no actual hair herself, and yet styles everyone else's.* I tried desperately to reign in my disbelief. It didn't work too well. "I have no idea what any of this is about," I burst. "Is there a *reason* you've never liked me?"

The charming autumn afternoon paused as Gloria pushed herself upright and crossed her arms. In the shadow of her shop canopy, dressed in her habitual black and gray, she looked like the most flamboyant reaper to ever hold a scythe. Not that she needed one: the look in her eyes was sharpened to a feather's edge.

"You think I waste my time disliking you?" she challenged me icily.

My hands flailed as I tried to be reasonable. "Well, do you start fights with *everyone* who walks by your shop? Do you care if *they* visit the castle or grow potted plants?"

"*I* didn't start the fight. *You* did. Ask anyone!"

"All I did was walk by!"

"Then I guess you better watch where you walk, hadn't you?" Gloria tossed her feathered crest. "Grow up, Red. Drop the innocent act."

"I already told you, I have no idea—"

Gloria stepped back into the shadow with a look of disgust. "Just stay away from the castle," she said, before striding into her shop and slamming the door behind her. "You can't turn *everything* into your own story."

For a moment I remained on the sidewalk, stunned. *If somehow she is caught up in Owl's murder, you'd think she'd be less obvious about it. What is it about the castle she's so determined to keep secret?*

* * *

Even though I managed to open my shop after all the delays and gossip, I didn't actually do much business. Between hunger and a serious squabbling-with-Gloria hangover, I think I scared off all but the most stalwart of my customers. I certainly knew better than to try making any potions while in that state; my old master, Paracelsus, had literally burned the words *your attitude affects your results* into the wall of his lab. Instead, to pass the time, I busied myself with cleaning, glaring at stains and dust bunnies. I actually stayed open later than I'd meant to, caught up in my own whirlwind of thought.

The sun had long since set by the time I slunk up the apartment stairs and kicked off my boots. William was still out, probably telling Thorn and everyone else in town all about Luca and the elf history conspiracy.

Let him stay out, I thought irritably. *He hates it when I make a racket, anyway.* And there *was* a racket. I clanged and banged just about every pot I owned as I made myself some butternut squash pasta, dumping handfuls of rosemary into the butter sauce for strength.

And when it was finally quiet and I sat at the table to eat, I made it through about three chewy mouthfuls before the noise started up again. This time it was Officer Thorn thundering up the stairs with her customary grace.

Rather than greet her, I said querulously, "William let you in, I suppose? I'm surprised."

"I'm surprised he could hear me knocking after all that din," Officer Thorn agreed. "I could hear you all the way across the square, Red. No, no, no pasta for me, thanks. I had dinner at the tavern. Though it does smell . . . strong."

"Har. Har," I said, though I doubted the officer truly appreciated her own pun; she didn't strike me as someone who cared much for the properties of herbs.

"That's why I'm here, actually." Officer Thorn sat across from me at my tiny kitchen table, tucked into the front corner of the apartment. I eyed her; she'd waved away my offer of pasta, so her statement didn't make much sense to me until she added, "You know where I've been?"

"No."

"Huh. I figured that was why you were mad."

"I'm not mad." I glared at her—and quickly lost that staring contest. I looked down at my pasta again. "I happened to run into Gloria this afternoon, is all."

"Well, you've got to learn some time," Officer Thorn said rather cheerfully, given the situation. "I've put Luca under house arrest. Shop arrest, I guess you could call it, since he lives above the bookstore."

92

"And how exactly is that supposed to help anything?" I set my fork down on the table with a clatter. "I thought you wanted to find those books. How—"

Officer Thorn held up one large hand. "We'll cross that drawbridge when we get there. Ha. Anyway, William told me all about it. Seems to me *you're* the one we really need for book-finding, not the scholar."

"I don't see how either of you can be so heartless about it. It's not as though Luca's going to run away, or steal the books out from under our noses or something. For goodness' sake, he could hardly stand being in the castle again. And now you're running around locking him up, which by the way is probably exactly what Owl would do if he were still alive!"

I bit my lip. Gloria had really unnerved me; I'd said more than I intended. But if it got Thorn to listen, maybe that wasn't so bad.

"Listen, Red," she was saying. "I know you don't agree with me. And that's fine. But that doesn't change the fact that this case is still dangerous. Didn't your dog hear someone in the castle?"

"He can probably hear *you*, you know."

"Probably not. He's busy." When I raised an eyebrow, she explained, "I'm having him watch Gloria."

"What happened to Ari and Stella?"

"I gave them a break when the salon closed for the day. Besides, sometimes I think they're just talk, and we need more than that right now." Thorn shrugged, and in the ensuing pause, I sighed. Though I poked at my pasta, I found I didn't feel like eating any more. Everything was so jumbled up.

"Trent did the spell," she continued after a minute, as though we were talking about decorations at a birthday party, not accusations of murder. "It's not a bad one, Red. Luca can still move freely between his apartment and his shop. He's got all his books right there with him. He'll be fine. He just can't get out the doors or windows, which is probably for the best."

She scratched at one ear and changed the subject slightly. "Do you know anything about his life before he worked for Owl?"

"Who? Luca? No." I paused, thinking. "Didn't he always live in town, like everyone else?"

"He didn't want to tell me about it," Thorn mused.

"Maybe that has to do with Owl," I pointed out. "Have you heard Dusty talk about him? I think he was abusive. Not to mention it sounds like he was blackmailing half—"

"I know, Red. I know. You don't think I've been doing nothing, do you?" Thorn didn't wait for an answer before continuing, "All attempts to find Owl's family have turned up nothing. Plus, Trent did a tracking spell, out on the road outside the castle. Looking for any magic or lingering emotions. It picked up on some strong stuff that went up along the hiking trails. Traces of glamours and the like."

That explained why we'd hadn't run into Thorn and Trent at the castle: they'd been trekking all over the mountainside. But I wasn't mollified. "So?"

"*So,* it's clear there was more than one person mad at Owl. I'm not closing up this case yet, Red."

"Good."

"Which means I need you to keep it together. Tomorrow Trent and I are going back out to the castle, to look through the inside this time. We need to figure out where the murder happened. I want you to come too. And then I want you to take a look at that getup that we found on Owl and see if you can learn anything about it."

I'd forgotten about the "getup" on Owl. Thorn's words startled me into recalling what Jade had said about the kitchen cloths. "Okay," I agreed slowly, musing. "I think I have some ideas that might help."

"Good. Trent's doing some spell mumbo-jumbo at the station tonight. Last ditch attempt to find anyone connected to Owl." Officer Thorn waved a hand. While I was glad William wasn't present to be offended, I understood her bemusement. To the uninitiated—which included me—the ways of spell-working often seemed time-consuming and inscrutable. But then, so did a lot of science, so I tried to keep an open mind. Thorn went on, "In the morning we'll come and get you after breakfast. One way or another, I want this thing solved."

12

Round the Neck

Contrary to the turn of the seasons, it seemed to me that the sun rose earlier than ever the next morning. I'd run out of my stores of baked goods, so I had to rifle through my overstuffed cabinets for some oats and dried fruit to make oatmeal with. (The person who could eat oatmeal without some kind of sweetener in it was a dark person, indeed.) On top of that, the loose leaves of my tea spilled all over the place as I was filling the strainer ball to brew myself a cup of caffeine. I frowned at the mess, feeling cursed. Most likely I was only cursed by my own lack of concentration, but knowing that didn't help my mood.

So I did what I always did when I was getting grumpy: I went out to tend my plants. Gloria had called them poison, but nothing could be farther from the truth. I had dozens, most in pots and other containers, all beautiful as far as I was concerned. In my days as a traveling alchemist, they went everywhere with me. In fact, most were souvenirs of my adventures. There was a cactus from the Shifting Sands that only flowered under the light of the full moon, and in an old glass tea kettle, a rare rainbow kelp that had drifted in from the open sea. I had all the usual herbs too, of course: basil, mint, rosemary, thyme. Usually I used them in my own cooking, but sometimes they were useful in stocking the shop, too. Alchemy mostly dealt with elements and minerals, but I'd always been drawn to living, growing things. Especially living, growing things that didn't care what their prickly neighbor did or who might have murdered whom.

"Thorn reporting!"

The familiar voice rapped out from the corner of the house. The officer beamed at me as she strode over to the back patio. "Good, you're out here already. Are your chores about done? Don't want you getting too rooted."

I straightened from an old barrel holding a tiny, wizened dragon's blood tree, and restrained myself—just barely—from emptying the rest of my watering can over Officer Thorn's head. It was far too early for puns. "I just need to run up and grab my cloak and my kit," I told her. "Is there anything in particular you want me to bring? I've got plenty of lights."

She nodded along absently, surveying my tiny backyard. "Those goggles of yours should do the trick. We're picking up Trent on the way there. He's still at the station cleaning up."

"Did he find out anything overnight?"

"Not a whit." The officer shrugged. "Maybe we've been too focused on the castle grounds and this book nonsense. Today's a clean slate."

"Fine." I set aside my gardening tools and ran up to my apartment, passing a groggy William on the stairs. No doubt he was out to learn what all the commotion was about—*or maybe,* I realized, *to report something about Gloria.* He'd been up later than me the night before, so we hadn't had a chance to talk.

Of course, my curiosity about a productive crime-solving conversation between Thorn and William was laid to rest when I tumbled back down the stairs, gear in hand, to overhear arguing.

"Don't know what you expect to find," William was grumbling. No doubt he was disgruntled to learn I'd be out for the morning; that meant he would be in charge of the shop, and since he was already up, he wouldn't be able to get out of opening. "The whole town knows about the investigation already, so whoever did it has had plenty of time to cover their tracks."

"I think the entire town is *involved* in the investigation," I said lightly, swinging my multicolored cloak over my shoulders.

"All hands on deck," Thorn agreed. "It's Guild procedure. But I've only told Red and Trent about our plans for today, and you know what he's like. Never met a Witch so good at keeping a secret. Oh, speaking of, you'll like this, Red."

I paused in adjusting my belt. "Will I?"

"Luca mentioned it yesterday," Thorn continued, unaffected. "Apparently, scholars all wear special pendants with memory charms on them. Some sort of weird club thing. They never take them off. I want you and Trent to look at Owl's and see if you can learn something."

"We could try," I said reluctantly. "But I bet the charm is to help them remember stuff like dates, not real-life killers."

"That's what I said at first." Officer Thorn clucked. "Sometimes I worry about that boy. Even if he isn't a murderer. Ah, well. Time's wasting—time to go."

I paused to thank William for watching the shop. It wasn't entirely his fault that Luca was stuck at home, after all, and being mad at everyone wouldn't get me anywhere. William stuck his tongue out at me. It only made him look cuter.

"All right, then." As I caught up with Thorn in the alley that would take us out to the Square, she rubbed her green hands briskly. "An officer of the law, an alchemist, and a Witch. Let's go see what we can find."

* * *

For all Officer Thorn's energy, we didn't make it far. In fact, we didn't even make it to the street before we were hailed.

Oh, brother. I'd meant to keep my bristling to myself, but I must have said something aloud, because Thorn put a heavy hand on my shoulder as the beauty parlor's side door swung open and two forms leapt out to talk to us.

"Officer, Red, we have to talk to you!" Ari and Stella waved us over to the shadows on their side of the alley, beaming, looking like they'd just doused themselves in glitter.

The fairies made a brief report to Officer Thorn—Gloria, it seemed, got up to very little aside from keeping the residents of Belville looking beautiful—and turned to me.

"Red, we need more copper-flake skin cream," they said.

"Okay, no problem. I can get it to you after—"

"And you wouldn't *believe* what Gloria's been saying!"

"Is that so." I rolled my eyes, knowing that it wouldn't affect them in the least. I'd long ago come to the conclusion that Ari and Stella sought me out not so much for alchemical concoctions as for a person to talk to. I couldn't blame them; Gloria herself was not the chatty type and making reports to Officer Thorn wasn't everyone's favorite pastime. Most of the sisters' prattle was harmless, but their timing was terrible.

"She keeps saying she's going to raise our rent when she *knows* we don't make that much money! And she said she's going to block off the alley, can you believe it? How would we ever get to your shop when we need things? She talks about it all the time though. We hardly ever get a moment to ourselves. *We* think she's all worked up about something *else*. And then the three-thirty hair appointment yesterday told us that it's because of a feud with the old bookseller!"

"Hold up there." Thorn shifted, as though tempted to take a knee while talking to the fairies. "Which bookseller? You mean Owl?"

With a chiming sound, which may have been a laugh, Stella manifested a pair of sparkling wings and flew right up to Thorn's eye level, tapping her on the nose. "Of course we do!"

"Why didn't you tell *me*, then?" asked the Officer.

"You're right here, aren't you?" Stella beamed sweetly. Maybe it was my cynicism carrying over from the night before, but the expression felt a bit false.

"Anyway," said Ari. "It's all just nonsense."

"We both know there's something *else* going on," the fairies affirmed together. "She gets this faraway look, and did you *see* the new necklace she has? It looks really old and valuable. Just the kind of thing a lover might give their beloved! Can't you just imagine? What if she fell in love and moved away and sold the shop?"

"That sounds a little drastic," I said, doing my best to see the reason in the situation. It was pretty well obscured by glimmer and pixie dust and over-dramatization. "Now, if you'll excuse us, Officer Thorn and I have some errands to run—"

"Oh, of course! But don't forget to come see us later, okay? You too, Officer! Your nails are looking great still! Byeeeee!"

With mirrored head tilts and waves, Ari and Stella saw us off. Thorn practically towed me out of the alley and halfway down the street before looking down with a grin.

"Errands. Nice."

"I've found that the best policy with them is 'less is more,'" I returned, settling my knapsack more securely over my shoulder.

"Isn't that the truth. Not that Ari and Stella aren't nice folks. And they *have* been pretty good at keeping an eye on Gloria."

Thorn paused, and I waited until we'd passed a large family of dwarves and foxkin to guess. "Thinking about what they said about Gloria and Owl?"

"It could be nothing," she said. "Gloria has feuds going with half the town."

I was about to agree, if reluctantly, when inspiration struck. "Wait—what if it's not a feud? What if Owl was her lover, and she has the pendant Luca was talking about?"

"Let's not get *too* ahead of ourselves, Red," Thorn cautioned. "We don't even know if Owl's pendant is missing."

"I know, I know," I said, as Thorn chuckled to herself. We turned off Market Square and headed down toward the police station. Beyond the squat wooden sentry, the forest loomed. And from the station yard, a stick-like figure waved. Trent.

Officer Thorn waved back and picked up her pace. "Come on. The game's afoot!"

13

The Heart of the Castle

"The magic says Owl died that evening, right before we showed up," Thorn summarized cheerfully as we traipsed into the woods. "The way I see it, anyone in town could've scampered off to the castle and gotten in a fight with Owl. Although," she added, an afterthought, "you're probably safe, Red."

"Oh thanks, seeing as I was just as surprised as you when we found him."

"Not to mention terrified of whatever the murderer was trying to feed his body to," Thorn remarked with satisfaction. Above her, a pack of geese squawked as they cut across the sky. I wished one would fly down and mess with her perfect hair.

"I was not." But, recognizing a useless conversation when I met one, I leaned around Thorn to look at Trent. "Speaking of those things. Luca thinks they were wendigos, maybe. How's that sound to you?"

"Beats me." Trent shrugged. "I checked the Belville Grimoire left behind by the last Witch, but it doesn't say much. Nothing about angry spirits or whatever. Just an old fey tale about a cursed castle."

"Cursed, or haunted?" I clarified, stumbling as we came upon the old bridge.

Thorn snorted. "Does it matter?"

"Definitely cursed," Trent affirmed. He reached up with one bony fist and cuffed the officer on the shoulder, saying, "You're lucky some of us pay attention to this stuff. Haunted means there's things there that don't want to be disturbed. Cursed means *you* could wind up being the next to haunt it.

"But," he added, after due consideration of this sobering fact, "I brought along some amulets. Figure we should be okay."

Heartening as Trent's presence might or might not be, all the hairs at the back of my neck rose as we clambered into the castle garden. The day had turned gray and heavy, and the fog seemed to chase us through the gap in the wall. Thorn marched us straight to the side door; she and Trent had been over the front door and its environs the day before. As we followed, Trent chucked something at me: a small satchel, it turned out, one that smelled of heliotrope and myrrh. Despite his lack of explanation, I assumed it was meant for protection and tucked it gratefully into a pocket. Like a well-oiled magitech machine, the three of us batted ever-present vines out of the way and got ourselves inside.

Trent and Thorn fell into a discussion of the ghostly figures while I looked around, listening not to their conversation but to the castle itself. Even the silence seemed to have a shadowed quality, like there was something looming just beyond it.

Something like Jade, I thought, a little uneasily. *I mean, he does live here. Doesn't he?* I had to admit I'd been disappointed not to see him the day before. He'd told William that he found it hard to approach people; maybe groups of visitors made him shy.

Or, warned the cautious voice in my head that sounded a lot like a certain familiar, *there's a more nefarious reason he didn't want a bunch of people to see him.*

"Red. Red! Are you coming or not?" Thorn's voice snapped me back to the present, and I followed my companions through the familiar hallway and into the castle's central, vaulted room.

"There." Officer Thorn turned and pointed in the direction of the front doors, which opened directly into the hall we occupied. "I want to start by taking a look at those doors."

Trent chuckled. "Good luck with that."

I could see what he meant: heavy vines wound their way along the door frame, one on either side of the massive entrance. Tendrils and leaves obscured the doors themselves. I bit my lip. "I don't think those vines have always been there. Have they?"

Thorn shrugged as she began walking toward them. "You're the one who's been in here most recently, Red."

"We didn't even bother looking at the front door. We headed straight to the back," I explained. "But now I wish I had looked around some more."

"Come to think of it, I did lead Team A during the sweep." Thorn must have been referring to her initial search for Owl after his escape; Trent and I exchanged an amused glance at her name for her conscripted helpers. "We came through here. I don't remember any vines at all."

"It could just be a sign that the castle's becoming wilder," Trent pointed out. "Maybe something about the murder or the creatures is upsetting the balance."

"Or removing the books," I realized with a stab of guilt. *Talk about playing with things you don't understand.*

"Or it could be a sign the murder happened here, and the body was moved outside afterward," said Thorn stubbornly. "I want a full examination of this mess."

For all his irreverence, Trent knew a call to action when he heard it. He flipped his hair back over his shoulders—today his T-shirt was emblazoned across the back with a broom and the words "clean up before you go," which seemed both oddly appropriate and mildly threatening—and focused intently on the nearest plant. His eyes glowed purple and it made me dizzy to watch.

I slipped my goggles down over my eyes and walked to the other side of the doorway to examine the other plant. My investigation took all of two minutes. Much as Thorn might suspect them, the vines looked like simple blackberry vines to me. I took some samples just in case, but there wasn't much else for me to do.

Thorn'd been watching Trent with crossed arms but shifted as I came near. "Well?"

"There's not much here," I said, pushing my goggles up. "No blood as far as I can see."

"We'll wait and see what he has to say. I want him to look in the greenhouse too, in case there's some link between the plants out here and in there." She jutted her chin at Trent before fishing around in the pockets of her prim uniform. "While he does that, will you check up on this for me?"

As she held it out, I realized she'd brought along one of the cloths that had covered Owl's body. I took it from her, careful to close the fingers on my gloves first. A quick survey showed some white fibers hidden in the fabric folds, but nothing else of note. Even without Jade's words ringing in my ears, I immediately thought of a kitchen towel.

Officer Thorn seemed to see where my thoughts were going, and she grinned. "I brought it along to see if I could find a match. But since I can't talk to the castle resident, it's a better job for you." Thorn raised an eyebrow at me. "Care to track down your ghost boyfriend?"

"He is not my boyfriend," I protested. "He isn't even a ghost."

Thorn shrugged—a bit conspiratorially for my taste—and waved me on.

I fought the urge to stick my tongue out at her, like William might have done. Tucking the cloth carefully into my knapsack, I headed deeper into the castle.

From the central hall, more than a dozen hallways branched out, blossoming into rooms and crisscrossing each other in labyrinthine patterns. Though I knew how to get to the side door and how to get to the greenhouse, I had no idea where to find the kitchen. Truthfully, my best option was to yell for Jade and hope he heard me, but I didn't want to do that while standing right next to Officer Thorn. I moved toward the back of the hall, where a staircase led to an open second story. My lightstick turned the green-tinted, dusty wood a cozy golden color. When I thought I was far enough from the crowd, I called out curiously, "Jade?"

"Rrred!" The voice came from above and then suddenly from ground level. Part of me was glad Jade remained invisible for whatever floating was involved in that process. "I noticed you arrive, but I wasn't sure if I ought to approach—you have a charm on you, I think? That is a good idea. Have you come for more books?"

"No, not yet," I answered, smiling at the interest in Jade's voice. It set me at ease to think that Jade wasn't malevolent enough to be held back by Trent's charm.

"So you wanted to visit me?"

"Sorry to disappoint you." William would have said I was being too friendly, but Jade made it so easy. I dug the towel out from my knapsack. "Actually, I have a cloth from outside, and I was wondering if you could take a look at it for me. You said they came from the castle's kitchen, right?"

There was no noise, and I felt a little silly holding a towel out into empty space. But when he spoke, Jade was as gallant as ever. "That is far from disappointing. I am glad to be of use. I can show you where it came from, if you would like?"

"Yes, please." I stowed the towel again.

Jade seemed hesitant. "Would you mind extinguishing your light? There is no danger, I assure you. Orr . . . if you prefer, I could take hold of your hand . . ."

"This is fine." I shook the lightstick, deactivating it, and stowed it in a voluminous cloak pocket. In the ensuing gloom, Jade's features became distinguishable. He stood off to one side, smiling at me. He was in sharper focus today, I realized. I could see the stitching in his cape and the strands of his hair pulled back from his face.

"Are you stronger here?" I asked as, with a little bow, he led the way down a side corridor toward the back corner of the castle.

"Perhaps a little," he admitted, angling himself so that he walked at my side, only fractionally in the lead. "There is tradition here which I may draw from."

"You know that makes no sense to me, don't you?"

"I have every faith that you will figure it out."

"Uh huh. Why is it I can see you so well, Jade? Why were you able to hold me in place when you told William you could only move small things?"

"That was also an effect of the castle." For a moment he looked troubled. "I am sorry to have hindered you, Rred. I'm afraid in the immediacy of the situation, I lost my head. It was my first thought to draw on the magics here to hold you, and—"

"—and to conjure up the fog," I finished. "That *was* you."

"To make the moonlight reflect." In the gloom, I could see Jade's smile flash.

"Not bad." I grinned, seeing that he was proud of himself. We crossed a threshold into a long, table-lined room with stoves at each end. "This is the kitchen, then?"

"Yes. The cloths would have been here," Jade said, striding over to a woven basket tucked under one of the tables. It was one of a series of baskets, all lining the wall. The one Jade gestured to was empty when I tipped it up to look. Curious, I poked into a few of the others; little but shriveled roots and lost spoons rewarded my effort.

"The other two here," Jade said as he watched me work. "I think they have charms like yours, is that right? I can sense them."

"By the front door, you mean? Yeah, that's Officer Thorn and Trent, the Witch. Actually, you might want to meet Trent—maybe he can help you. He'd be more help than William, anyway."

"Perhaps." Jade's voice was distant.

"Let me know if they come back here," I added as I continued working around the room, my goggles pulled down, glancing over every surface and hidden storage bin for any evidence. "You can do that, right? I'd like to be prepared. If Thorn comes around and yells and makes me jump, I'll never hear the end of it. She's already making fun of me about the creatures."

"I can." The absentness faded from Jade's voice. "Does the good officer know about you?"

I turned sharply from squinting at the dust on a door frame. "Do *you* know about me?"

Still at the back edge of the room where we'd started, Jade spread shadowy hands in a placating gesture. "I only refer to what I have read in the library about the island clans."

"I don't do the 'Seer' thing." I stopped, hearing my voice become abrupt. It was the same tone I used with William when he brought up my past. I loved my parents and my home very much—I wasn't running from anything. I just didn't fit in among mystics, that's all. And usually I made a point of not telling anyone I came from a family of Seers because I preferred *not* to explain it. "Is that why you came to me? Because—"

"Pardon me, but no, Rred," Jade interrupted.

"Okay, well, how did you know?"

"I hope you will forgive my assumption," Jade said after a moment. "I—I thought it was obvious. The way you move, and your hair . . . "

"Oh." I lifted a hand, knocking my goggles askew and sifting my fingers through said hair. No one had ever said anything about seeing the tiny glittery highlights in it before, not even Gloria, and hair was her business.

"And your name," Jade continued softly.

This time I sighed, then chuckled. "My moms used to call me Cinnabar. William said I should just use that if I wanted my heritage to be a secret, but I thought it was too on-the-nose for a professional alchemist. I didn't think anyone outside of the Islands realized that Seers in my clan name their children after colors."

"I've spent a long time in the library," Jade said as though apologizing.

"*Do* you think that's why I can see you so well?" Since the cat was out of the bag, we might as well examine it. "Because my family has dealings with ghosts, I mean."

Jade moved closer, leaning against a nearby table. "But I am not a ghost."

"Right, shadow, I know. I just thought . . ." I sighed. "This is why I avoid telling people, to be honest. It just makes everything more confusing. I've never fully understood all the traditions that go along with Seeing. I really wish I did."

By this point I'd entirely forgotten about searching the kitchen. There wasn't anything there to find, anyway; I knew that. What I didn't know was why I'd confessed to Jade. I'd never said as much to anyone—not even myself.

Jade moved closer again so that he stood next to me, distracting me from mindlessly picking at my gloves.

"I think that is why you can see me," he said very softly. My head snapped up, my eyes fixed on his. "Not everyone will perceive me, or ghosts, or other such things, as you know. Not everyone wants to know hidden truths. But you look for them and you let them show themselves as they are. Even if what they are is monstrous. That is not because you come from Seers, Rred, that is because of who you are.

"It is also—" Jade stopped, and stood still a moment. "Officer Thorn and the Witch are coming, I believe."

14

Symbols and Hearsay

"Aha! There you are," Thorn declared, striding into the shadowy kitchen like she was about to make an arrest.

"Geez, it's not like I was on the run from the law," I muttered, clutching my arms around my middle, blushing, and generally acting extremely guilty. Rather than listen in to our conversation, Jade had politely disappeared.

"You should've been," Thorn informed me. "Why'd you bust a hole through the greenhouse yesterday? I told you to look for books, not destroy the castle."

I winced. "That must have been William. We were surprised by a trapdoor, and he wasn't pleased."

"I'm not pleased either, with the breach in security. It was as much as Trent could do to make a patch. We couldn't even put it in place yet, because the new glass has to cure. So now I have to come out this way yet again. Why didn't you turn on the lights?" Officer Thorn concluded. She waved at Trent, who conjured dancing lights with a snap of his fingers. I cast my eyes around the room even though I *knew* Jade was gone.

"Haven't seen a kitchen like this since school." Trent began nosing around, poking his head under tables as though looking for used gum or graffiti. "How old's this place, anyway?"

I cleared my throat. Yet again, I'd failed to get any castle-related intel from Jade. "Luca might know."

"We're about done here for today," Thorn said as Trent continued prowling. "Trent here says nobody but me touched the front door. Anything on the cloth?"

I filled her in on the little Jade had said and then fell into musing. "So the vines could mean nothing after all. I wonder if Owl really *was* looking for the books. If he was, it's kind of sad, when you think about it."

"He was dead right next to it, Red. What more do you need?" Thorn snorted. "What's sad is that he chose a life of crime."

That's what I meant—he got so close but so far. But I didn't feel like arguing the point, particularly because I wasn't that interested in feeling pity for Owl.

In the silence Officer Thorn glanced across the room to see the local Witch poking his head into an ancient stove. "What are you doing? Looking to get yourself made into a pie?"

"I was just looking at these weird symbols." Trent's voice was muffled, and when he pulled his head back, his bangs and nose were sooty. "Looks like something I saw in World Cultures once. Figured maybe they're important, and look, behind them was this."

Rather than walk across the room, Trent lobbed a small rectangular object through the air. With a deft movement, Thorn caught it before it hit her square in the face. In the ensuing cloud of ash, she coughed and shoved the thing at me.

"Another of the books," I realized, tracing my hands over the darkened bark cover. I wasn't exactly happy to see it. In fact, I was starting to get a bit suspicious—even resentful—of the way these things turned up.

"Go on then." Thorn prodded me, literally. "What's it say?"

"More about the Drus, probably. I'd rather look at it in better light—no offense, Trent." I could hear my mother saying *magic lenses don't count for everything, you'll still ruin your eyes by squinting, Cinnabar,* as though she was leaning over my shoulder just like she had when I was eight years old. I wrapped the book in an old scarf from my knapsack and tucked it in a hidden pocket.

Trent shrugged and his dancing lights waggled over his head as though they agreed with his lopsided grin. A thought occurred to me and I asked him, "Would you mind copying down the symbols you saw? At this point, to make any sense of this, I think we're going to need all the help we can get."

Thorn nodded authoritatively. "Excellent excuse to stop by the book store, Red."

"I didn't mean—"

"No, no, it's no good protesting. I'm interested in what more the scholar has to say for himself, anyway. We've done good work here, so we've got the time. And I still want you to come back to the station with me afterward, to look at the rest of the getup on Owl. The family's had the customary day to get back to me by now, and I can't wait much longer."

"I'm gonna pass on the bookstore," Trent said. "I've got something cooking in the cauldron back home that I've got to get back to."

"Just you and me, then," I said to Thorn. "And, I can't believe I'm saying this because I thought William was the only one who won't mind his manners, but you had better be nice. Just because you think Luca is a suspect doesn't mean you shouldn't be civil!"

* * *

"Listen, if you want to really prove your innocence," said the Officer an hour later, with a distinctly aggressive tone to her voice, "then you better start helping out with the investigation. Time to step up to the plate. Some might say . . . tee time."

Thorn winked at me over the bookshop desk, which she had lumbered behind to tower over Luca, who slipped further off his stool by the second. I glowered.

"I *warned* you about this," I reminded her. "I'm not making tea for anyone who can't be nice. Look at Luca! You're scaring him!"

"Well, what are you?" Thorn put her hands on her hips and stared down her long nose at the scholar. "Are you a rabbit or are you someone who wants to clear their name? Granted, I'm not so sure you *can* at this point, lad. But you could do us all a favor and confess everything you're holding back."

"Um . . ." Luca's gaze was fixed firmly to the floor. The newest book from the castle lay in plain view on the counter, like the last cookie left at a banquet of ravenous wolves. "I do want to help, really I do, but it's just . . . see I don't know anything about the third book, especially since I haven't looked at it, and I don't know yet what the symbols mean and I'm not even sure what Owl thought the books would teach him and—and—" Briefly his gaze flicked up to me. I did my best to look reassuring, but I was so annoyed at Officer Thorn that I wasn't sure it showed. Luca stammered, "Were you able to find his pendant at least?"

I answered first. "Not at the castle, but we haven't—"

"That's for us to know and you to never mind." Before I could say more, Thorn cut in. "Now why is it you think the necklace is so important?"

"Well, you see, well—everyone has one, every scholar I mean, he always told me never to take mine off. If you don't have it on, then you aren't—aren't really a scholar. That's what he said. So I really don't think he would ever . . ."

"You don't think," said Thorn, "that he might give it to his girlfriend, for example?"

Luca's hood nearly slipped off, he turned his head so fast. His eyes went as wide as saucers. "Owl had a—had a partner? Wh-who?"

"Gloria. But that's just gossip. Though she *still* hasn't explained why she was at the castle that day," I said to Thorn, crossing my arms.

"That's enough discussing evidence in front of a suspect," Officer Thorn reprimanded me. She clapped Luca on the shoulder. If he hadn't caught himself, he'd have gone headfirst into his desk. "Forget about all that. Let's have a look at that book, shall we?"

Luca hesitated. "It's the third one, for sure," he said as he glanced over the title. Clearing his throat, he began to read:

> *Prince Kalos of the Ring of the Moon was known to say that the most important aspect of the sweet-cherry was its original meaning, back in the time of the beginning of the Drus. Then, the flowers symbolized abiding, returning love. The Prince was young; his mother the Queen knew better, that the sweet-cherry's royal connotations were important too. When the elves began fighting, the Queen remained neutral. But the Prince was known to be against the Stagers, who had re-purposed the symbol he loved so well. And therefore, thought the people, he*

was on the side of the sweet-cherry burners. The Prince was decried for being misguided, thoughtless, and wild. One day one of the highest-ranking of the elves came to the castle of the Drus seeking shelter. A hunting party had gone awry, she said, and she feared for her life. She was one of the Stagers, accustomed to Drus support. But at the castle gates at the base of the oldest sweet-cherry left in the forest, she met with Prince Kalos. The Prince refused to let her in. He told her that the Drus wanted no more of this elven discord. When she begged, threatened, and pleaded, each time he said no. And for this, the elf cursed him.

"Doesn't make much sense to me," Thorn observed.

"Probably because you still haven't read the first two." I bit my lip. *A cursed prince. Like we need more melodrama.* "'Stagers' is the name the books give for a bunch of elves trying to squash an internal rebellion. Does it sound at all familiar?"

The officer shrugged. "There was an elf community higher up on the mountain, way back when I started out at Belville Station. Small affair, though. Don't recall them having any name for themselves. That's something this one ought to know."

Luca flinched, but Thorn merely waved her hand at him without making contact. When the moment had passed, he rustled through the desk drawers to produce a scrap of paper and magitech quill. "I'll make a note to look up the elf names in the Belville history collection," he said as he scribbled. "But like I told you, Owl never kept much about them."

"We know." Thorn watched Luca carefully as he wrote; no doubt William had shared his suspicions with her in full.

Luca's hidden face was hard to read, though, and he offered no further comment. At last, Thorn turned to me. "On to the station, Red. We haven't got all day!"

"I have to stop by my shop for some extra sample vials. I'll meet you there," I promised. Thorn saluted and the door shut loudly behind her. The silent bookshop reeled, readjusting to her absence. I cleared my throat. "Hey, are you doing okay? As well as you can be, I mean?"

Luca tossed his quill down amongst the loose papers on his desk. For a moment he bit his lip. Then he smiled at me. "I'm okay. Thanks for asking, Red. I mean, it's not really *so* bad, you know? I have an excuse now to stay inside and . . ."

He waved his hand at the piles of research around him, and I took it he didn't mean "clean." I chuckled.

"Mostly I just—it bothers me how much I don't know, Red," Luca added suddenly. "Owl always knew everything. I never really realized how much I . . . just don't know."

I paused, setting my hand on the desk. "I know, but it's okay, Luca. We're going to figure it out. Besides, no one really expects you to know all this town history stuff by heart, not yet, and Owl left you at a disadvantage. If you get stuck, maybe try sending Cairn a note? It'd have to go through Thorn, of course, but it might be worth it. Cairn seems to know a lot about local history for someone who's a transplant like me. Maybe it comes from selling all those antiques."

"Thanks." Luca straightened, and his teeth flashed as he smiled again. "I'm really glad you're here."

Again I hesitated, and Dusty's words came back to me. *Ask what it was like before you came.* But I didn't like it—didn't like thinking that something about me had created some kind of change in Owl, or in Belville. I was just an alchemist. So, for

117

the moment, I just smiled at Luca and slipped out the door.

* * *

Going from the bookstore to my shop was a straight shot, one I normally could walk in about ten minutes depending on foot traffic. But as the side street ended and Market Square opened up to my left, something bright crimson drew my attention.

My stomach was growling, and my head was spinning with thoughts about Officer Thorn's myriad demands and accusations, not to mention the new installation of the Drus story. I had to blink several times before I understood why I'd stopped. Causing disruption in the shoppers in front of me, Gloria had cut a path straight out from her shop and into the park. She stood there now, her forehead against the trunk of an oak tree. The leaf-strewn grass around her lay empty; no one in the Square was about to go ask Gloria what was wrong.

My mothers always told me that I had a tendency to ask the wrong questions.

My feet directed themselves toward Gloria of their own accord. I'd say it was about fifty percent sympathy that motivated me, honestly. With the fairies' rumors still ringing in my ears, I was plain curious.

"Gloria, is everything okay?" I asked as I came under the oak's canopy of bare branches.

"What do *you* care?" Her voice was low, but it cut through the quiet evening easily enough. In the cold air, not only her breath but the plumage atop her head seemed to smoke. "Hoping for something to report back to the officer?"

"Listen, not everything has to come back to that." *Though apparently it does for* you, I thought. I tried to rein in my voice and give it another go. Gloria seemed more upset than usual, and I wanted to cut her some slack. "I just wanted to be neighborly, that's all."

"*Neighborly?* In this town? Please! Everything anyone around here knows about neighborliness could be contained in a book about half a page long." She whirled away from the tree trunk, and as she did, I caught sight of a wooden circle swinging from her neck. The shiny brown stood out against her dull black clothes.

"Oh." I focused on the necklace, ignoring her comment about books. "Where'd you get that?"

"This? I've always had this." Gloria's hand went to the pendant at her breast, and she narrowed her eyes as she looked from it to me. "Why? What are you trying to say? You think I *stole* it?"

"Let's be serious," I said, taking a step back. Her eyes had a black sheen to them, and I couldn't be sure if that was emotion or some kind of magic. "Gloria, don't you think you're going a bit overboard with all the accusations?"

"*I'm* not the one making accusations. Not that you'd understand." Gloria sniffed and turned away. "Everything always works out for you. I know your type. But sometimes . . . for the rest of us, things just don't work out."

For the first time, I heard the hurt in her voice, underneath the venom. It was like catching a glimpse of someone who'd been locked away. "Gloria, I don't know what's going on, but . . . where I'm from, they have a saying. 'If it hasn't worked out, you haven't walked far enough.'"

Again she snorted, black puffs of smoke obscuring her frown. "That's ridiculous."

I had been about to walk away after her rude reaction, but I paused. "You know, Gloria, you're not as alone as you think. I'm new here too, after all."

"Of course I'm alone," she snapped back. "I'm completely alone . . . *now*."

15

Body of Lies

"There you are," Officer Thorn deduced as I straggled into the police station at last. "Two more minutes and I was about to launch a search party."

"You would have found me pretty quick just by asking the concerned citizens of Belville," I replied, shutting the door firmly behind me. "Must everyone here know everything?"

"Only about what their neighbors do. We need you for unraveling the deeper mysteries. It's official—there's no word from any family of Owl's, so I'm moving ahead with the physical examination. I have my own checklist, of course, but see what you can find first."

Physical examination. I knew what that meant. She wanted me to look at Owl's body, to see if there were any strange substances or clues hidden among his clothes.

Ignoring the officer's cheerfulness, I set my work bag on her reception desk and began suiting up. The actual process—pulling down my goggles, straightening my gloves and lab coat—was not as important as the mental one. I'd seen corpses before, and there had been no love lost between myself and Owl. But the world had gone topsy-turvy, and I needed that moment of silence to prepare for the task ahead.

Once I was ready, I followed Thorn deeper into the station. Normally I preferred not to go inside Belville's tiny police station at all, and I certainly wasn't the only one. Like the Hut, the station was a residence inherited by each new officer that came to Belville, and yet it seemed to echo Thorn's personality perfectly. (*Were all police officers like Thorn?* I wondered briefly and shivered at the thought.) The front room served as a reception area, with a large desk and a few stiff chairs for those who couldn't be convinced to stand at attention. The wood-paneled walls boasted an extensive collection of awards, medals, historic articles, and the occasional magical knickknack, no doubt a trophy of some past case. Thorn's office, entered by a side door, doubled down on the impressive atmosphere with an *extra*-heavy, sparkling-clean, pin-straight wooden desk. Beside that room was the broom closet and a set of stairs running down to the basement, where the occasional unlucky criminal was kept—also the scene of Vic's death at the hands of Owl and his unknown accomplice. Mentally I said a prayer for Vic as we made straight for the examination room, which took up the back of the station.

Tools and reference materials decades-old lined white walls, walls that seemed to lean in, longing for secrets. The only furniture in the room was a high table, square in the center, supporting Owl's body.

"I took a brief look right after we found him, and Trent did all his spells last night, but that's it," Thorn said matter-of-factly. "Everything else was subject to approval."

"Who *was* Owl's family?" I asked, not so much procrastinating as struck by sudden curiosity. And, okay, procrastinating too.

"No clue," Thorn said. "And they really were good for no clues, get it? Ha. Anyway, it's a secretary over at the Guild office in Pine who does all the looking up relatives, and they weren't able to find anything. Plus there was nothing at his apartment, no wills, no letters, not so much as a postcard."

"So he had no one at all?"

"Not a single person. Had the final report via magitech wire when I got back from the bookshop." The officer considered Owl for a moment, then said conversationally, "Maybe he wanted it that way."

"He probably did," I agreed. "The question is, was Owl hiding from his past? Or was he trying to hide his present?"

"Now's the time for science, not philosophy," Thorn said, rubbing her hands. "Once you're done looking, I'll finish up the Guild's checklist. But I don't mind saying, Red, that anything you can come up with will probably be twice as helpful as all that. 'Specially since you're the one who can ID any suspicious materials."

I nodded and moved forward. Never in a million years had I ever thought, upon becoming an alchemist, that I'd be examining bodies at a police officer's request. But I did have better tools than Thorn. *All I have to do,* I reminded myself, *is apply the scientific method. One step at a time. Just like any experiment.*

"Life is an experiment," my old alchemical master liked to say. What would he have said about death?

At first glance in the bright light, I understood why Thorn had said Owl seemed "made up" or in a costume. A faded paisley cloth covered his pale head, and underneath it, gray curls obscured the tips of his pointed ears. Owl himself was known to be nearly bald; it had been something of a joke in town. While Luca always kept his robe's hood up, Owl habitually wore his down, and his head gleamed in the candlelight he used to illuminate his shop. Less charitable people compared them to the new and full moon.

I decided to continue this line of investigation, starting from the crown of the head and moving down. That meant examining the fake hair first. In my goggles, it showed decay and breakage, even more than might be expected from real hair. Rolling some between my fingers, I realized it resembled the cotton-like tendrils of some plants. I could find out which species or at least which family, but that would take time. Pulling out one of my extra vials, I took a sample of the gray fiber to test back in my lab.

Next I moved to the cloths themselves, picking them off the body and setting them to one side. They covered Owl's dark robe haphazardly; if it hadn't been for the fact that Thorn had squished them between her shoulder and Owl's body, the cloths would probably have been lost in the run from the castle.

Aside from these oddities, Owl looked perfectly normal. "Normal," for him, had included a haggard look many in town attributed to too much time amongst dusty books before we realized it was due to something more criminal in nature. His boots were new, but muddy. His hands were clean. His glasses were perched on his large nose, and his eyes were closed. But as I pulled aside the mop of plant fibers, I saw what Thorn already knew: someone had hit Owl from behind with something heavy.

Like I said, I was no medical examiner. I skimmed over the injury, breathing deep to calm my nerves. Then I moved over the rest of the body, looking for signs of hidden trinkets or, for Luca's sake, signs of a scholarly necklace. I even broke out a small but powerful magnet from my toolkit, scanning the body for any iron. I found none.

Finally, I stepped back and straightened my crooked back. Wiping my hair from my face, I told Thorn, "There's not much here for me to work with. But I will say, his skin *is* unnaturally cold. Are we sure that's not due to the spells Trent did? No? Okay. I couldn't find the necklace Luca mentioned. So the rest is up to you—aside from this," I said, holding up the vial of fibers.

"The grandma wig?" Thorn asked, stepping forward to look at what I'd removed.

"The unidentified plant matter," I corrected. "There's a lot of plants that could look like this, if you dry them and run them through a heckle. Don't worry about it." I waved a hand when Thorn scrunched up her eyebrows at the unfamiliar word. "The point is, I might be able to narrow down what kind of plant it was, if that's helpful."

"Everything's helpful," Thorn declared with a toothy grin.

I pushed my goggles up to my forehead and grinned back at her, albeit wearily. "I have no idea where you get your energy from. I'm going to go grab dinner from Lavender's. Do you want to come?"

"Negative. Checklist, remember?" Thorn held up her guild manual. "While you eat, why don't you think up reasons Luca wanted Owl to look like a grandma?"

"You're making assumptions," I said. "I doubt Luca would have done something so macabre. Besides, maybe whoever did this wasn't going for 'grandma.' Maybe our murderer doesn't perceive color. But, sure. I'll add it to the list of things

125

to ponder."

* * *

Lavender's Tavern sprawled across the far corner of Market Square, presiding over all the town's business. It was *the* place to be, for travelers and locals alike; Belville wasn't big enough to support two such establishments. There was a little diner and a pizza place on the Square, but Lavender's reigned supreme. Rumor had it that the tavern had been there since the town began, and Lavender had been running it all the while. Lavender herself, a warm and welcoming and very ample woman, neither confirmed nor denied this claim. She appeared like a middle-aged human, aside from shimmery edges and the occasional feather in her hair—and eyes that matched her name. No one knew for sure where she'd come from, but everyone was reasonably certain she had fae blood.

Mystery aside, the one thing Belville's residents knew for sure about Lavender was her culinary skill. I didn't eat out often because I enjoyed cooking at home, but if I did find myself without a meal, Lavender's Tavern topped my go-to list.

By the time I got there, a combination of sunset and autumn wind had chased everyone inside. In the main room, the hearths blazed, firelight flickering along the exposed beams of the ceiling. Voices filled the space beneath those beams, colorful, sparkling voices of people enjoying good company. A waft of garlic and butter met me at the door.

"Red," Lavender called from behind the bar. "I was just thinking how I ought to tell you how *wonderful* your new warming powders have been. I can't keep them in stock."

"Thanks, Lavender!" I had to shout across the crowd. I surveyed the tables before picking a path into the room. "No delivery today, though. I was hoping for dinner."

"We're running short of room, as you can see, love."

"No problem." My eyes locked on a familiar red plume, and I made my decision. "I'm going to go sit with a friend."

Lavender just smiled approvingly and returned to piling tankards and steaming plates onto a serving tray. I couldn't say exactly why I was so willing to confront my neighbor; normally I preferred to avoid her, and now this would make two showdowns in one day. Maybe it was the examination of Owl still lingering at the back of my mind. In the face of death, weird squabbles seemed a lot less scary.

Plus, Thorn *had* asked me to think about who would have wanted to dress up Owl. And with Gloria currently heading my suspect list, maybe it was time to figure out if all the rumors about her and Owl were really true.

Especially because, if I could get Gloria to top *Thorn's* suspect list, then Luca would be free.

Gloria glowered in the darkest corner of the room, her scorched skin understated in the shadows. Her legs were crossed tightly beneath the table and she picked at her fingernails rather than finishing her half-eaten meal. As it became clear where I was headed, her head rose slowly, her eyes narrowed into slits.

"You know what?" she said as I sat down. "I really don't care anymore."

"Good," I said.

"Yeah. If you want to be a mannerless dope and sit where you're not wanted, there's nothing I can do about it, is there?"

"Nope." Channeling Officer Thorn's oblivious cheer, I

waved a request for dinner at the nearest server. Over his shoulder I caught sight of Ginger, a werewolf who ran the bakery, sitting with Cairn; *maybe I should have gone to sit with them and gotten info for Luca,* I thought regretfully as I smiled in return for their waves. But my decision had been made. I turned to Gloria. "I have to say, I still really like that necklace you've got on. Is it part of a new line you're carrying at the beauty shop?"

Gloria looked at me like I was a seasick worm. "Like you'd ever step foot in there."

"Maybe I would if you sold cool wooden jewelry like that."

"Please. You think nerdy scientists' goggles are the height of fashion."

"You sound like William. I guess maybe it's time I look into accessorizing."

"What is it with you and this necklace?" Gloria broke first, her hand coming down flat on the table.

"What is it with *you* and that necklace?" I fired back. "Come on, Gloria. I've known you for months now and you only ever wear black."

"I've always worn it," Gloria insisted. But a cloud passed behind her eyes, and her free hand closed around the pendant, like it might get away. "And anyway I don't see what business it is of yours what I wear."

"It's none," I shrugged. "I'm just curious." We both fell quiet as the server, a slim dark fairy, shoved a heaping plate of tamales and a mug filled with milky tea onto the table before the crowd whisked him away.

"Perfect. I love how they remember what I like, even though I don't show up very often," I said conversationally as I drew my dinner closer. My mind raced. Should I come clean to

128

Gloria and admit that the necklace might be evidence in a murder?

When Gloria remained silent, I had no choice but to edge closer to the topic on my mind. "Have you heard all the rumors going around town?"

"Ari and Stella said something." Her gaze flickered. "Why do you care?"

"I'm just making conversation." To counteract my rising frustration with Gloria, I took a bite of corn dough and cheese—heavenly. My good humor returned at once. "And you know how Ari and Stella always seem to know everything."

"They don't know anything," Gloria snapped. But then she paused, and that flicker passed over her face again.

The flicker intrigued me. Gloria acted almost like some people I'd seen under spells. If their will was strong enough, they'd question the spell, even as it compelled them to do things. And Gloria's will was *incredibly* strong—that I knew first hand. Maybe it was strong enough that she'd break through the spell and finally admit something.

Experimentally, I took another bite and watched her. The crowd around us was loud as ever, but from the impatience in Gloria's fingertips on the table, it was clear that she found my silence deafening.

"They're telling people I was in love with Owl," she said after a few minutes. It came all in one go, one breath she'd been holding. "And that he was killed by frost creatures while we were out on some kind of rendezvous."

"Huh." I tried to contain my disappointment. I'd hoped for a more news-worthy breakthrough.

Gloria narrowed her eyes at me, her face more aquiline than

ever. "Don't act like you haven't heard that too. But it isn't true—not that that matters."

"If that's the case," I said over another forkful, "then what *is* the truth, Gloria?"

"Seriously?" She stared me down, but I knew the trick this time. I won. She rolled her eyes. "He wanted my shop."

"*Owl?*"

"Ask Dansforth if you don't believe me."

Dimly, I recognized "Dansforth" as the name of one of two real estate agents who worked out of a tiny office on the other side of town. They'd sold me my building—that seemed ages ago now. "What was he going to do, move the bookstore?"

"Who cares? He probably just hated me because of my—my family, not that *you* would know about that. All I know is, he spent all summer trying to get me on the town council's blacklist and run me out of business."

"Seems like quite a coincidence, timing-wise," I remarked, mostly to myself. If Gloria was telling the truth, it was a sobering tale indeed. Gloria wasn't the cuddliest neighbor, but *Owl* as a neighbor could have been much worse.

"I have nothing to do with any of this," Gloria said as she leveled a glare at me. "You think I let Owl out of jail just to kill him? Credit me with *some* brains, won't you?"

I have to admit it: I was rattled, and I let her get under my skin. I blurted, "In that case, why have you got his necklace?"

"This thing? You think this is Owl's?" Gloria looked down at the pendant. Abruptly, she yanked the thing over her head. "I never wanted anything to do with him. If you knew anything about phoenixkin, you'd know that. Most of us are actually asexual and aromantic. In fact, if you really must know, technically we can change gender too. So I have absolutely *no* need for a bonehead boyfriend, much less one who wanted to run me out of town, just like the rest of you jerks."

"Whoa, slow down," I said, holding my hands up as though to stymie Gloria's sudden eloquence—not to mention her uncharacteristic freedom with personal details.

"I have no idea where this came from," she continued, slamming the pendant down on the table. "I don't care about it at all. I just wish you all would leave me alone."

She met my gaze and held it. No flicker.

My eyes slid to the pendant. Had *that* been what was putting some kind of spell on her? Or had I been imagining her internal struggle?

"Gloria," I said slowly. "I'm sorry. To be honest, I didn't know what to think."

She snorted and. "Whether I was guilty or not, you mean."

"Not really. I just can't get a read on you in general," I admitted with a small smile. "I mean, come on. You're beyond glamorous by Pastoria's standards. Why bother staying in Belville and putting up with petty fights when you could go anywhere?"

It would have been more accurate for me to say *picking petty fights,* I thought, but Gloria must not have noticed the factual slip. She grunted noncommittally.

"You keep that stupid thing if you're so interested in it," she told me after a moment, with an absent wave toward the pendant on the table. She finished her drink in one long swig and stood. "Oh, and Red? Tell your wolf-dog to stop following me."

She was gone in a moment, turning heads as she swung her hips toward the door. I eyed the pendant left in her wake. It looked innocuous enough: a simple wooden disc, about the size and shape of a coin, but with beautifully curved edges. Try as I might, I couldn't shake the feeling that I probably shouldn't touch it.

Eventually, though, I gathered up the remnants of my courage. I gobbled down the last of my dinner, scooped the necklace into a lined pouch, and made my way up to the bar to pay. I realized with a resigned sigh that as soon as I got home, I'd have to fill in William the "wolf-dog" in on all he'd missed. Not to mention set up a distiller and chuck in the strands of plant from Owl's body. It had been a long day, and it looked like the night would be even longer.

16

Ghostly Warnings

I had made it halfway through brewing a cup of tea and shaking off nightmares the next morning when the revelation hit me. That banging I could hear—it wasn't the echo of the footsteps of terrible creatures in my dreams. It was someone pounding at my second-story kitchen window.

"William, wake up!" I hissed as I stalked through the kitchen, eyes straining for any sign of our visitor. Who would be at the second story? An overeager woodpecker? A flying frost monster?

William's head popped up the moment I said his name. But his shape never moved through the golden morning shadows in the apartment. Instead, he yawned from his window seat. "It's your shadow, Red."

"What do you mean it's my—oh." I blushed and lowered the tea strainer in my fist as, with my free hand, I threw open the wooden frame over the sink. "Jade?"

"Rrred." His voice flew into the room, full of relief but urgent nonetheless. "I'm very sorrrry to barge in on you. I couldn't think of what else to do. There's been trouble at the castle."

133

"Trouble? Is someone in danger?" I set my things on the kitchen island and reached for my cloak as the thoughts kept coming. "It isn't Luca, is it?"

"No." I couldn't see Jade, but I was aware of him shimmering over my shoulder. "It is your neighbor, Gloria."

* * *

Of course it wouldn't have been Luca—he was safe at home under house arrest. Still, my mind struggled to make sense of my morning. Jade continued rambling. "I discovered her this morning when I noticed a strange presence on the grounds. She wasn't doing anything, Rrred, not even moving. Only breathing. She is stuck there, and I cannot move her. I came to you as quickly as I could."

As I threw on my cloak, grabbed my kit, and ran outside to collect Officer Thorn, Jade hovered just behind me, as though he really was my shadow. I hit the street, which was empty and still, aside from a light on at the antiquities shop and the scent of chocolate wafting from the bakery. *No Ari or Stella yet,* I noted. The fairies weren't particularly early risers. Hopefully if I wasn't back in time, William would know what to say to them. For the moment, I shouldered my bag and loped down the street.

In no time, Thorn was marching along beside me. "You did right coming to me first, assistant," she said. "Did your ghostie say anything about those monsters lurking around? I don't like the sound of any of it. I'm getting the Witch."

I stopped in my tracks. The first tree limbs of the forest waved above our heads. "Thorn! Do you really think we have the time to waste?"

"*We* aren't wasting it," she decided, shouldering her club. "I'm going to rouse Trent and meet you there. You and your ghost boyfriend will be fine, yes?"

I nodded my assent and turned to run. As I did, Jade whispered in my ear, "I'm not a ghost."

I waited until we'd pulled up just inside the break in the castle wall before commenting. "What, no complaints about the other part?" With a short laugh, I caught my breath and turned to business. The rising sun hadn't quite penetrated the castle walls; the gnarled trees and shrubs around us shivered in the dark. The last thing I wanted was mist creatures on our trail. That's if they weren't already after Gloria herself. I reached into my pocket and lit a lightstick at once. With the light, I could only faintly see Jade's outline, but I was willing to bet I'd be able to feel him. So I held out my hand. "Take me to where you found her?"

"Of course. Thank you, Rred."

Jade's hand was cool and soft in mine. He picked his path carefully through the overgrown garden, not heading for the castle, but for the back of the property, where an old gazebo haphazardly rested. Despite Jade's care, I found myself clinging to his hand as I did my best not to trip over roots and vines. The freezing breeze on my legs reminded me I was still wearing pajama shorts under my cloak, and sturdy boots alone couldn't keep the season at bay. *If it is just the season that makes it so cold here,* I worried.

Jade slowed as we passed the gazebo and neared the rear wall, my light dissipating the night's fog. "Herre," he said, drawing my hand up to point for him. "The landslide is fresh. I'm afraid she may have been caught in it and injured."

The air around us was indeed full of the smell of damp,

disturbed earth. The mountainside above us had cascaded over the castle wall, bringing rocks and saplings with it. And as I stepped around the mess, following Jade's lead, I finally caught sight of Gloria.

At first glance she looked almost like an ancient depiction of a reclining goddess, half sitting, half laying amongst the rubble. But my lightstick illuminated twigs and dirt in her ruffled crimson feathers, and her dark skin was smudged to black. The expression in her eyes was nothing short of murder.

But at least her eyes were open and alive. She proved as much by looking me up and down. "You look ridiculous."

"I could say the same to you," I returned, stepping over the dirt at her feet.

Her eyes latched onto the knapsack at my side. "Do *not* tell me that you are the local rescue team now too."

"I'm not. I just happen to be—friends with the spirit who lives here."

"You're friends with the things that live here?" Gloria still hadn't moved, aside from her face. Her glare slackened, sliding from disdain to distrust.

"Well—there's several things that live here, as far as I know. I'm hoping you didn't meet some of the worse ones yet." I'd been looking her over discreetly but hadn't yet found any signs of blood or broken limbs—or ropes, for that matter. I wasn't sure *why* she was stuck. "What happened?"

"The creatures *were* here earlier. They are gone now," Jade said helpfully from several paces back.

Gloria's gaze darted around me. "Who was that?"

"That was Jade," I told her. "So you can hear him, then? Good. We can talk about that later. Tell me what happened."

"When did you become boss of me?"

"Gloria, I'm trying to help."

"Fine." Her gaze drifted from my face. Still, the rest of her body remained . . . frozen. She sighed. "I don't know what happened. I was out for a hike like usual, and then I was here."

Oh boy. We're going to be here forever, I thought with a sigh of my own. I took a seat on a boulder beside her and arranged my cloak over my lap, smoothing out my frustration. "Uh huh. So you like to go for early morning hikes? Alone?"

"It gives me perspective." Gloria glared at me. "I'm not stupid about it, like *some* people. I never go at night and I stick to the trails I know."

"And I guess you were on the Crystal Falls trail?" I held her glare: I knew a thing or two about the trails around Belville. I used them often when gathering ingredients.

Gloria broke eye contact first. "Yeah. The exposed rock section."

"Right above us." I leaned back, peering up through the wounded woods beyond the castle wall. "Okay, that part makes sense. But are you sure you didn't notice whatever caused the landslide? It must have been huge."

"I didn't notice anything. Like I told you." Abruptly, Gloria's voice dropped. "Red, cut the nonsense. You have to tell me. Why can't I move?"

"I'm not a doctor, as you pointed out yourself. And . . . honestly, I was hoping *you* would tell me that. Are you in pain anywhere?"

From the castle grounds, a rumbling sound too loud to be Jade interrupted Gloria. With a blast of sharp-edged wind, Officer Thorn and Trent arrived on the scene, hopping down from Trent's flying broomstick like mail carriers with an

137

express delivery and a bonus on the line.

"I am now," Gloria muttered.

"And here I was hoping that by catching a ride on Trent's broom, I'd be able to beat you after all," Thorn announced to me as she strode up. Trent hung behind her, giving me a little salute when I looked his way. Thorn continued, "So, what's all this? Looks a bit like rock bottom for you, Gloria, doesn't it?"

Gloria glowered.

"All right, don't take the joke," Thorn shrugged. "What's the problem, then, Red?"

"We're not sure," I answered with a glance sideways at Gloria. "She doesn't remember anything from when she fell, and as far as I can tell, she isn't injured."

"Then it's obvious. Right?" Thorn stepped up and laid her long fingers along Gloria's exposed wrist, then waved Trent over as well, saying, "Sweet justice, she's cold."

I frowned. "You don't really think it was the mist creatures?"

"I think she's lucky the sun came up when it did," Thorn replied.

Trent, who had been muttering under his breath with his eyes closed, suddenly turned his gaze on Gloria. For a brief moment, even his pupils shone purple. "There is some kind of magic there," he affirmed. "I'm not really great at IDing magic types yet. It's sort of a bright red color, which doesn't make much sense."

"Great. Red magic. Mist creatures." Gloria pursed her lips at all of us. "I can't believe I have to listen to this."

"Or worse," Thorn added. She stood and scratched thoughtfully at one ear. "Once we fix you up, it could well be the jail cells for you."

"For what?" Gloria's nostrils smoked. "Hiking alone?"

"Returning to the scene of the crime," said Officer Thorn.

"I wasn't trying to get to the castle. I was just on the trail!"

"That," said Thorn, "is exactly what a murderer might say."

* * *

Neither justice nor medical assistance was about to happen at the rear end of the cursed castle, so between the three of us, we figured out a way to carry Gloria back into town. Gloria was part-elven, tall, and well-endowed, but Thorn managed to lift her up smoothly enough. Her limbs fell stiffly over the officer's arms. Thorn was lucky Gloria didn't have the motion control to poke her right in the eye.

Our party was silent on the way back through the forest. I found myself deeply unsettled by Thorn's idea that the mist creatures had caused Gloria's immobility; the idea called to mind images of spiders injecting prey with poison before slowly eating them.

And really, could Gloria be the killer? I'd been so sure that she'd exonerated herself the night before. But of course, she could have killed Owl out of spite just as easily as out of passion. What was it she'd said—Owl hated her because of her family, somehow? The pendant niggled at me, too. She'd handed it over so easily, once the spell or whatever had been broken. I hadn't had time to tell Thorn about that yet.

A nearby voice pierced my thoughts. "Help!"

Thorn stopped dead. The smoke of Belville's chimneys lay just down the hill in front of us. But the voice came from our left.

"Someone, help!"

Trent cocked his head. "Think it's a trap?"

"Well, there's three of us and only one faint voice," I decided, tired of their hesitation. *There's a reason some traps work,* I admitted to myself as I turned off the road and began climbing the forested hill in the direction of the sound.

Thorn and Trent crashed through the undergrowth behind me, amid Gloria's loud protestations. If this was a trap, there was no way we were going to sneak into it. Realizing this, I called out, "We're coming! Where are you?"

"Red? Is that you?" The voice filled with relief, but I still didn't recognize it. "Over here! Below the—"

"Ledge," I called to Thorn and Trent as the berry bushes gave way to a rocky outcrop. We all skidded to a halt. Peering down, we saw a person lying in the dirt several yards below us, hidden from the road and all hope of passersby.

"Thank goodness," said the person below. Peering down into the shadow, I made out a yellow dress with embroidered apron, gray hair, and wide eyes.

"Cairn," I realized, just as Thorn came to the same conclusion. She set Gloria down and began clambering down the slope. I followed, asking as I went, "Cairn, how in Beyond did you end up out here?"

"Oh, Officer, Red, I'm so glad you heard me," Cairn was saying. "And is that Trent, the young Witch? Now, isn't this luck!"

"Don't pick her up," Trent called down to Thorn. "I can lift her if she's hurt."

Gloria made a muffled comment we all ignored.

I'd been fearing the worst too. And yet when Trent mentioned the possibility, my blood ran cold. "Cairn, are you okay?"

"I'm fine," Cairn said to me and to Officer Thorn, already

kneeling beside her. But it was clear from her strained smile that she wasn't, and when Thorn pointed this out, she burst into tears. "Oh, I'd promised myself I wouldn't cry," she sobbed. "What kind of helpless old woman must I look like? I—I'd promised myself I'd be brave about it . . ."

"Cairn," I said gently, kneeling on her free side. "It's okay. You can cry if you need to. We don't think any less of you." While Cairn nodded and struggled to regain her breath, both Thorn and I surveyed the scene. I couldn't see any traces of blood. The air was freezing, and it wasn't just the shadow. I glanced at Thorn to see if she noticed it too, but Thorn's gaze slid to Cairn's legs, tangled in her skirts. I understood what the officer was thinking. Like Gloria, Cairn was talking and she didn't seem bloodied, but we'd yet to see her lower half move.

"First things first," I said firmly, to reassure myself as much as Cairn. "We need to make sure you get the care you need. One thing at a time. Can you see me okay? Does my voice sound normal?"

Cairn swallowed and, very carefully, nodded.

"Good." I smiled encouragingly. Like I'd told Gloria, I was no doctor, but I'd done my share of emergency roadside first aid. "Can you wiggle your fingers and toes?"

To my immense relief, Cairn held up her hands. They were dirty and scratched, but otherwise fine. Then there was a pause, though, and my heart sank.

Cairn smiled at me grimly through her tears. "You've always been such a smart girl, Red. You already know, don't you? I can't—I can't feel my legs at all. It's just so, so, so . . ." She closed her eyes and shuddered. "So cold. Like something crept up and turned my feet and knees to ice. I'm afraid, Red. What if I've been cursed?"

17

Examinations

Like many small towns across Pastoria, Belville didn't have a true doctor's office—just a thriving home herbalism practice, a vet who took in magical animals, and my own arsenal of potions. Serious cases usually involved a lot of fervent "this'll tide you over" healing spells and someone flying—literally, most often—to Highridge, which had an infirmary. I'd expected Thorn to lead our small party back to the road and from there to the police station, but she seemed to have other ideas.

We'd clambered back up the small cliff and she'd picked up Gloria once more, while Trent lifted Cairn using magic. Thorn's eyes glittered as she looked down at me. "I bet the scholar knows more than he's said about this. And those creatures."

I spluttered. "You really can't think—"

But yes, it turned out that the Officer *did* think that cutting through the forest and heading straight for the bookstore was a good plan. In fact she insisted we do just that, despite my protests.

And, to be honest, it *was* a shorter trip that way. Not to mention that the bookstore—or rather, Owl's empty apartment—had more free space available than the station. And I had to appreciate that if Luca did know more about the castle than he was telling us—a big *if*, in my opinion—the sustained guilt of living with innocent victims of the castle's curse would wear him down pretty quick. I could see how Thorn thought she was making a good strategic move.

As soon as we showed up, though, Luca was ready to do everything possible to make our patients comfortable. Like my own shop, the bookstore had an apartment above it—actually, two snug apartments, two stories each, tucked side by side. One had been Owl's, but Luca had the key and offered it up without another thought. Thorn had already combed the place for any clues, and Trent had put numerous spells on it when Owl broke loose, so we knew the place was clean. Trent did still mutter something about it being "morbid," using a dead man's apartment as temporary medical quarters, but Thorn was having none of it.

"It's not like he died here, at least," I whispered to Trent as Thorn deposited Gloria in the third-floor bedroom and returned to help maneuver Cairn onto the couch in the second-floor living room.

"I know, I gotcha." Trent nodded as, with the gesture of one hand, he lowered Cairn into place. With the other hand he blocked the apartment doorway, physically holding Luca back. "I was just saying, that's all."

"Can I get you anything?" Luca asked from the hall. "I have more blankets at my place. I just got them out of my trunk for winter. I think I know where Owl kept his. Unless Officer Thorn went through it already? She probably knows where everything is. Can I put on a pot of tea? It's not as good as Red's, but it'd be hot. Did any of you have breakfast? Do Gloria and Cairn need any medicine?"

"Luca." I, too, barred Luca's entry to the narrow apartment. Essentially, he'd unlocked the door for us, and we'd streamed in only to dam up the entrance. This was a decision made with unspoken unanimity. Not because of any suspicion of Luca, but because it had become rapidly apparent that in times of crisis, Luca was a hoverer. "What we need is quiet, and some time to sort things out. We still don't know exactly what happened to either of them."

"I don't know anything. I know Thorn said she wanted to ask me questions but I'm not sure I can help." Under his hood, Luca's light eyes looked stricken. "I can look something up in the scrolls downstairs if that'd be useful—"

Trent rolled his eyes, and I swatted him. "You know what," I said to Luca, "I do think that'd be helpful. Remember what you were saying about wendigos? Could you look into that kind of thing? Make sure you keep your sources out, though, in case Thorn asks how you know. She thinks maybe the creatures can make people freeze up. We still have to hear Cairn's story, but," I confessed, lowering my voice, "I'm worried that the cold at the castle and the cold affecting Cairn and Gloria are somehow the same."

Luca rocked from side to side, bouncing on the balls of his feet. "That's what I'm worried about too," he admitted, and then darted down the stairs.

"Nice. You sure Thorn wouldn't mind you saying all that?" Trent watched Luca's robe disappear speculatively.

"Who knows. But I *do* think it'd be a big help. And I wasn't just trying to get rid of Luca, if that's what you mean by that 'nice.'"

Trent shrugged like that would have been a valid reason, and the gesture made me bristle.

"He just wants to help," I found myself saying defensively. "Which I think says a lot, given how Officer Thorn has treated him. By the time we have things settled here, I bet you he'll have a whole dissertation prepared on the mist creatures."

"Oh, joy," drawled Trent. My only response was to shove him again. It made me feel a little better, at least. Together, we joined Thorn at Cairn's bedside.

Owl's decor screamed musty old bachelor: dark walls, deep carpet, messy piles of books, and furniture for one, covered in some kind of faded corduroy. A staircase tucked behind the tiny kitchen at one end of the room led up to the bedroom Gloria now occupied. The entire apartment curved at the edges to accommodate the architecture of the building. It felt exactly how I would imagine being in a nest in a tree might feel, and somehow it smelled very much like that too: dusty, and dry, but also pleasantly piney.

The dark and dust didn't make it easy to examine Cairn, though. Thorn installed me at the head of the couch with an extra lightstick trained on our patient while she ran through her guild checklist and Trent did some spellwork.

"Nothing," Thorn murmured at last, drawing more blankets over Cairn. "Curse it. I never did take to the science-y bits of training."

"It's not all that magical, either," Trent mumbled. The two sounded so alike in their frustration that I had to hide a chuckle behind my hand. "On Gloria the traces were pretty clear. But this is all muddied up."

Thorn tugged at her ear. "Maybe the creatures aren't as

strong away from the castle. Soon as we're done here, I'm interrogating the scholar again."

"Assuming it was creatures who did this," I reminded her. Looking down at Cairn, I asked more gently, "The cold isn't spreading, is it?"

"No." Cairn spoke with her eyes closed. "Thank you, Red, for your kindness."

"Don't mind that for now. You've done plenty for me in the past," I said with a smile. I shifted, kneeling beside Cairn's head, while Thorn threw herself into an armchair and Trent perched on the coffee table. "Can you tell us what happened?"

"I—I think I remember it all." Cairn's eyes fluttered open, and she focused on me. Everyone else fell silent; Cairn was known around town as a venerable storyteller. As long as we let her talk, she'd tell us every little thing we might need.

* * *

Cairn began with one rattling breath. "I opened the shop early this morning. But I didn't bring in the mail myself. A moon or two ago, I hired a nice little schoolgirl to help me look after the register—one of Dusty's nieces, she is, and a very pleasant helper. She stops by each morning on her way to school to say hello and hand me the mail, and then in the afternoons she helps with the ringing up. I've—well, you know how it can get sometimes, running a store by yourself, Red. I've grown to look forward to her stopping in, so these days I always leave the mail for her to pick up.

"Today in the mail was a letter." Cairn's mouth was drawn tight in concern; her hand slipped down from the cushions to find my sleeve. "Of course, it wouldn't make sense to you yet.

"I should have started the story a lot earlier—years ago. Let's see . . . just over a decade ago, back in my days as a traveling merchant. I happened to fall in with some scholars at Rote University, you see, and they would sell me old trinkets or curiosities from time to time, and for a very good price. Sometimes, if they knew where I was on my circuit, they'd even send along packages of things in the mail and collect the payment later. Scholars are drawn to antiques, my uncle used to say. How true! Now, in one of the last packages they sent me, there was a little wooden amulet.

"That was years ago now. I didn't think anything of it at the time. We see all kinds of jewelry in the antiques trade, and this was plain by any standard. But even plain things sell, and this never did. It almost seemed to . . . forgive me, sounding like a superstitious old lady. But it seemed to give a bad feeling to whoever picked it up. I'd been here about a year when I began to grow suspicious of the thing, so I took it over to Owl, to this very shop. I thought, since it had come from scholars, maybe he might know something about it. He said it had a charm on it—a powerful memory charm, he said. Nothing untoward. But I had grown to dislike the thing and Owl had trouble with his memory even then, so . . ."

Cairn waved her free hand, and let it fall back onto the quilts piled atop her middle. "It seems so strange and far away now, to think once I was friends with Owl. That any of us were friends with him. I suppose we never really knew him, did we?

"I gave him the amulet. I never thought of it again, all this time, until this morning," she resumed, frowning. "There was a letter from the scholars in Brass. Someone had been looking through their old records, it seems, and realized that the amulet had been sent to me by mistake. It's a terrible, demonic thing, one which prompts the wearer to do unspeakable deeds, if they wear it long enough. It never should have left the university."

Cairn shuddered. "I just couldn't bear it, thinking of what I might have done, bringing such a thing here. Then I thought of how Owl had died in the woods, and I had—I had just seen Red leave that morning . . . you know I'd never spy on you, dear, forgive an old neighbor being nosy. And so, so worried. What if there was a murderer out there, in the forest? I went to find you—that's why I was out on the road. But I thought I heard something off the path, and I was struck with such horror, thinking what if it was *you,* dear, and so I ran over to see, and—all at once I was so dreadfully cold."

"And, of course, you found me soon after." Cairn reshuffled herself, taking a few deep breaths. "I remember very little from my fall, thank goodness, except I am certain there was something reaching out for me. It meant to catch me, I think, but it only grazed my skirts."

She shivered against an overstuffed orange pillow, and repeated, "Thank goodness you found me. I'm so sorry, Red. Will you promise to destroy that thing if you find it? And could you ever forgive me?"

"Don't be so hard on yourself, Cairn," I said at once. Lifting up on my knees, I gave her a quick hug. "You had no idea about any of this. If anyone's to blame, it's Owl."

Thorn tugged at her ear and directed her question at me rather than Cairn. "Think the scholars' amulet and Luca's pendant are the same?"

"Could be. Which reminds me, I got the pendant from Gloria yesterday. I think I put it in a pocket . . ."

"How is Gloria?" Cairn asked. "I hate to think my mistake has put so many in danger."

"Gloria can handle herself," I said, poking through my pockets. The fact that I was still wearing pajamas became apparent once more.

"Run along home and get it, Red," suggested Thorn. "Just be careful. Meet me at the station. I've got to talk to Gloria, then Luca, and then I'm going to make some calls. Trent, you're on guard duty."

"You mean nurse duty?" Trent shrugged and grinned crookedly. "Fine. But if Gloria recovers enough to throw something at me, I'm blaming you. Oh, and Red? Will you grab some warming potions while you're at your shop?"

"Sure," I said, rising. "In fact, I'll do better than that. It's time to get—"

"Don't," groaned Thorn. "Not that dog."

Despite my better judgment, I grinned. "The sooner you figure out how to help everyone and end this, the less chance you two have to fight."

18

Bad Blood

Despite Officer Thorn's flair for barking out plans, we were still very much in the dark. On my way out of Owl's old apartment, I stopped by Luca's desk in the bookshop to catch him up to speed, something accomplished in about thirty seconds.

I leaned against the desk, appreciating its sturdiness, as I wrapped up. "Trent's going to stay here with them. I think he's already gauging which of Owl's things to animate into a nursemaid."

I made a face at Luca as I said it; I wasn't a fan of animated objects. There were ethics involved, which, in my experience, somehow end up backfiring on the nearest scientist (that is, *me*) rather than the spell-happy Witch. But Trent would learn his lessons in his own time.

Luca nodded along, but he was clearly still mired in an older part of the conversation. "Cairn thinks the scholar's pendants are actually something bad?"

"Well, we don't know for sure if you and she are talking about the same thing. I have Owl's, by the way, but I left it at home. When I get it, we can clear up that part of this mystery at least. Wooden disk on a braided cord, with a symbol etched in it?" Experimentally, I described the necklace for him. Again, he nodded. I bit my lip. "Luca, are you sure the necklaces are a good thing?"

"Yes! I mean—well—I guess I don't know. I have one too," Luca said. His fingers rustled at his neckline for a moment before he managed to pull the necklace out from beneath his clothes. As I leaned in to examine it, I realized that Luca's dark skin was covered in deep mossy-green tattoos. *Maybe that's why he always keeps his hood up.*

The necklace he held out looked a lot like Owl's, but the symbol was different. I knew as much at once, because I recognized the one on Luca's: it was a diamond with a curling branch extending from the rightmost corner, a symbol used often in alchemy to designate the process of filtering.

"Luca . . . I hate to repeat myself, but are you sure it's a good thing?" I asked, leaning back.

He stowed the necklace beneath his shirt once more. Never had the cord left his neck. "I've never wanted to murder anyone, if that's what you mean."

"Of course not," I assured him. But with Thorn's suspicions so strong, neither of us smiled about what should have been a lighthearted joke. *Maybe the filter represents a sort of protection charm,* I thought, making a mental note to ask William. *And maybe the necklaces* are *similar, but somehow Owl's was corrupted.*

"I brought out everything I could think of that relates to cold creatures," Luca said, gesturing to a mountain of jumbled scrolls, pamphlets, and encyclopedias on the side table behind his desk. "I'm afraid I don't really know if any of it will be of use. The shapes and snarling you saw at first could be anything from wendigos to rogue werewolves, whereas cold spots usually result from hauntings, and actual cold-curses often indicate an elemental creature of ice or snow, so that could be something entirely different. And then there's what you said about Owl being—being marked or dressed up somehow? I keep trying to tell the officer, I'm not sure how that fits in."

"Me neither. But—"

A jingle at the door interrupted me. "Red!" a familiar voice said. "Not here in your unofficial capacity, are you? 'Cause I just spent all morning avoiding Officer Thorn."

"Dusty!" I turned to greet Luca's visitor, hand on hip. The gnome looked exactly as he always did, completely unruffled and ready to fix the nearest broken thing. "What do you mean, you're avoiding Thorn? You aren't on the run from the law, are you?"

Dusty scoffed, hitching up the wrench on his shoulder and nearly knocking over a haphazard book display. "On the run from people telling me how to live my life, more like. Every time I see her lately she gives me another talking-to about going with you folks to the castle. As if it was my fault you put a hole in the greenhouse glass!"

I glanced at Luca, hiding a grin behind my hand. "Well, you *are* the one who let me run into a trapdoor all by myself."

"Ha! Next time you really will be on your own," said Dusty, but he said it with affection. As he strode through the shop, he continued, "'M here for Owl's place. Don't mind me. Got an alert about a busted pipe upstairs and figured I'd fit it in before lunch."

"Oh—oh dear—Trent must have—" Luca flailed helplessly as Dusty and I looked on. A drip of water *plink*ed onto Luca's ancient cash register. Over the tiny puddle, Luca looked at Dusty. "You're sure you don't mind?"

"What? Bein' in the apartment of a murderer? Don't mind that any more than I mind coming into the shop of someone under house arrest," Dusty said with a wink at the scholar. "Don't you mind what folks in town are saying, lad. It'll all blow over."

"It will," I agreed, staring Luca down until he looked like he might possibly believe us. "And in the meantime, I'm going to leave you to it. Good luck!"

* * *

Any guilt I might have felt about leaving Luca to his Officer- and Witch-induced troubles evaporated when I neared my shop. Gloria's beauty parlor was dark. From the sidewalk outside my own window displays, I saw the fairies perched on the sales counter while William stared at the register with his shoulder to them.

Clearly, guilt was no longer necessary. Karma, in the form of mediating a magical-assistant-related tiff, had made quick work of my deeds.

"Oh look," William began even before I'd opened the door. "Red's here. You can bother *her* now."

"Red!" Ari and Stella flew over to me at once, literally flying, something that ratcheted up my anxiety several notches as I watched their little slippered feet barely miss my glass jars and mineral samples. "Oh Red, we've been so, so, *soooo* worried!! Something awful has happened, we just know it! When Gloria never came this morning, we came straight here! We've been with William all morning and he hasn't said *anything* useful!

154

Please, oh please, say you can explain what's going on?"

"All morning, huh?" It was easily lunch time now. I glanced at my assistant. Just as he'd been giving the fairies the cold shoulder, he refused to notice my sympathetic grin. "I'm really sorry you were alarmed, Ari, Stella. We—"

"Where is Gloria? Did you find her? Did something awful happen? Why didn't she come to open the shop??"

I cleared my throat. "We did find her, and she's safe at the bookshop now. She'll be okay." *Hopefully,* I added silently, and hurried on, "If you want more details, I'm afraid you'll have to go to Officer Thorn. In the meantime, maybe it'd be best to contact everyone who has appointments with you? They're probably wondering what's going on, too."

"The bookshop?" Stella's pink eyes were huge. "Did she go there to be closer to Owl's memory?"

"The appointments!" Ari shimmered, getting gold dust all over my floor. "Oh no, we never thought of that!!"

"And they scared off all *our* customers, too," William grumbled in the background.

The distraught fairies turned as one. "Oh, no, we couldn't! Your customers must be very brave to put up with *your* attitude all the time!"

They said this very sweetly, and for a moment I wasn't sure if they meant it as a compliment or an insult. Or if it was simply the truth. But when William snarled, I knew which *he* thought it was, and decided to head him off.

"Everyone, please," I said, gesturing with both hands for peace. "Gloria is recovering from a hiking accident. It's nothing to do with Owl, as far as we know. Like I said, Thorn can tell you more. For now, focus on keeping up your shop, okay?"

"You're right!" The fairies turned to me, full of the light of hope once more. "Oh, Red, that's exactly what we'll do. Gloria would want us to keep up the shop. It'll be like nothing even happened! We'll fix it all up, just wait and see!!"

"Well, I didn't exactly say . . ." It was too late; Ari and Stella had already floated out the door. As the bells announced the door's closing, I sighed.

In the fairies' absence, William's silence was palpable. I crossed the room and perched on the counter they'd vacated, reaching out to stroke his black fur. He always acted like he was too good for pets, but I knew better. And when he didn't shake me off, I knew exactly how rough his morning had been.

I sighed again as I looked around my shop. The skies outside were cloudy, and William had never turned on the interior lights; most likely, Ari and Stella hadn't given him the chance. They must have showed up right after Jade and I left.

"I'm sorry," I said at last.

William sneezed.

"I kind of forgot about Ari and Stella," I admitted.

This time he growled. "Did you forget you have a shop to run, too?"

"No. But some things are more important than business. I know Thorn says that just to get on our nerves, but the fact is, she's right."

"I don't care if she's right," William snapped, glaring at me over his shoulder. "Why don't you see that this isn't fair, Red? You didn't come to Belville so that you could run all over town fixing everyone else's problems."

"Is helping out your friends *not* part of settling in to a new place?"

"Exactly how hard are you planning to settle?"

156

I paused. "Alchemists are nothing if not great at distilling."

William huffed and rolled his eyes, but this time his huff was not as threatening as before. "You're ridiculous."

"You sound like Gloria. And speaking of, I'd like you to come and see her, and Cairn too. A lot has happened this morning, and we could use your help."

"Sure," said William. As I struggled to recover from my shock at this bit of civility, he added, "At ten gold pieces per visit."

"William!" He eyed me with that beady stare until I gave in and laughed. "Let me remind you that Luca *has* offered to pay me for my help finding the books."

"An offer you refused. Don't think just because I'm stuck here all day that I don't know what's going on. This is all that scholar's fault in the first place."

"Actually, *none* of this is his fault, and it's you and Thorn suspecting him that's meant that I have to get so involved," I said firmly. "You ought to try giving people a second chance sometime. We aren't all perfect magical beings like you."

"And how well will that have gone when it ends up with you stuck in some pit at a haunted castle, or frozen by a mist creature, or worse yet, dead?"

"I can look after myself. You know that."

"So be it. If you're that determined to learn at cost to yourself." William shook his ears. He'd said what he needed to, and his mood turned a corner.

Sensing this, I smiled, and gave William a rundown of everything I knew. As I spoke, an idea occurred to me. "I have to grab that necklace and go see Thorn, but how about we all meet up at the bookshop this evening? We can have a council of war."

"So you continue to include the number one suspect in your planning?"

I bit down on the particularly sassy comment which came to mind first. "We don't have much choice now that the Officer has put Cairn and Gloria there. Besides, *I* don't consider him suspect number one, I consider him someone with valuable insight into the castle. How about I'll work on being safe, and *you* can work on giving people a break?"

I left my moody companion and charged up to my apartment to begin searching pockets.

And maybe, finally, eat that breakfast while I was at it.

19

Council of War

That evening in the bookshop, I struggled to regain control of my reality. It helped that Officer Thorn had ordered a delicious herbed quiche and potato casserole from Lavender's Tavern for everyone. What didn't help was the fact that, despite an afternoon of searching, I hadn't found the necklace Gloria had given me. It had to be in the lab somewhere; I planned to turn the place upside down once I was done with my plant experiment. That would only take another night, but I didn't like the thought of that necklace loose in my lab.

But for now, I reminded myself, *I have everyone in the same room ready to brainstorm, not to mention all of Luca's scrolls at our disposal. There's nothing we can't solve. As long as we can sort out our priorities and work together.*

"I can't believe any of you want to prosecute some ancient cold spirits," William grumped from an ottoman. "You ought to focus on what Owl was looking for, because it's obviously something dangerous enough to linger around town for."

"A murder is a murder, and now two of our own have been attacked as well. The culprit is still out there and needs to be caught, spirit or no," Thorn declared as she paced the overcrowded aisles.

"I've been researching, and I was thinking maybe we could try to catch one of the creatures to question it?" Luca's voice was lost almost before it made the trip over his desk.

So much for consensus, I thought. I watched them all from a perch atop a free-standing waist-high bookshelf. It'd been miraculously empty when I came in, and I couldn't resist the opportunity. More than likely, it had once housed the pile of research material now crowding Luca's desk.

"And another thing," said Thorn, rounding on Luca and William. "How is it you don't know what's causing that cold?"

"I haven't seen it," sniffed William. "Someone didn't see fit to invite me this morning."

"You have to remember," said Luca, "the castle and the Drus who built it were their own little world. They existed entirely separately from Belville, and they liked it that way. Plus with the way Owl treated—"

"We'll have a better chance after I identify the plant-wig," I said, before Luca could incriminate himself any further by complaining yet again about Owl and elf history. "That was supposed to draw the creatures in, right? I put it in the distiller yesterday evening. By tomorrow morning, if we're lucky, I should be able to say what it is. That should give us more to go on."

William sneezed. "That shadow was probably confused, saying that the creatures were drawn to the getup on Owl. I've never heard of plants of *any* variety calling down evil fog spirits."

"Shadow?" Luca looked puzzled.

"Jade," I clarified, and added to William, "I thought we were trying out second chances? That means not disregarding what people say."

"We can't disregard anything when there's practically nothing to begin with," Thorn broke in. She'd begun pacing again, having already wolfed down her breakfast-for-dinner. Only her shiny black hair and sloped shoulders were visible over shelves overflowing with books. "We started out with an escaped, murderous criminal and a mysterious accomplice, and now we have a dead criminal with no signs of a fight. Just a magic castle and some ages-old war story. More and more, this looks like—"

"Hold on," I interjected. "You're theorizing without all the facts. You just pointed it out yourself: we don't know what secret the castle is hiding. I say we focus on that."

"Um," said Luca, when all eyes turned to him. "That could be good. I've been working on it and I think I know how to find the rest of them." He pushed the three books we'd collected over his desk toward me, as though hoping I'd corroborate his findings. "Remember how there's a symbol for each one, and the symbol for the next book is on the last page of the previous one?"

I nodded, shushing William's scoff with a pointed look.

Luca continued, eyes lighting up despite his predicament. "The symbols are also clues about what room they're in. At least, that's what I think. See, the first book has this symbol, a sapling, which could mean a new beginning in Drus culture and a doorway is a perfect place for that. Then there's the second one, which I thought could be a bunch of pages, but could also be bricks. Maybe it was meant to represent both. Now the third book had a stand of trees, which again when you think of the Drus, could mean community—"

"Hence kitchen, the most communal room in the house," I murmured.

"Exactly! And now," said Luca, flipping through the third book, "we have the symbol for the fourth: crossed axes. At first I thought that was just a commentary on the story, but in the context of the other symbols, I think it might mean the garden, out among the fruit trees by the wall. What do you think?"

"I would never have noticed it. Couldn't have axed for a better person to have those books," Thorn quipped. "Criminal or no."

I groaned loudly as I turned to her. "Puns aside, do you see how letting Luca out of his shop might be helpful? If we're going to find the books, it helps to have a scholar present."

"Of course," said Thorn, and just as I was about to celebrate my victory, she added, "because I plan on coming along too."

"Great." I glanced around the room. "Tomorrow after I finish up my plant experiment and grab that necklace, we can go to the castle and find the three remaining parts of the story."

"All in one day?" Luca asked.

"If we can." *The sooner the better*, I thought. "With your brains, Thorn's luck, William's protection, and my toolkit, we should be able to find anything."

* * *

The matter was soon settled. It wasn't anyone's favorite plan, but it was the best we could come up with. Before William and I headed home, I went upstairs to check on Gloria and Cairn—and maybe, as a last resort, to ask Trent for a little magical help finding that necklace. But I found all three deeply asleep, Cairn still shivering and Trent sprawled across the floor, so I decided to let them be. Most likely I'd dropped the necklace near my experiment during the set up, anyway. I hated to run to magic over such a simple matter, something I ought to have been able to solve myself.

William and I walked silently through the streets of Belville. The evening had been another long one, and most of our neighbors were asleep or snuggled up in front of crackling hearths. I did notice, as we passed the beauty shop, that Ari and Stella had already brightened the windows with magic lights and strung up cheerful garlands. I rolled my eyes, smiling to myself. Gloria was in for some hard work as soon as she recovered.

Beside me, William bristled. With a low *woof,* he said, "What are you doing out and about?"

At first I thought he was talking to the lamppost on the corner in front of my store. "William, what—"

"Good evening, William, Rrred," Jade said.

"Oh." I smiled. My searching eyes settled on Jade as he bowed from a patch of shadow before our front door.

William huffed. "Got another attack to report?"

"No, I do not, fortunately. But I wanted to inquire about your patient. And," Jade added, looking at me, "to offer my assistance in any way you may need it."

"Well, we do need all the help we can get. Come on, we usually use the back door," I told Jade, keeping my voice light while wondering how someone little more than a "shadow" could have such a deep effect on the butterflies in my stomach. As the three of us trooped around the side of the building, I asked, "You said you saw those creatures around when you found Gloria, right?"

"Yes," Jade answered. "But they left with the morning light."

"Were they there for her?" William asked. "Or are they always there?"

I hadn't thought to ask that question. Appreciatively I ruffled William's ears as we turned around the back of the shop.

"They have always been there, as far as I know," said Jade thoughtfully. "But more and more lately, I sense them. Like wolves howling beyond the windows."

"Hmph. Is there someone—or something—they want?" William sat on the back patio and looked unerringly at Jade.

"That I couldn't say. I do not think they would be discerning," Jade admitted.

"Like a curse," I murmured, thinking of Trent's thoughts about the castle.

"More than you realize," William said. "Your friend Jade can't talk about why they might be there. Can you?"

This last query was directed at Jade, who shuffled apologetically. "I can not."

"I figured. That's it for me, then." William promptly yawned and turned tail, not going into the shop but instead sauntering out the other side of the small yard for one of his nightly solitary rambles.

Part of me thrilled at being left alone with Jade, but my mind was still turning. "You know, we found the third book—just yesterday, when Trent and Thorn were there with me. And . . . it talks about a cursed prince. Someone deeply connected to the castle, and to the Drus. It made me think. Jade, you *are* that prince, aren't you. You're Prince Kalos?"

Jade's outline, which I could see with clarity in the cloudy night, abruptly distorted and fizzled like a magitech wavelength interrupted, and I realized my mistake. William had said Jade *couldn't* talk about the curse. Jade had said it himself a few nights ago. "Oh, no," I said, throwing in a few curses of my own for good measure. "Don't answer that. Forget I said it. You don't have to—"

But Jade didn't seem to be listening. "I . . . I am not that perrson any more." His smooth voice was cracking. "I am no longer . . . whole . . . only . . ."

"Jade. Jade!" Well and truly alarmed, I sprang forward, reaching out.

". . . a shadow . . ."

"I get it, stop talking," I demanded. My fingers found the edge of the cape and I clung to it, moving closer as though my own personal gravity would keep him from fading altogether. "Just stay with me, Jade."

". . . Rrred." Jade's head was bent low, his lips at my jawline. Slowly he seemed to anchor himself in the present once more, his presence becoming more solid. Suddenly I was very aware of his hands on my waist.

"Just be still for a moment," I insisted quietly. I couldn't feel his breath: shadows didn't breathe, I supposed. But the fabric of his clothing felt real enough, and I twisted it in my hands. Watching him almost disappear left me shaking. Maybe it had been a much harder day than I'd thought.

After a moment, I added, "I'm so sorry. I didn't mean to get you in trouble."

"It is not yourr fault. There is much I would tell you—"

"Don't you dare," I interrupted, tugging at his shoulders. "I almost lost one friend and a neighbor today. I'm *not* going to lose you."

Jade's laugh was whispery as it slid over my cheek. "Only a

neighbor, hmm?"

"You'd understand if you'd met Gloria," I chuckled. Thinking of her brought me solidly back to earth. I moved away a little. My body felt very warm under his touch, too warm for such a chilly night. "That said, I really appreciate you helping her, Jade. And coming to me. Without you, who knows what could have happened."

"I was merely lucky," Jade said, settling back to smile at me. "Had I not been paying attention, I could have missed her. My senses, my tie to the castle—neither are infallible."

"Oh, you *aren't* perfect?" I grinned, grateful for the distraction of teasing him. His eyes shone against the clouds overhead. "Well, you're still very helpful. We're planning on coming by the castle tomorrow to look for the rest of the books, by the way. I can't shake the feeling that something about this case is hiding in plain sight."

"Just please, Rred, make sure you find it before it finds you."

"I'm doing my best," I promised. "And—if you want to help tomorrow—if you can—you'd be welcome to."

"I can at least help you find certain areas in the castle," Jade said. "I will make sure to desist as soon as I feel any danger."

"You'd better."

When the pause lengthened and I made no move to go inside, Jade hesitated too. Then he took a step closer. When I held my ground, he took another step and all at once his arms were around me and he hugged me tight. I returned the gesture, trying to will the blush from rising into my cheeks.

"Thank you, Rred," Jade said as he stepped back once more. "Thank you for your concern for me. And do not worry. Every curse must have its limits."

20

Wins and Losses

Every curse must have its limits, Jade had said. Unfortunately, the same held true for experiments.

Every alchemist in Beyond, from serious potion-makers to idealistic dreamers hoping to create gold, must secretly have had a thing for miracles. I certainly did. The more I learned about scientific processes and step by step procedures and what actually went in to making all those fun powders and potions, the less room there seemed to be for miracles. The world filled up with facts, not magic. And yet I had a suspicion that it was in the tiny spaces *between* the facts where true miracles occurred.

All that to say, ninety-five percent of me knew that very little would come from my distillation of Owl's plant-wig. But five percent hoped like mad that it would somehow break the case wide open.

As I slipped down to the lab the next morning, I noticed the back door blinked with a subtle indigo light. I knew from experience that the glow indicated a spell William had placed on the door. Nothing could make that ex-familiar get up early, but he'd still wanted to be sure I wasn't going anywhere without him.

Smiling and still not fully awake, bathing myself in caffeinated fumes, I set my morning tea at one edge of the workbench and began donning the protective gear necessary to check the distiller. It wasn't truly dangerous—only hot, and heat could be dangerous enough, as the desert-island child in me knew well.

William's spell blinked along with my progress as I checked my Ever-Hot Burner and the liquid levels in the distiller. As far as I could tell, nothing had gone wrong overnight. My experiments rarely did; one of the benefits of having a night-wandering companion was that, when he came in at last, William would check things over for me. He was no alchemist himself, but he could tell when there were flames or smoke where there shouldn't be.

Once, I'd asked William where he went on his night journeys and why they were so important. His response had been a scoff. Over the years, though, I had gathered that familiar magic was easily depleted and had to be replenished by association with the element or source of the spell that had created the familiar. Despite his decidedly earthly attitude, William's source seemed to be the stars themselves. And I'd come to realize that simply maintaining the complex wards on the shop—and, admittedly, myself—was about as much as my gruff companion could do.

One thing at a time, broke in the voice of my old alchemical master. My stomach growled, voting that the "one thing" be breakfast. I traced the words in the reference book with my finger, forcing myself to focus.

"There," I murmured aloud, pleased with myself. The

chemical properties listed in the book matched perfectly with what my distiller had given me, which was a rare victory: experimenting was a constant battle against impurities. "Let's see . . ." I looked back up to the top of the page, which listed the plant family and all species included therein, as well as any other pertinent facts. "Alpine flax. Ha! But I thought that kind of flax only grew way up on mountain peaks . . . yep. So how in Beyond did anyone in Belville get their hands on some?" Belville was surrounded by mountains, sure, but it would be a hard few days' trek to get near the peak of any of them.

I straightened up from the book, frowning. *If I have time, I can run over to the florist's and ask before picking up everyone to head out to the castle.* The flower shop was on the way to the bookstore, so it would be easy enough. I wasn't confident that they'd be able to help—flax wasn't a popular cut flower, and alpine flax was even less so, since the fresh flowers required a lot of hiking—but talking to them would at least strike off another item on the list.

"Now, then. To search." I turned to tidying up my experiment, figuring that by tracing all my steps in reverse, I might find where I'd dropped the necklace. The lab had to be cleaned, anyway. I was pretty pleased with myself . . .

Until precisely an hour later, when my experiment was cleaned up, my lab was overturned, and I *still* hadn't found that stupid necklace.

* * *

"You could've woken me earlier to help you look," William said.

"I don't think the search needed *two* groggy people bumbling

169

through the lab." I ruffled William's ears as we walked, ignoring another growl in my stomach. I'd picked lunchtime for our book expedition so that I could catch the morning rush of potion pick-ups before closing for the day—something I'd only barely managed, after frantically searching for lost jewelry all morning.

William dogged my heels as I headed to the bookshop, even waiting patiently while I paused to talk to the folks at A Petal in Time. Rumor had it they were vampires, but they were very sweet nonetheless.

Sweet, and not helpful. "No luck," I told him as we resumed our trip.

William accepted this in silence. Perhaps he'd realized that we were in the midst of an attentive public, and whatever we said was sure to be repeated all over Belville.

"Sorry, we're closing—oh, Red, William, hi," Luca greeted us with a smile of relief. "I've had the hardest time chasing people out. First no one wanted to come in, now suddenly everyone wants books on fairy tales and monsters. I keep trying to tell them Belville *isn't* haunted and Cairn and Gloria will be fine, but—"

"But people are foolish," William finished. When I shot him a reproving look, he shook his fluffy ears. "What? It's true. So are we going or what?"

"Hold on a moment," I replied. "Luca, how are our patients? Is Trent upstairs? And have you talked to Thorn yet today?"

"About the same, yes, and no," Luca said, checking off each answer on his fingers. "Trent said she might call in a doctor from across the lake, though. I just have to finish locking up here, and then I'm ready. We just—um—we have to tell Trent to lift the house arrest spell so that I can actually go outside."

I winced. "Right. Don't worry. While you close up, I'm going to run upstairs for a moment. William, will you keep a lookout for Thorn?"

"Why?" grumbled my companion as I began to thread my way through the shop. "You gonna rob the Witch?"

"Har har," I called back over my shoulder. "No, but since we're going to be together all afternoon, I was hoping you two could get your bickering over with now!"

Without waiting for William's response, I bounded up the back stairs. The door to Owl's old apartment was open, but the moment I crossed the threshold, I was met by a smoke sprite with one finger in front of its face.

"*Shhh!*" the sprite hissed at me. I skidded to a halt.

"Trent?" I peered around the living room.

"*Shhh!*" insisted the sprite.

"Sorry about that." Trent came tumbling down from the bedroom stairs, sending his own sprite into a tizzy. "There was lots of noise coming up from the bookshop, so I tried a few spells to make it quieter for Cairn. Nothing really worked."

"She's sleeping, I take it?"

"You know Priya, who runs the curiosities shop next to Cairn's? She came over this morning with some herbal teas and other goop and said she'd keep an eye on Antiquities For All. I guess the tea or something was to help Cairn heal."

As Trent disentangled himself from his disapproving sprite and waved me out into the hall, I said, "You *guess?*" I didn't really suspect Priya of poisoning Cairn, but clearly if she'd wanted to, Trent wouldn't have put up much of a fight.

"Fennel, fairy's cup, mugwort," Trent rattled off. He closed the door in the sprite's face and grinned at me. "I know what it *was*, Red. I just never got into herbology. I'm more into

171

animation."

"I can tell."

"Anyway, that's not everything. Just now, Gloria started yelling. She can move now. But," Trent held up a hand, stymieing my excitement, "now that she has feeling, she realized she hurt her spine in the landslide. So I'm keeping her in place for a bit."

I blanched. "Is it serious?"

"Naw," said Trent, and while his casual hand-wave failed to be reassuring, his explanation did ease my fears somewhat. "It's bruising mostly. I gave her some stuff for it—stuff from your shop, actually, the stuff you brought over yesterday. She'll be fine, once she gets over her wounded pride at someone having to help her out."

"And once she rests," I added firmly. "Maybe you should give her some of that tea, too. Still, though—that's great! Maybe the creatures' effect is only temporary. Speaking of, you'll have to let Luca out of the house so we can visit the castle. But anyway," I said, finally getting to my point, "I wanted to ask if you've seen anyone hoarding any alpine flax. And also, I need your help finding a necklace."

"Negative on flax. Isn't that a weed?" Trent made a face. "The necklace I can help with though. I can scry for it, if I get all my tools set up. You do have a really good idea what it looks like, right? Cool. Yeah, I can do that. But I have to warn you, a lot of people carry obsidian or black tourmaline these days—you know, to ward off scryers."

I paused. I didn't have to think about scrying very often; William took care of such protection. And I hadn't wanted to admit that a *person* might have taken the necklace.

"Come on, Red." The cheerfulness in Trent's voice sounded

unlike him, and very familiar. "The least we can do is try, right? But as far as letting Luca go goes, we have to check with Officer Thorn."

Officer Thorn. That's *who he sounds like.* I followed Trent down the stairs, trying to shove aside my uncharitable thoughts about police officers brainwashing newbie Witches.

21

Among the Trees

Part of me was terrified that Officer Thorn's "solution" to lifting Luca's house arrest temporarily would be a ball and chain. Fortunately, she seemed content to rely on a promise that she'd be watching Luca closely—not to mention the threat of her club. Trent waved away the force field across the bookshop door, and we marched out dutifully in single file: William, me, Luca, Thorn.

We arrived at the castle and scrambled through the outer walls in record time. William stood for no sight-seeing, and Officer Thorn was in fine form, raring to go. For a moment we paused in the garden, William glowing as he checked the perimeter, me surreptitiously looking through the dark shadows under the old fruit trees.

"Here's the orchard," Thorn declared, just in case we hadn't noticed. She looked down her nose at Luca. "Where's the book supposed to be?"

"Among the trees," said the scholar brightly.

William looked to either side of us, at the dual rows of overgrown trees which ringed the circular wall, and sneezed.

"Looks like we're starting here and making our way round," I decided, before anyone could complain.

In fact, it was a lovely afternoon for a walk. The sun shone bright, even within the castle grounds, and the old timber didn't seem so menacing. The rustles surrounding us were the small and happy kind that come from birds and small furry animals rather than terrifying mysterious creatures. We soon developed a system, spreading out into a line as we walked under the twisted tree branches. With only an arm's length between each of us, and all four of us squinting ferociously at the ground, looking for axes, it seemed only a matter of time before we found the symbol Luca expected.

Of course, the plan did have one flaw. In staring at the ground, we forgot about the rest of the garden. Officer Thorn, the tallest and broadest among us, suffered for this first. She let out a yelp and brought her club crashing down on her attacker, scaring half a dozen sparrows and a robin and thoroughly crunching up some rotten wood before we all realized what had happened.

William sniggered. "If you find it so hard to search and walk, maybe you should just keep guard."

"That tree moved!" Officer Thorn shouted, brandishing her club at all the remaining trees for good measure.

Luca made a sound that wasn't quite a cough. "Um, I don't think the trees in the garden are magical. There's no evidence of fairy rings, bark faces, leaves in specific numerical clumpings, or—"

"Are we searching, or are we here for an afternoon nap?" William demanded.

"Everyone focus," I said, having a hard time concealing my own amusement. "And maybe look up once in a while."

175

Thorn grumbled but fell back into line. Silence descended.

By the time we were a quarter of the way around and the offending tree was well behind us, I was feeling pretty expert, despite having not found anything. Thorn had relaxed back into joking with Luca and William snuffled at mushrooms keenly.

By the time we were halfway round, however, spirits had begun to flag.

When we were about two thirds of the way around, in the area of the garden where Thorn and I had seen the shadowy creatures several nights before, a definite pall hung over the party. Thorn's club swung insistently at her side. None of us noticed birds or small furry animals or mushrooms anymore.

It was William who finally found it. Only a stone's throw from being back where we started, when even Luca was beginning to droop, the shaggy familiar let out a *woof* of triumph and surprise.

"There," he said, scuffing at the grass and crinkly leaves with his front paws. "There's something right under there."

Luca fell to the ground at once to help William clear the dirt. Together, they revealed a gray stone lid, the kind that might be used to close an old well or outdoor icebox, or more romantically, to hide buried treasure. This one had been carved with crossed axes. Luca sat back on his heels and beamed. "This is exactly it. Perfect!"

William eyed the excitable scholar and moved out of hugging distance before answering. "You going to open it or what?"

Luca tried, his fingers scraping over the rough stone. He looked up at me, but I was already kneeling at his side, drawing a vial of weak acid from my belt. "Maybe it was sealed, or maybe it's just dirt," I said as I shooed his unprotected hands away. Using the talons in my gloves to guide the acid, I quickly had the rim of the lid loosened. Then, after cleaning my gloves carefully, I managed to maneuver another slim volume out of the opening.

"Book four," Luca read as I handed the book to him. He held it up like a proud parent. "Shall I read it aloud?"

"Have at it," Thorn said, gesturing with her club as she kept watch.

Luca sat back on the cold grass, cleared his throat, and began to read.

> *There was a creature in the forest, one which above all others, the Drus feared. None among them would speak its name, for to do so was to invite death. This creature was considered to be an avatar of destruction; it dwelt among the fallen trees, where age and decay gave way to mushrooms and minerals. It so happened that the elf whom Prince Kalos refused to harbor knew of the Drus' fear. But the elves had no such superstitions about this creature. Thus it was that in her rage, she set upon the Prince an elf curse. She decreed that his inner nature, merciless and reprehensible as it had shown itself to be, must be aligned with this creature that represented destruction to the Drus. And so, because Prince Kalos had turned away the elf sorceress and doomed her to face her enemies, his body would become like the creature which he most feared, and his outward face would be forever relegated to the shadows.*

Definitely Jade was my first thought. My mind lingered on the bit about shadows. *But what in Beyond is the creature they're talking about? Is it the same thing as the mist creatures?*

As though sensing my thoughts, William whined. "It could mean any number of things," he said. "All sorts of creatures have been associated with death and destruction."

"Would've thought they'd name their greatest enemy," Thorn grunted. She didn't seem too impressed with this new chapter of the story.

"They were too scared of it," Luca explained. "I'm almost certain that whoever wrote these books was Drus themselves. So naturally, they would believe that to write the name of the creature would be to invite bad luck, or—or worse."

William scratched behind one floppy ear. "Sounds like all sorts of bad things were happening to them already. Why worry about naming a creature on top of all that?"

"We don't know the end of the story yet," I pointed out.

"We know the castle's abandoned, and the prince is haunting it," William argued. "And don't tell me you didn't think that maybe the creature in the book is the same as the creatures trying to get Owl, Red. I know that's what you were thinking."

Luca's ears had pricked. "Prince?"

"We don't actually know anything about the prince for sure," I countered uneasily. Something in me didn't want to give away my suspicions about Jade—not yet. Not after the way he'd reacted to my talk about the curse the night before. *He said he wasn't whole anymore. The curse split him in two . . .* "Let's focus on finding the fifth book for now. What's the symbol, Luca?"

Suitably distracted, Luca flipped to the back of the book in his hands. "It's a . . . hm. These shapes in the foreground, they might be robed figures. They seem to be gathered around a pole—a tree, rather. That's probably the moon above them, since they're nocturnal."

"So is it prayer or party?" Thorn grinned.

"Could be anything as far as I'm concerned," I said, staring at the picture. "The symbols we use in alchemy are way more straightforward."

William broke in. "They're not praying. Most lunar cults *sing*."

"Of course," breathed Luca. "It's a choir."

"All right then." I stood, brushing off my leggings and boots. "Looks like our first stop should be the music room."

* * *

The front door of the castle remained solidly closed, so we circled around to the side door. Luca and I pried away the vines that, as usual, had grown over the wood.

"Even the plants around here are suspicious," Thorn muttered as she shifted from foot to foot, ready with her key. "Hey, Red, what did you figure out about that wig?"

"Alpine flax," I said, realizing I'd forgotten to update the Officer.

"As in, the fibers used to make linen?" Beside me, Luca jerked awkwardly and nearly inhaled a vine.

"Yeah," I said, reaching out to steady him. "Why? I figured it must have come from out of town, since most people in Belville spin with wool."

"Yeah, why?" Officer Thorn echoed. From the keen interest in her eyes as she towered toward Luca, she clearly hadn't forgotten her suspicions of him just because he'd been helpful on the book hunt. "You know anyone using flax around here?"

Luca yanked at the plants, clearing the doorway at last. "Erm

179

. . . no."

"I already asked at A Petal in Time. They rarely carry it," I volunteered.

Luca seemed to sense us watching him; he glanced at me from under his hood. "I was thinking . . . if someone knows about alpine flax and keeps it on hand like that, maybe they know about the Drus too."

"Why?" William sneezed. "Because they happen to like plants?"

"I just thought—plant use like that is pretty rare here, and maybe up on the mountain—"

"Maybe they *are* Drus," Thorn interrupted, tapping her club against one of her shiny, knee-high boots.

Torn leaves fluttered about Luca's feet like confetti. "You think the murderer is Drus?"

"That would explain why they rely on death-creatures to clean up their dirty work," William said.

I eyed my companion, unsure if he was stirring the pot or being serious. "I thought they were too scared of the creatures to deal with them."

"I'm just saying, we shouldn't rule it out," William replied, his nose in the air.

Luca was still processing this turn of events. His words came out jumbled. "I guess . . . maybe the Drus moved away, up the mountain . . ."

Officer Thorn was absorbed by her own line of thought. "Elves and Drus. They were having some kind of war, right? What are the chances they're still having it now?"

Silence reigned until Luca startled, realizing that the question had been directed at him. "I—I don't know. Owl never said anything."

"But *you're* an elf," William pointed out. "Right? Do you need Owl to tell you everything?"

"*William*," I reprimanded.

"I don't know," Luca was repeating, shifting from foot to foot. "I mean, I guess if you said that the Drus Prince is still here in the castle, maybe he might still have a reason to fight some elves, but it wasn't *all*—"

"This prince," Thorn interrupted, looking at me, "isn't by any chance your new boyfriend, is it?"

I blanched. "He is *not*. I mean, it's possible that Jade is the prince, yes. But—"

"And you never knew anything about any Drus at the castle," Thorn continued, this time to Luca. Her words were laden with pointed skepticism.

Luca had still been rambling about elves, mostly to himself, although William was giving him a funny look. "Um—what? Oh. No, I didn't know anything about the Drus until Red brought me the first book and we read it," Luca insisted. I had a feeling he'd repeated this statement often in the past few days. "And I still don't think they were hiding any sort of martial power or anything like that. The books are just a history of their downfall—"

"Exactly," said Thorn, batting a stray vine from her nose. "I'm going to need you to find the rest of them double-time."

"Choir symbolism, double-time, ha," I said weakly. Unwilling to say anything more, I turned back to the door.

The books painted the Drus as innocent victims, but was that truly the case? Officer Thorn clearly thought of the Drus as mysterious, dangerous strangers, and Luca thought of them as research material. But I thought Jade was Drus, and he wasn't either of those things . . . well . . . not entirely, anyway.

181

And it didn't help that he wasn't present to assuage any of these new fears. I shook my head and focused on the task at hand. I bit my lip. "Let's get this door unlocked, first of all. Later we can theorize all we want."

To myself, I added, *Let's just hope the truth doesn't turn out to be the last thing we'd wanted.*

22

Faces in the Shadows

Outside, the afternoon light began to wane. We made it to the music room with no trouble—in fact, too little trouble, as far as I was concerned. We carried lights and stayed together, so I hadn't expected any interference from ghostly creatures; but I had hoped to see Jade. Short of running around yelling his name, we certainly made enough noise. Surely he would have noticed our presence in the castle. Maybe he had to refrain from helping in our search because of the curse? Or maybe there were more nefarious reasons he didn't want to encounter Officer Thorn . . .

But it wasn't helpful for me to worry, so I tried to focus. The music room, off to one side of the castle, was about as welcoming as a cursed castle room could get. A large upright piano stood sedately at one end of the room, illuminated by green light coming through a bank of ancient windows. Music stands clustered around some string instruments in one corner. A sofa, presumably meant to hold a rapt audience, was pushed up against the wall across from the piano, and above it shelves held knickknacks and small instruments that were perfectly stable. Near the piano, a large cabinet held rolls and rolls of what was, presumably, sheet music. Naturally, Luca made for that particular piece of furniture first. Meanwhile, Thorn poked around the shelves, and William glowed as he stared down the piano.

"Anyone found anything promising yet?" I asked, eyeing William in particular as I hung back by the door.

Thorn shrugged. "Who knew there were so many types of whistle?"

"There's lots in here!" Luca's voice was muffled, as his head remained buried in the cabinet.

I crossed my arms. "William?"

"What?" He snapped out of whatever trance he'd been in with a full-body shake. "Nothing. Some old enchantment to make it play music, but the magic is faded."

"Let me see that picture again," said Thorn, crossing over to where Luca knelt beside a growing pile of scrolls. "Is there anything in it about *where* in the room we'll find the book?"

William snorted. "As if symbols would be that specific."

"Maybe," said I, for the sake of peace-keeping, "what we need to do is establish a grid system. William, you can start on that corner beneath the windows. I'll start here by the door, and—"

"I found something!" Luca's head rose and he held a paper aloft in triumph. We all stood in tense expectation, staring at him. As if realizing what we expected, Luca added, "Oh. It's not a book, sorry. But it's something else!"

William looked my way and rolled his eyes. "Who'd have thought."

"Be nice," I shot back before picking my way toward Luca. The wooden floorboards around him were strewn with music.

"What is it?"

"It's sheet music. But for a choir," Luca added hastily, before anyone could point out he was practically drowning in notes and chords. "It has words. See? Primary sources like this provide great insight into a culture—"

Thorn snagged the pages from his hands and read in snippets. "'O beauteous moon' . . . 'sweet low branches of sweetest-cherry tree' . . . 'when we were out dancing and the seasons turned' . . ." She wrinkled her nose.

"The fact you can even read it, or that we can read the books for that matter, proves the Drus didn't live too long ago," Luca continued as if nothing had happened. "They must have been writing sometime *after* the Tower of Anti-Babble, when sorcerers came together to make all languages of Beyond intelligible. That was only seven centur—"

"Hold up." Officer Thorn put up a hand for silence and read, "'Silver rays guide gilded revenge/To protect one's home is no violence at all'? 'Bring death to those who dare break in'? This isn't sounding like a peaceful lunar cult to me."

"W-well," stammered Luca, "that's only one song. You could have chosen any number of others—"

"There's sheets of the stuff," said Officer Thorn, shuffling through the choir book. "'Righteous fate,' 'justice served,' 'gone and dark as the night at new moon.'"

William glared at me. "How do you do it, Red? How do you *always* find the cursed homicidal ones to mess with?"

"Hey, I'm not the one who found the castle. Blame Owl—"

"Owl's not here," Thorn said, snapping the book shut. "Because he was murdered. Need I remind you? No," she said to Luca, who had reached out for the music. She tucked it into the breast pocket of her uniform. "I'm taking this as evidence. And I say we hurry and find that fifth book before sundown."

"Well . . . I liked Red's grid idea," said Luca, rallying. "I guess I've already been through the bookcase. I can start here."

"I've got this corner," Thorn declared, moving back to her shelves. "Hop to it!"

After that, there wasn't much to be done but buckle down and look.

Given my previous experience searching the greenhouse, I decided not to try to outsmart the ancient Drus. Rather than look for something I thought might hide a book, I resigned myself to examining *everything* very closely. I started in the corner itself, right down at floor level. The door frame met the siding there, and ornate wood abounded, crying to be checked out. *Any one of these carved leaves or coils of vine,* I told myself, *might hide a secret compartment.*

There wasn't much art on the walls, because the walls themselves were works of art. As I moved up the wall, leaves and vines gave way to flowers, trees, and faces, too. They peered out at me from the foliage, each unique. They didn't seem bloodthirsty or bent on protecting their sacred story. From my travels, I knew that some cultures in Beyond believed in keeping the dead close by placing a picture or symbol in an important place. I wondered if it was the same for the Drus—if all these carved likenesses had been added to the wall as part of a remembrance. If so, it seemed a very touching one.

Or a macabre and dangerous warning, if one's mind worked the way Officer Thorn's did.

I paused, leaning on the door frame. I'd only made it a short way, but I needed to clear my head. *What is it about this mystery that's getting to me?* I wondered.

Maybe it was that nothing was what it had appeared to be. Innocuous books hidden behind symbols. A murdered victim disguised. Creatures in the night obscured by fog. Jade himself, a ghostly presence, split in two.

Across the room, Luca was practically crawling atop the piano to reach some drums hanging on the wall. I smothered a laugh, not wanting to distract him—but it didn't work. In the silent room he heard me, twisted, and slid off the piano with all the grace of a drunken goose.

William, alerted by the racket, turned and sneezed. "That's what you get for climbing on the furniture."

"Red did say to make a thorough search of your corner," Thorn pointed out. She beat me to Luca's aid by virtue of being closer and picked him off the ground, where he was tangled in the scrolls he hadn't put away. Though she tried to dust off his robes, Luca was having none of it.

"There's something special about that one," he insisted, gesturing toward one of the drums and looking very much like he wanted to climb the piano again.

"You're covered in dirt!" protested the well-dressed officer.

"If you're that determined, at least let us help," I told Luca as I also chuckled at Thorn's dismay. I crossed the room and pulled the heavy wooden bench out from beneath the piano, bracing it with my hands. "Here, climb on this. Not the rare and probably ancient instrument. Cairn would have a heart attack if she saw you!"

Luca obliged with a nod. Despite a bit of a wobble at the start, he soon had his hands on the drum. Matters came to a brief standstill as he realized that he couldn't simply pull it away from the wall. But with William's eagle eye assisting from the other side of the piano, Luca soon managed to maneuver the instrument off its hook.

He collapsed down onto the bench with the unwieldy drum in his arms. It was as large as his chest, curved and polished finely. I had assumed it was made of bone and skin, as many drums in the desert are, but found to my surprise it was a very thin piece of circular wood curved in on itself. And inside that curved lip, Luca found a little book.

"The fifth one," he said, eyes alight. "I didn't really think we could find it. This was such a good idea, Red!"

"Hold off on the congratulations," Thorn demanded, "and read the dratted thing."

"Oh—okay." Luca cleared his throat and read the book aloud.

The magic of the Drus was entirely related to the trees they lived in. They used the sweet-cherry pit to create tonics of long life and fast healing, and they prayed to the moon for insight and fortune. None among them could hope to make, or further still to remove, a curse such as the one the elf had placed upon the Prince. Elf curses were known to be rare, but for their rareness, they lasted forever. Unless the conditions of the curse were met, the Prince would forever be split in twain, and the Society with him. The conditions set by the elf were these: that every burned sweet-cherry tree, symbol of the Stagers and of the goodhearted Drus alike, be restored to its former good health. Such conditions, it was seen at once, were impossible to meet. The forest had been irrevocably changed. Where once were creatures who lived in quiet harmony, now were creatures who lived in slaughter and preyed upon death.

"That's it, then," said Thorn even before Luca was done. "The forest was overrun with whatever critters the Drus feared, and so they started using them to strike back at anyone who disturbed them."

I cleared my throat. Much as I hated to pass by an opportunity to shift the blame to a faceless mist creature, I couldn't condone wild speculation. "That's taking a lot of leaps, Officer. We still don't know for sure that the mist creatures and the Drus' nemesis-creature are the same—"

"What are you waiting for, Red, a mug shot and a detailed description?" William said. Clearly—for perhaps the first time ever—he was on Thorn's side. "If we want to solve this, we're going to have to make leaps."

"Can we at least gather all the evidence first?" I protested. "There's still another book out there!"

"It could be the book-gathering that made the Drus angry," Thorn pointed out. "Say, what do they look like? Surely the books have pictures of them."

"Hm?" Luca looked up only when Thorn tugged at the book in his hands. "Oh, here. There are pictures, yes, but they're very simplistic. Almost abstract, I'd say, much like the symbols themselves. In fact there's some evidence that the entire thing is symbolic, if you ask me. I doubt there's anything *real* attached to the books, other than the story itself."

"You've been saying that from the beginning," I pointed out. "Maybe now, Officer Thorn will listen?"

"Officer Thorn will listen when she's caught the murderer and there's no more dratted mystery," Thorn retorted.

"The only problem," said Luca, gesturing to the book Thorn

189

now perused, "is I'm not sure what this new symbol is. It seems marred, maybe by moisture or—"

"Let me look," insisted William, as though he was the expert on Drus symbols.

"Everyone can look." I felt like a preschool teacher. "We can take it home with us and spend all night looking at it, if you like."

This got Thorn's attention. "Take it home? Now?"

"Yes." I gestured to the bank of windows, which were now black. "You yourself said looking for the books could be dangerous, remember? And now it's evening already and we still have to get back to Trent and Cairn."

Thorn looked torn.

"For once, Red makes sense," said William. "Let's get out of here and get some dinner before we become dinner for something else."

23

Return

The walk back into Belville was a quiet one. Thorn was frustrated by the delay in the case—that much was easy to tell; she swung her club so hard that she left scuff marks in the road. William preferred to make all his walks in a musty silence, unless Dusty happened to be nearby. Luca, I believed, was wrapped up in contemplation of the symbol for the sixth book.

He'd shown it to me as we left the castle. I'd been distracted, still trying to peer into darkened corners—but honestly, there hadn't been much to see. While the fifth symbol had been a scene with a moon and definite figures, this sixth symbol was more like, well, some abstract symbol. And like Luca had said, the ink on the page was smudged, as though someone had wiped a handkerchief across it. The main body of the symbol seemed to be two circles stacked on top of one another, the bottom one larger than the one on top.

"Maybe it's a snowman," Luca mumbled. He literally walked down the road with the book in his face, at an angle as he squinted at the ruined picture.

I reached out and moved the book away from his nose. "Isn't that bad for the ancient parchment or something, to have you breathing all over it?"

"That's another thing," Luca said. As though there had been no time intervening, he picked up the thread of his lecture in the music room. "The book can't be any older than seven centuries, but this paper *is* in a really old style, the kind of stuff made thousands of years ago by druids. You see, it isn't really parchment—parchment is kind of like leather, essentially, it's skin."

"I know what parchment is made of, Luca." I laughed, half waiting for him to trip over his own feet. Thorn and William resolutely ignored our good spirits.

"Right, so *this* paper is actually a primitive sort of real *paper,* you know, something made from trees. Which makes sense when you think of Drus society. It's not very processed at all, which is why it's thicker and yellower than paper we use today. And you would think that means it's really old, but on the other hand, this kind of paper would break down pretty quickly, especially in a wet environment like that basement with the well. I mean, the folly."

"Guess they taught you that in Book School 101, huh? Care and keeping of old works?"

Luca grinned back at me. "Something like that. I mean, there is a *reason* the bookshop is so dry and dusty, you know."

"I figured you and Owl were just terrible at cleaning."

"I won't say you're wrong." Luca hesitated. "But do you get my point? Like, if these books are hundreds of years old, why haven't they disintegrated more?"

"I get it," I assured him. "I just don't know what to tell you. I could take a page and put it under my microscope to look at

192

the original fibers and try to count tree rings, but that would only tell you how old the trees were, not how old the paper is."

"Yeah." Luca looked thoughtful for a moment, and then turned back to squinting at the pages in question. In the dark. On an uneven road.

Swatting the book away from his face once more, I asked, "Didn't anyone ever tell you that's how you ruin your eyes? Or worse, break a leg falling over yourself in the street?"

"You could make me a pair of goggles like yours!"

"Really? You want goggles like mine?" Gloria's derogatory comments rang in my mind, right up there with William's. But then again, I supposed, nerdiness wasn't exactly something Luca avoided. "Well, it takes forever to melt down the special glass that's in them and get the enchantment done, so you're going to have to wait."

"Then maybe you should have it," Luca said. "I mean, you have all the tools and everything. I know you can't tell how old the pages are exactly, but maybe if you study the book and tell me everything you find, there'll be some piece of evidence we never thought to look for. You know?"

"Truuuue." I drew out the syllable. "But you realize that some of those tests might involve burning up pieces of the paper, right?"

Luca's mouth tightened, which was about as close to blanching as his dark face ever got. "Um, well, you don't have to do that much, do you? Like maybe just a teeny tiny corner off one of the back pages?"

"I'll be very judicious," I promised, unable to hold back a laugh at the way he suddenly clutched the book in his arms. "But anyway, the symbol should be our main priority, right?

I can look into the other stuff, but we have to remember to focus on that."

Luca fiddled with the book's bark cover. "I still think it looks like a snowman."

"That's ridiculous," I said before I could think better of it. Luca exclaimed in mock hurt and swatted my shoulder, making me laugh. "Okay, maybe it's not *so* bad. After all, the creatures do bring the cold with them . . . maybe we have to confront them to get the last book."

"Let's hope not!" Luca shivered. "This whole thing with the creatures and the—the murder is too much. This was just supposed to be some secret research, you know? I mean, sure, Owl was always really weird about the castle, but . . ."

"But you never thought people would die over it, much less that you'd get accused of murder over it," I concluded, my voice going soft. I reminded myself that Luca had been the closest of us all to Owl, for better or worse. On top of everything else, he was still dealing with the biggest shock. "Hey, do you really believe what Thorn was saying might be true? About the Drus using the creatures?"

"I . . . Honestly, Red, I don't see how the Drus could still be around." Luca chewed on the inside of his cheek, his eyes cast down. "If it was them and their creatures, and Owl knew what they were, he would have just faced them down. That's how he was, you know. He just seemed so . . . so untouchable."

I moved closer as we walked, putting my arm around Luca's shoulder. "Maybe that's just something he wanted you to think. All the secrets and the aloofness, that might have all been for the same reason." *The reason being that he was a greedy, wolfish jerk,* I thought but didn't add aloud. It was clear that Luca's feelings for Owl were mixed. And how could they not be? He'd worked for the man for years, from the sound of it. I realized suddenly that I wasn't even sure how long Luca had been at the bookstore; it seemed like he'd just sprung into being there.

"I know," Luca was saying. "And I know he didn't want me to know, but I still feel like I should. Does that make sense? I feel like the answer is staring me in the face and I just don't see it."

"That makes total sense," I told him. "But don't worry. We're going to figure it out."

* * *

"All right," said Trent a few hours later, spreading his hands and nearly hitting William in the face. "So . . . this is cozy."

Instead of splitting up when we got to town, every single one of us had filed into Luca's shop to see Cairn and Gloria and Trent. I had hoped to at least send someone away to get dinner, but alas, Trent had a huge pot of stew cooking as we walked in. It smelled of bay and sweet potatoes, and it tasted amazing. I'd wolfed down my bowl standing, which was for the best, because there was no longer any sitting room in Owl's tiny apartment.

Gloria was awake but refused to come downstairs, not that any of us wanted her to do so, given the condition of her back. Cairn, too, was up and smiling benevolently at us all from her spot on the sofa, letting us force second and third helpings of food and tea upon her. I'd taken up a spot near her head, and Trent perched on the sofa arm near her feet. William sat beside him, and Luca sprawled on the carpet nearby. Thorn took the only armchair, very much the presiding dictator. In the middle of our awkward circle, Trent's cauldron smoked and shed ashes all over the floor.

"Witches," William muttered, jerking his muzzle out of Trent's range and using his tail to flick ashes off his paws.

"I'm sorry," Trent retorted. "Is there a reason *all* of you have to be here while I scry for Red's necklace? Maybe you'd like to do the scrying yourself?"

William snorted. "I don't see why you need a huge and dirty instrument to do it when a sorcerer could use—"

"Show me the sorcerer who can scry half as well as a Witch can," Trent challenged. Something in his voice said that he'd prefer to meet said sorcerer outside in the street, maybe at twelve noon for a quick-draw duel.

"Can we save the spat?" Thorn interrupted. "That necklace is important evidence."

"It's—it's actually really interesting," Luca said. "You see, sorcery is often criticized for being all about big shows and pacts. Witchery, on the other hand, is generally about day-to-day affairs, and people in particular—"

"Luca, you're not making yourself any friends," I said, watching William's eyes narrow into slits.

"Yeah he is," Trent corrected with a lop-sided grin. He rubbed his hands together and, finding himself with more elbow room this time around, got down to business. "'Kay, here goes. Red, you have that drawing I wanted, right?"

I handed over a scrap of paper from my notebook, being careful to avoid the cauldron. It wasn't actually hot—the 'fire' beneath it was in fact a spell of Trent's and so were the ashes and smoke. Still, it's always best to respect another professional's space.

Trent accepted the paper and barely even looked at it before

196

dropping it into his cauldron, where it sank. With my goggles on, judging by the ripples, I figured the cauldron must be full of water treated with silver to give it a mirroring effect. I noticed petals mixed in the water, as well—*eyebright,* I guessed. Scrying was one of the many things I would never be able to do myself, but that didn't mean I wasn't curious.

Trent drew a sigil in the water's surface while mumbling to himself, something I had seen magic practitioners of all types do—and honestly, something not too unlike alchemy. Next he stirred the water clockwise four times. Then he lowered his face over the cauldron and became very still.

Not a single one of us moved. I didn't think Trent was even breathing. He focused until even the water went motionless, the particles suspended in solution reflecting the firelight.

"Red," Cairn whispered.

Not wanting to disturb the others, I leaned down to her very carefully.

"Red," she repeated. "When you find that necklace, you *have* to destroy it."

"Are you sure the one I had was the one you had in mind?" I asked, thinking belatedly that I should have shown her the picture I drew before Trent ruined it.

Across the cauldron, William cleared his throat.

"Positive," Cairn said, putting her hand on mine. It was the most I'd seen her move all evening, except to eat. Despite our best efforts and the time that had passed, the cold was still getting to her.

"It'll be okay, Cairn," I whispered.

"You have to promise—"

The surface of the water in the cauldron rippled as Trent breathed out. "Got it," he said, leaning up.

"Where?" Officer Thorn demanded.

"See for yourself." Trent motioned to the water. With a sly look at William he said, "Unlike *some,* I can make it so other people can see the picture too. For a while."

We all leaned in, as though the cauldron was a life preserver and we were seconds away from drowning. The image Trent had conjured up was three dimensional, and it showed more than just the necklace—in fact, the pendant wasn't visible: instead, Trent's magic showed us the area around it. It was almost as though we were looking into a little world within the cauldron. A little gnome-aquarium.

And the gnome within it was whistling noiselessly as he walked down the pitch-black road into the forest.

24

A Curse on the Loose

I was the first out the door.

And as Jade had pointed out, my speed wasn't normal. I could walk at a normal pace, and usually I did just to blend in. But when I wanted to run, I could *run*. As in, out-pace-a-horse-and-go-on-for-hours running. It was a blood thing. Some folks had magic in the blood, some folks had green skin or pointy ears or long life spans; I had glittery hair and super-speed.

That was why I didn't stay in Owl's living room, arguing with Trent and Thorn about how many non-witches could ride a broom at a time or if we could risk teleporting to Dusty. William wasn't capable of such magic, and I had no need to bother Trent for it. I was on the road before anyone thought to yell after me. Their calls faded as I streaked through town. All I could hear was my own breath and William bounding along behind me. Once, on the road, he'd confided to me that he used his bond with me to travel as fast as possible, even though it wore him out, because he "knew you'd get over your head in trouble otherwise."

And that was why I ran—why I worried. The first thing I thought when I saw Dusty on that road headed to the castle was that the castle at night would mean death to a gnome alone.

When I caught up to him, he was just under the cover of the trees.

"Dusty!"

The starlight weakly played across the surprise on his face. Aside from that expression, he looked exactly as he always did, dressed in baggy work clothes and carrying a multi-purpose maul on one shoulder.

"Red!" A welcoming, even wondrous grin split Dusty's face. "What are you doing out here? Where'd you come from?"

I couldn't help it: I laughed. Many's the time I'd wondered how Dusty managed to appear wherever he was needed to fix something, and here he was asking *me* a question about travel when that was the furthest thing from what mattered.

William skidded to a halt next to us, leaving a wake of upturned dirt behind him. His fur bristled and glowed as he settled on all fours. "Never mind that," he told Dusty, speaking for me. "What are you doing going into the forest?"

Dusty looked between us and shrugged. "Heard Cairn had some trouble out by the bridge, and thought I better go check to make sure it's still sound. Tank burst over by the grocer's yesterday after I fixed Trent's leak, so I've been too busy with cleanup to take a look 'til now. Finally got done today and I wasn't tired yet, and I still have some lights, so I figured, might as well take the chance while I've got it."

He waved one of the lightsticks I'd given him. My heart melted. I tried to speak in a rush, to get out all the important facts before Officer Thorn showed up and started ordering us all around. "Dusty, it wasn't the bridge, the bridge is fine. Cairn'll be okay. *You,* on the other hand, shouldn't go out into the woods alone because there's dangerous creatures at the castle, and according to a spell Trent just did, you have—"

"Aha!" Thorn's voice interrupted me as she hopped down from the back of Trent's sagging broom. "Imagine *Red* telling a person not to go out into the forest!"

"Not the relevant issue," Trent called, dismounting rather more gracefully.

"Right." Officer Thorn turned, hands on hips, to Dusty. "You, sir, have been avoiding the law. But it's all over now. Time you turn yourself in and hand over the cursed pendant."

* * *

Dusty took a step back. "Pendant? You think I have some kind of necklace or something?"

"He's only been avoiding you because you're bossy," I told Officer Thorn, stepping up. "It's not like he's a convicted criminal."

"Jewelry first, explanations later," Thorn insisted. "The first thing you learn in the Guild is good sense comes to those who follow orders. Turn out your pockets, Dusty."

"Sure." Dusty set down his tools and began emptying first his coat pockets, then his shirt pockets, then his pants pockets, then a secret pocket in one of his boots, then another coat pocket he'd forgotten earlier; and just as I was wondering if we'd be there all night long, Thorn let out an exclamation. She grabbed something out of the growing pile at Dusty's feet.

Personally, I had to admit I was impressed she'd seen it among all the loose screws, leftover nuts, rubber bands, bits of fluff, nubby pencils, and various tools.

"He's more pocket than gnome," William grumbled quietly as we waited for Thorn to finish maneuvering her discovery into a charmed evidence bag.

"Oughta be," Trent said proudly. "I renewed the spells on most of those pockets myself."

"In fair payment for fixing a leaky roof!" Dusty added, leaning around Thorn's bulk to see us.

I chuckled, not so much at Trent and Dusty as at William, who had probably thought he'd go unheard.

"There," declared Thorn, as though we'd all been waiting silently for the end of her performance. She thrust the bag out at me. "Is that the necklace, Red?"

I stepped closer, squinting in the dark. Through the enchanted muslin, I caught sight of the rounded wooden pendant with its strange, twisted symbol. "Yep, that looks like it."

"What necklace are we talking about?" asked Dusty. "I don't keep any jewelry. Just gets in the way."

"You certainly aren't keeping this," Thorn agreed as she shook the bag at arm's length. It may have been only wood and cord, but she handled it like it was pure mercury. After everything we'd heard about it, I couldn't blame her. "This is going in for testing. Where did you get it?"

"I'm telling you I didn't," Dusty protested.

"Then how'd we find it on you?"

"Leave him alone," William snapped at Officer Thorn. "You think he's playacting all this surprise?"

"He could be protecting someone." When William and I turned to glare at Trent, he shrugged. "What? That's how it always is in stories, right?"

"You stay out of this," William growled. "You're not involved in the investigation."

"Ex*cuse* me?" Trent couldn't glow the way William did, but his hair lifted off his shoulders. "It's a job and a half just keeping Cairn's heartbeat normal! I've used up so much magic on this 'investigation' that I could barely fly us out here! Don't tell me—"

"I'll tell you what I think," Officer Thorn interrupted. For once, I was glad she did. Everyone stopped fighting or gaping to pay attention. "I think the tests—when Trent can do them—will prove that this pendant has been at the heart of the crime the whole time. Say it started out as a trinket of Owl's. So he gives it to his new girlfriend, Gloria, so she'll remember him when he's gone to jail. Together, they kill Vic. Then the necklace and the creatures take over her mind—don't give me that look, Red, Luca gave me five different books yesterday about demons that whisper to their victims through cursed jewelry—and she kills Owl, takes to haunting the castle grounds herself. Tries to get rid of the necklace by pawning it off on Dusty, and gets attacked in the meantime."

William rumbled. "Are you saying Gloria got herself attacked on purpose? That's stupid."

"Gloria gave the necklace to *me*," I protested at the same time. A beat passed. William and I looked at each other, equally shocked to hear one another defend our cantankerous neighbor. "She didn't remember how she got it either, just like Dusty. And how come it didn't affect Owl, if it's so cursed?"

"Owl was plenty evil, if you'll recall," Thorn reminded me.

"I still don't see what any of it has to do with me," said Dusty in the silence.

"That depends," said Officer Thorn in her best official voice, "on whether you were an innocent bystander or an accessory."

Dusty sputtered. "I told you, I don't carry jewelry!"

"No, but you'd be an excellent candidate to steal some back, wouldn't you?" Thorn paced the road between us. "Say Gloria regrets giving the necklace away. That very night, she makes a plan to get it back. Who can she go to? Not William, of course. Who else has access to Red's shop?"

"Dusty hasn't been at my shop—"

"No, but he *was* at the bookstore the day you lost the necklace," Thorn said. Dusty gasped, and she turned on him. "Ha! You thought I didn't know that, didn't you? Trent told me all about it. You came to fix a flooded kitchen, but you dallied downstairs. Now why might that be?"

"To complain about *you*," I said in frustration when Dusty wouldn't speak.

"I'm sure criminals have all kinds of complaints about the law," sniffed Officer Thorn. She looked down her long, crooked nose at Dusty. "One other thing. Why doesn't anyone know where you live?"

"'Sa gnome thing," said Dusty, shifting on his feet.

"Is it? Well, then, so is spending a night at the station."

"Thorn!" I cried, incredulous.

"Red," said she, and her voice had the air of finality. "He's evaded the police and has no known address for house arrest. This is our best precaution until we've had a chance to examine the evidence. You ought to be glad. This could be a break for your friend Luca. If this pendant is as cursed as everyone thinks, then chances are, whoever was in possession of it three days ago is the one who murdered Owl. That's supposing it wasn't your lover and his army of mist creatures!"

* * *

I stood, rooted to the road, as Thorn and Trent walked back into town with Dusty in tow.

Once they'd disappeared into the night, William shook himself. "There isn't anything you can do about it right now, Red. We'll have to hope the Witch's spells, whenever he gets to doing them, will come up with the truth."

"Oh, there is *absolutely* something I can do right now," I replied through gritted teeth. The thought hadn't occurred until William had said something. Sometimes I thought he did that on purpose—challenged me with the negative view, just so I'd get a jump on something positive. "'Lover,' indeed. 'Army,' ha!"

"Red, I am not going to help you break into the police station."

"Not that." With one last look at Belville, so silent and unassuming in the cloudy night, I turned to face the forest.

"I am also not going to a haunted castle with you at night."

Ignoring William and his list of *nots*, I took as deep a breath as I could and bellowed, "JADE!"

"In fact," William continued, "if you do go, I will give you up for lost right now."

"JADE! COME OUT HERE!"

"Then I will go back to the shop and start divvying up your things."

"JADE! I KNOW YOU CAN HEAR ME!"

"He probably can't."

"Thank you, Captain Obvious," I said to William, exasperated. "I was hoping some confidence would do the trick, but I should have known better, with *you* around. Curse it! I need to

205

talk to him. Literally everything Thorn has said this evening has been ridiculous. Jade's the last one who can make any sense of it. Maybe he knows about the pendant, if it really is a Drus thing and not a scholar thing. Maybe—I don't know—"

"We're not going to the castle to talk to him," William repeated firmly.

"I *know*. Why do you think I'm standing here yelling? JADE!!"

"What makes you think he'll come out now when we didn't see him all day when we were actually there?" William huffed. "By all means, continue yelling if it makes you feel better. We can see which of us goes deaf first."

"Oh, gods and goddesses!" By that point I was so upset I was ready to kick the nearest tree or, better yet, punch a hole right through whatever murderous mist creature we might encounter at the castle. Instead, to my embarrassment, tears began pooling at the edges of my goggles.

I have no idea what I was thinking. I yanked the goggles from my head and wiped my eyes on my sleeve. William wisely refrained from comment. In the silence I realized how ragged my own breathing was and how cold the night had become. *Dusty in jail, and Gloria bedridden, and Luca* still *a main suspect? That wasn't how any of this was supposed to go. It isn't right.*

The frost creeping over the tips of my fingers felt exactly as bitter as the knowledge, deep in my heart, that somehow this entire investigation had gotten away from me.

But before I could pitch headfirst into that particular well of self-pity, from the road behind me I heard a small cough.

25

At the Heart

Jade was visible, if patchy in the starlight, as he bowed. He stood in the road behind us, as if he had just come out from town for a walk. I froze, thinking of how I'd been shouting in the wrong direction and now was in puffy-eyed, red-cheeked misery.

"Am I . . . am I late?" Jade asked, his voice mild.

"Oh, no, right on time," said William, full sarcastic mode engaged. "The gallant gentleman arrives, not during the fight nor when called for, but when his ladylove sheds a tear."

"I am *seriously* going to need you to shut up," I hissed, stamping at William.

Jade, meanwhile, stepped back in surprise. "Are you crying, Rred?"

"I am not!" Realizing that I sounded like a four-year-old child, I decided this meeting needed to get on track. "Listen, Jade, do you have a minute? Because some things have happened, and we could really use whatever insights you have."

"Of course I have time," Jade answered. "But you should come away from the forest. The creatures at the castle . . .

they grow bolder all the time."

"Just invite yourself in, why don't you," William muttered.

I glared down at him. "If you're going to be rude, Jade and I will go talk at the tavern."

"You mean you'll be seen by everyone in town talking to yourself," William retorted.

"I don't care," I said. "How do you think it will reflect on you, since you live with me?"

Jade, who had been watching this banter, spoke gravely. "Is it me, or is this more bickering than is normal?"

"It's been—it's been a long night." I sighed. "Come on. Let's go back to the shop, and I'll fill you in."

* * *

"A cursed pendant," Jade murmured. He and I sat at my kitchen table over a pot of tea. William had perched himself like a chaperoning gargoyle on the back of the sofa, staring us down. I buried my nose in a cloud of honeyed chamomile and ignored him. Jade, who didn't seem to actually drink tea but who had been very understanding of my need to make some, continued musing aloud. "Perhaps that is why the creatures are restless. They grow not bold, but desperate to retrieve it."

When I was silent, William spoke. "You think it's true, then?"

"I couldn't say," Jade replied.

"Aren't you supposed to be Drus royalty or something? Who *else* would be able to say?"

"Hush, William." I was tired and keenly aware of the fact that we had to tread lightly when asking Jade questions. And, on top of that, even more aware that despite this danger, Jade had been the first person on my mind to talk to. Why had I bothered him if he couldn't help? What was wrong with me all of a sudden?

When William's response was to stomp off to his window seat and curl up with his tail to us, I sighed and said to Jade, "I'm really sorry about all this. It just came out of nowhere. Officer Thorn is convinced Gloria and Dusty are behind it, even in on it together somehow, but I—I just—"

"It doesn't entirely make sense, does it?" Jade asked softly. He sat in the darkest shadow of the room, the corner beside me—near enough to reach out and touch. A smile flittered around his lips as he added, "You wish to protect them both, don't you? Even your standoffish neighbor."

"Hm." I couldn't manage a full chuckle, but I returned his smile. "I wish I could, but it feels like I'm at my wits' end. Have you . . . you said you'd seen Gloria around the castle before, right? Was she with Owl?"

"Yes. In the past, she would come often to the castle, though only as far as the gazebo."

"Really?" I bit my lip, remembering Gloria's voice as she mentioned the "things" living at the castle. "You didn't ever—didn't ever talk to her, though?"

"No. It is not me she met. I admit I was wary of her presence, and I wonder if she could sense how . . . how twisted the castle has grown."

"You were wary?" I glanced up at Jade, whose impassive gaze was fixed on me. It took me a moment to realize what he might mean. "Oh! Because she has elven heritage?"

There's no way Gloria's family had anything to do with the elf curse, I thought. *She's a stranger here, like me.* If her elvenness was Jade's reason to hesitate, then his reaction was outdated. But then, so were a lot of things about Jade.

As if sensing my thoughts, Jade inclined his head. "Not my finest moment. But it became clear she knew Owl. I believed them to be friends, which was enough reason for me to avoid her. But now I think perhaps that, too, was an assumption on my part."

"Hum." I swished the liquid in my cup, almost burning the tips of my fingers on the hot porcelain. "You knew him a long time, I guess? Did he ever seem like the pendant was getting to him? Creatures whispering evil things in his ear, or whatever?"

"There could only have been one creature whispering in his ear." Jade's voice had gone very hard, and though I didn't fully understand what he meant—was he saying Owl was self-centered?—he continued, "I believe Owl was a victim of his own cruel ambitions. I will not say it was justice—indeed, I could not even guess who struck him down—but truly, it was the end Owl created for himself by his actions. I do not think he was driven out of his senses, if that is what you mean. Perhaps he knew enough to keep himself safe from the pendant's curse. He was a very clever man."

"Wow, Jade. I don't think I've ever heard you speak that way about someone," I said, watching him.

His eyes flickered up to mine. "Forgive my vehemence."

"Of course," I assured him. "You certainly weren't alone in feeling that way about him." Even Dusty, I winced to remember, had spoken out against Owl. "But Jade . . . I should probably tell you that if the necklace thing turns out to be a bust, Thorn's next idea seems to be that *you* did it. Killed Owl, I mean. You, or some other Drus, somehow."

"I . . ." Jade hesitated, shuffled next to me. "I did not think any Drus remained. And if they did, I do not think Owl is the one they would wish to kill."

I startled. "There's someone *else* mixed up in all this?"

"I couldn't say."

"Don't tell me you mean they'd be mad at *you?*"

Jade was silent for a moment, returning my gaze. Then he said, levelly, "It is hard to know who they would blame. The matter is a difficult one, particularly because *you,* Rred, have become part of it. I think Owl knew that also. Even when you first came to town, he tried to warn me away from you. But by then it was too late. In his egotism, he made an uncharacteristic mistake."

"Oh." I blinked, and again my slow thoughts struggled with this. *Why should my presence make any difference? Because I'm an outside observer? Maybe I shouldn't have put chamomile in my tea. Did Jade just imply Owl could have used me to get to him?* "Well . . . I had hoped to see you, today at the castle. But if it was too much—"

"It wasn't that," Jade interrupted gently, laying his hand over mine as if to prevent me from blaming myself for asking. "I wanted to see you. But I couldn't come close. I don't know why; perhaps the Officer, knowing of the pendant, employed some kind of protection against cursed objects."

"You aren't an object," I pointed out. "But I guess it's possible Trent gave her a charm."

Jade smiled. His hand on mine tightened. "I came into town this evening to ask how your research went. And to offer any help I can."

"We found two more books, but we still have one left," I told him. "Thorn thinks that looking for the books is riling up the creatures. Or maybe some kind of ancient nature magic, you know, with all the vines. I don't know how that fits into her many theories, but she also thinks—she thinks the creature the Drus feared above all others is the same as the mist creatures now." When Jade remained silent, a slight frown on his face, I asked, "Do you think that's possible?"

"I . . . I am not sure." His voice was faint, but he soon rallied. "But I can look into it for you, Rred. I can try to see what they look like and report to you."

"Thank you, Jade. That'd be wonderful. I never did get a good look, that first night."

Jade smiled as if he knew what I wasn't adding, that he had been distracting me. "I will go now and see. You should get some rest, my friend. And . . . Rrred?"

"Yes, Jade?"

"I want you to know," he said before he left, "that I have full faith in you."

* * *

The next morning I showed up at the station with a basketful of almond pastries from the local bakery, run by a werewolf named Ginger. He was temperamental, but absolutely expert with sugar and dough, and I was devoutly thankful for his presence in town. I'd been too distracted all night to bother doing any baking myself.

Thorn let me in to see Dusty without much comment. Dusty himself, however, was full of comment about his situation.

"An' she won't tell me when this'll all be over an' I have *work* to do. But she keeps goin' on about how to find me if I leave an' I keep trying to explain bout the Principle of Society an' how it's always best to be invited out but she just stares at me an' says she only has my word for it. Which," Dusty ended sulkily, "*I* think you could say about the whole darned thing. Whoever said I liked Gloria, anyway?"

I made what promises I could and made sure he was reasonably comfortable. But those words echoed in my head. *We only have your word for that.* Dusty was right. That could be said about every step of this mystery, not just Dusty's explanations of the finer points of gnome culture. Even the books could be biased or giving us the wrong information. The only things I knew for sure were the results of my own experiments and Trent's spellwork.

And for once, Thorn was not encouraging. "Put a hold on all investigations," she told me as I emerged from Dusty's cell and passed by her desk. "Wait and see what we get from this pendant. You're too emotional, Red."

I nodded and mumbled something that wasn't a promise.

If Thorn had left things there, maybe my day would have gone differently. Maybe the whole investigation would have been different. But Officer Thorn's never been one to pass up an opportunity to be bossy.

"In fact, you should stick around your shop today. I might even ask William to—"

"Ask him to what?" I'd been walking while she talked. I'd almost made it out of the station altogether. But when she brought up William, I stopped at the threshold of the front door. And as I turned back to look at her, my blood began to boil. Actually, I think it had been boiling all along, ever since she put Luca under house arrest, and that was the moment it finally erupted.

"Why don't you just have Trent put a spell on me," I said, loud enough to be heard in the street. "Why don't you stick me in a cell with Dusty? Hm? I'm surprised you didn't lock me up while I was delivering baked goods. I'm surprised you haven't locked up the entire town! How many people do you need to put under house arrest, Officer? Everyone except Gloria?"

"That's not being reasonable," said Thorn, jabbing a finger at me as though she could pinpoint the exact word where I'd gone off the rails. "I *did* have someone watching Gloria. The fairies."

"As if they ever do anything *but* watch her!"

"Listen, Red, I know you're upset. But the plain fact of the matter is that Gloria had a good excuse at the time, and your friends did not."

"She was out on a desolate road in the middle of the forest, at *night,* after having missed an entire day of work! What in Beyond could have been a good excuse? How come you didn't just arrest her then and save Luca all this trouble?"

Thorn shifted. She looked left and right, as though there might be eavesdroppers in her empty, magically-protected police station. Then she hauled herself up and stalked right over to me, pulling closed the door I'd opened partially on my way to leave.

"I wasn't going to tell you," she said, her voice low. She had to hunch over quite a bit to come close to whispering in my ear. "As a rule, I don't get involved in property disputes. Not until they get ugly, that is."

I glared at her, stepping back to avoid her cream-cheese-and-bagel breath. "What are you talking about? I don't have any dispute with Gloria."

"*You* don't." Thorn chuckled, which I considered very poor taste. "She was meeting with the real estate man, Dansforth. Pondering her options. That's exactly what she said. They had to meet out of town to avoid suspicion."

For a moment I sputtered, remembering my own conversations with Gloria. She'd mentioned the alley once; she'd mentioned Dansforth. "Did she actually say her dispute was with *me?*" Thorn paused, and I charged ahead. "It was with Owl! She told me herself, he wanted her shop!"

Thorn pulled back. "Eh."

"'Eh'? Don't 'eh' me!" I retorted, bristling.

"I'm sorry, Red, but that's all I can say about it. You might be right, but unless Gloria's hiding a *lot* of information, there's no evidence of Owl having designs on her shop. There's no evidence of anything Owl did. Don't you think that's frustrating for me, too? The plain fact of the matter is we have to *hope* his murderer had to do with the pendant or the castle, because otherwise there's nothing to go on at all."

Even though I was mad, I understood her point. She could investigate the emotions of living people, but she couldn't fathom the plans of dead people. "Wait— what about Vic?"

Thorn crossed her arms, but her expression softened. "I haven't forgot about him, believe me, Red. How could I forget about my fellow officer? That's why I have to be so hard on the suspects. You know what they say. Play hard and you'll be—"

"Don't you dare—"

"—Victorious."

26

Key to Crime

Rather than go back to my shop and help William open, I trekked to the other side of Belville to visit the bookstore. Even though Thorn had made good points, I was still steaming, and the cool walk through crispy leaves helped me calm down. Plus, there was no chance I'd go meekly back to my own store after the things Officer Thorn had said. I'd let Gloria sit on her mysterious grudges and real estate deals for far too long.

Before I could make it up the back stairs to check on Cairn and Gloria, though, Luca stopped me by excitedly holding up a very old encyclopedia from behind his desk.

"I figured it out," he informed me, beaming.

That got my attention, vague as it was. "You mean you know what the mist creatures are?"

"Well . . ." Luca hesitated. "No. I'm not sure. But I know what the Drus thought was so awful! Did you know that there's a unicorn for both dualities?"

"A what." I was fully distracted from petty arguments, thanks to the feeling of ice running down my spine. *Relax*, I instructed my nervous thoughts and itchy feet.

216

"A unicorn. Both dualities, you know, like both poles, or opposites? Now, you know the light one, right? Well there's a dark one too!"

I stared at Luca, utterly bewildered and still feeling defensive. Under the weight of the silence, Luca crumpled.

"I guess it *is* all theory," he said, setting his book down on the desk. "Probably just made up by someone who liked drawing different kinds of unicorns. I shouldn't have brought it up, I'm sorry."

"Hey, Luca, don't say that." I walked over and put my hand on his shoulder, setting my own worries aside. "I'm just slow this morning, that's all. A lot has been going on. Walk me through it, okay?"

"Okay." Luca smiled up at me shyly, as though making sure I meant it, before relaunching into his explanation. "I found it in this book late last night. I never thought of it before because it's *super* elusive—we don't even have a name for it, and I don't think anyone has seen one. But in this book it says they're the opposite of normal unicorns, that is, instead of guarding life, they guard death. It makes sense in a way, right? Then I thought about that Drus text talking about mushrooms and destruction and how, today, we recognize that decay exists essentially as the flip side of the coin to life . . ."

Luca went on, discussing his evidence and the correlations he'd drawn. I have to admit I stopped listening. I'd heard of dark unicorns. I'd always thought they were a fairy tale my mother liked to tell. She used to say, "unicorns come in all colors, Cinnabar," and I'd reply "whatever," because I thought she was just trying to make me feel better about being different.

But if that's what Jade's physical body had been cursed in to

217

. . . did it make sense? I wondered. *Does that mean that there's* another *creature running around the forest, or haunting the castle?* I remembered his words from our latest conversation. *"It is not me she met."* What if Gloria had run into Jade's other half?

"Luca," I said, interrupting his stream of thought. "I think you're on to something. But do you have any pictures of what it looks like? Is it actually dangerous, do you think?"

"Dangerous?" Luca paused, as though he hadn't thought of that. "I mean, on one hand, I guess most people would say no. The source talks about dark unicorns being reclusive and passive mostly. But on the other hand, *everything* can be dangerous, right? It just depends. If one was mad I'm sure it'd be terrifying, just like a normal unicorn would be."

Oh, Luca. A sudden wave of sympathy for my timid friend came over me, and I missed the chance to make a remark.

Luca kept talking. "'Dark' doesn't mean 'evil,' of course. Not even the Drus would be that simplistic about it. But I still think it's the creature they were scared of, because it represents the opposite of what they were used to. You know, they lived a really long time, so they didn't deal with death very much; they worshiped the moon, which is a kind of light worship; and even though their entire culture was reclusive, they were actually really communal amongst themselves. Plus they love trees and flowers, which moss and fungus kind of take over, which could be pretty disturbing for a tree-loving society when you think about it. I mean, a lot of that stuff *is* pretty gross."

I swatted at his hood. *"That stuff* being mushrooms and mosses that are actually really useful in potions, you mean?" When he chuckled, I smiled and said, "You seem like you have a better handle on Drus culture now, too."

Luca nodded. "I reread the five books we have about a million times last night. I can't really sleep lately. Might as well research, right? Oh, plus, I found this." He reached across his desk to a scroll on top of a pile. After knocking over said pile and determining that he had the wrong scroll, he tossed it aside and began hunting around the dusty cash register. From a gap between the desk and the nearest bookshelf, he withdrew another crumpled scroll.

"Here, look," he said, unrolling the compromised parchment with expert care. I leaned over, tilting my head to make sense of the closely-written text. It seemed to be some kind of inventory. "'Moon Cults of the Past Ages,'" Luca said proudly, indicating the title at the top. "This is just a copy of the original, of course. They didn't include any pictures. But there is a description of a society called the Moon's Ring, which I think is the same as the Drus. The author describes them as a subspecies of elf, but that's really old language. They probably wouldn't be talked about that way today."

"Wow, Luca. When you come through, you *really* come through, you know that?"

"It only took me three days." Luca grinned up at me, equal parts bashful and self-deprecating. I shook my head, but returned his grin.

"Better slightly late than never," I reminded him.

"I guess. But think about it, Red. If the elves saw the Drus as essentially their 'younger siblings'—which at the time they probably did, because elf culture has a history of being patronizing that way—then you can see how the elves *really* would have been mad at the Drus for not helping them out in their political war. And you can see why the Drus would have been deeply divided, too."

219

"Yeah," I said slowly, thinking it over. "I guess I see that. Hits closer to home, and all."

"Exactly." Luca sounded as pleased as if he'd just been awarded first prize at the county fair.

First prize for investigating a power-hungry murderer, I reminded myself, my smile fading. "Luca, does this mean you think that the murderer might be Drus after all?"

"I still don't see how there are any still around. Aside—aside from maybe Jade, like you said." Luca's hands drifted down to the desk, re-crumpling his scroll. "I don't know, Red, I've just been looking stuff up without thinking about the—the murder. But it's not like—um—it's not like Owl was speared or anything. With a horn. And honestly, if you think about it, the elves have a lot more to hide in this story than the Drus do."

"Maybe someone didn't want Owl uncovering the history." *But I doubt Owl's first thought upon breaking out from jail would be to expose an ancient dispute,* I reasoned. *Maybe he thought he was getting power, but someone else knew otherwise.* This line of thought started to make my head hurt, so I turned to thoughts of another person with things to hide. "I have to run upstairs to talk to Gloria. Keep up the good work!"

* * *

"I do *not* need your help, Red," spat Gloria.

I sighed as I paced back and forth at the foot of her bed. I should've known that asking her directly about Dansforth and Owl wouldn't get me anywhere.

"I'm just saying," I told her, "if I *were* you, not that I am, but if I were, I'd be a little more cooperative."

"Cooperative. With *you*." Gloria looked at Trent, who stood at the head of the bed with the breakfast she'd refused to eat. He grinned and waved like they'd just met.

"We are trying to help you," I said, for what felt like the fifth time.

"By keeping me here?" Gloria's eyes narrowed as she turned back to me. "How about you do something *actually* helpful?"

"Like what? What could be more helpful than trying to give you food or prove your innocence?"

"Like finding who attacked me out there, that's what."

I ran my hands through my hair. "Listen, Gloria, we've been over this. All we know is what you've told us, which wasn't much. You made it sound like it was an accident and then the creatures showed up."

"It wasn't creatures who stole my keys." Gloria looked between me and Trent as if to be sure she had our attention. "I had the safe keys for the salon on me during the walk. I *always* wear them on a chain clipped in my pocket. But when I looked through my coat yesterday, I couldn't find them."

"Wait, you got up and searched your stuff?" Trent frowned.

"I had to! I thought—" Gloria paused, then rolled her eyes. "I thought Ari and Stella would come asking for them, if they're keeping the shop open."

"They haven't?"

When Gloria didn't answer my question, my gaze slid to Trent, who shook his head. "No visitors."

"I wouldn't want to see them anyway," Gloria muttered. "Gods, they're probably giving out cuts and treatments for free. The point is, someone stole my keys, and it must have happened while I was out. And that means someone else was *there*."

"Which means you were attacked rather than self-sabotaging," I murmured aloud.

"What?"

"Nothing," I said brightly. "Any idea who this other person was?"

Gloria stared at me, her black eyes narrow. "No. I don't. Just do a scrying spell for the keys and find the thief yourself. I know you can. You kept me up all night last night doing it for that stupid necklace."

Again my gaze slid to Trent. His pale skin stood out against Owl's musty red wallpaper, and yet his expression was unreadable. "I do still have my stuff here," he said, shrugging.

"Do you have the energy for it, though?" I asked. "I imagine looking at the pendant takes priority."

"Thorn's bringing it over this afternoon. I'll be fine between now and then." When I moved to help him bring his gear up to the bedroom, he whispered to me, "I might have exaggerated a little last night. Truth is, Cairn wears a couple weird old health charms that are helping keep her steady. I'll be *more* fine doing this and getting a little tired than I would be if Gloria threw a fit and blew flames in my face."

"Don't be rude," I reprimanded, keeping my voice down so as not to wake Cairn. "Phoenixkin don't do that. I think."

"Yeah. Gloria would be the one to try, though." Trent grinned.

We soon set up the cauldron in the corner of Owl's old room. Gloria watched from the bed like a displeased queen as Trent stirred the water and dispelled all traces of the spell the night before. He made her sketch out her keys, as I had done with the necklace, and then he settled in to work.

I glanced over at Gloria while Trent slipped into his trance.

Again I thought of what Jade had said about her, that she often went to the castle alone. Had Owl had some hold over her, something aside from the whispers of romance or feuds? Or had she been meeting Dansforth all that time? I'd never seen him come by her shop at all. In fact, Gloria never seemed to have any visitors, aside from clients. Somehow, she'd managed to live in town while remaining completely isolated. Surely that couldn't be entirely her fault.

"Hummmmm." Trent shook his head, making me jump from my reverie.

"What is it?" Gloria demanded. "Who stole them?"

Trent ignored her and looked at me. "Red . . . I think you got this one."

"Great. Thanks." I shifted, holding up a hand to silence Gloria. Glancing into the cauldron, I wondered who could have intimidated Trent so badly. Roving mountain giants? A band of thieves in the forest?

The scene in the water took a moment to filter through my brain. It was full of sparkly lights and mirrors. I sat back, my breath hissing through my teeth.

"The keys are already back at the salon."

27

Safekeeping

William always warned me that fairies "polish" the truth. They wouldn't lie, exactly, but they knew how to make you see what they wanted you to see. And I was so, so tired of not seeing what was going on that I stomped over to the beauty shop ready to do the one thing I could think of to cut through all the distractions: confront them directly.

I caught Ari and Stella just as they finished up their pre-lunch appointments. Waves of rose perfume and sparkly hair enveloped me as the customers flooded out and I rushed in. The shop took me aback at first. The mirrors had always been there; but the few times I'd been in before, the shop had been decorated in a calm, cool style, with sleek black accents and leafy plants. Now, the place was a riot of color. Flowers tumbled off of every surface and fairy lights littered the ceiling. It looked more like a pixie discotheque than an upscale salon.

Stella was on me at once, her hands on my long ponytail. "Red! Oh we're so glad you came in, do you want a haircut? We could do so *much* with you! Imagine long flowing tresses and balayage and maybe pink highlights—"

"—no, gold glitter—" Ari hovered by my shoulder.

"Stop!" I yanked my hair away from the fairies and turned to glare at them. Both floated a foot off the ground, the breeze from their wings nearly knocking over the window display of glass bottles of shampoo. I wondered if Gloria had a "no flying in the shop" policy. I wondered, too, how long Gloria had been fighting to keep back the fairy lights.

"You don't expect Gloria to come back at all, do you?" I asked Ari and Stella, crossing my arms. "You were hoping that fall would do her in."

As one, the fairies widened their eyes. The effect, in the dancing colored lights of the shop, would have been comical if we weren't discussing a serious crime. "Oh, Red, how could you ever think such a thing!!! We would *never* wish that on anyone! We've been so worried—"

"Save it." I held up a hand. "Tell me why you have Gloria's safe keys."

The two exchanged a glance.

"She gave them to us," said Ari.

"Yes, we're looking after them for her," said Stella.

"She had no idea you had them." I ground my teeth, choosing my next words carefully. "Maybe you didn't want her dead. But you *did* want her gone, didn't you. You wanted to frame her for everything that happened with Owl. Were *you* the ones who found that necklace out at the castle and gave it to her? Were you the ones who charmed her so that she couldn't move? That sure explains why her symptoms are different from Cairn's. You got close, but you couldn't quite replicate what the creatures do."

Ari and Stella settled on to the floor and looked up at me with a new expression across their faces. A sly one. "You can't prove any of that, Red. In fact, who do you think would listen to you? Do you really think Officer Thorn cares what you have to say? If she did, then she wouldn't always be bossing you around, now would she?"

In tandem, they took one step closer. I held my ground. "Back off. You can't do anything to me with William right next door."

"Are you sure about that?" The fairies asked sweetly. "Are you sure he isn't *tired* of having to run after you all the time?"

Visions of William being towed in my wake as I ran, being grumpy and turning tail, being left behind to stew raced after one another in my mind's eye. I *did* disrupt his life quite a bit. I remembered how put out he'd been about having to deal with the fairies, and about dealing with Gloria—

"This is what you've been doing to her," I realized aloud. "This is why she hates everyone in town. *You're* the ones telling her that everyone's out to get her. So what happened? Did she figure it out? Did she become too difficult to manipulate anymore?"

Suddenly Ari's face was not pink, but red. "It would have been just fine with everything the way it was."

Stella, too, wasn't glittering so much as gleaming, knife-sharp. "We didn't *need* to take over the shop. We were pushed into it."

"Because she started suspecting the truth," I repeated, glaring at them both. "You know what? You don't intimidate me. You should be ashamed of yourselves. Gloria has never done anything wrong. She even let you live here!"

"Maybe she was keeping us captive," suggested Ari.

"Did you ever think of that?" Stella challenged. "No, you come in here just like her, wanting to make victims of us!"

226

For one split second, I considered the idea. Then at once I realized I'd fallen into their trap again. I scowled. Stepping up between them, I did something my mother used to do when she was exasperated: I snapped my fingers in front of their faces. It didn't do anything in particular. Once upon a time, the gesture might have been used to dissipate spells, but those days were long gone. Mostly it kept me from the even more immature response of kicking their shins. And, thankfully, it rendered them temporarily speechless with indignation.

"Give it up," I said forcefully. "I don't want to hear any more stories from the two of you. You're done. You can go to Officer Thorn and explain everything, or you can clear out. Now."

"You can't fire us. Only Gloria can fire us. Are you trying to take over her shop?"

"Gloria is none of your concern. You try to see her, and I'll have Trent curse you both with purple spots."

"We have her keys!"

"And I," I said, drawing a small case from my pocket, "have a lock-picking kit. I don't care in the least. What's it going to be? The station or the road?"

In their anger, the two fairies looked exactly alike. All the pink and gold and frills faded away. They glowered at me, but they didn't try anything else. I'd gambled a bit mentioning William but, as it turned out, his protection really did save my hide. With no ability to charm me solid or talk their way out, Ari and Stella stood before me as exactly what they were: cowards.

I stood firm. Ari and Stella wavered, blinked, and then the fairy lights and flowers were gone. Two neat suitcases sat at their feet. Like little dogs, the suitcases trailed out the door with Ari as, wordlessly, she left.

"We may have left Gloria out there," Stella told me on her way out, "but we never did anything to the old antiques lady. And we never gave Gloria the idea to go out to the castle as much as she did in the first place. Maybe that shadow that follows you around is more dangerous than you think."

"Don't bother coming back. Everyone in town will know what you've done," I said, mustering enough bravado to hide the way her comment struck a chord. She sneered at me, but, like her sister, she left.

"Phew." I took several deep breaths and looked around me at Gloria's shop. It now appeared exactly as it had before, cool and sleek. Most of fairy magic is glamour. Ari and Stella had only conjured up appearances, not changed anything real. That was how they could take it all down and pack up using magic, too.

In the silence, I wondered if I'd been too harsh. I wasn't usually the one who dealt with magic creatures—usually that was William's job—so I was surprised at how easily they'd left. *But they were the ones who chose to leave rather than come clean.* I brushed away my doubts. Fairies were known to be rovers and tricksters. It was a stereotype, one I hadn't wanted to believe, but at its core was an unsettling truth: Ari and Stella would be fine. Angry, no doubt, but perfectly capable of landing on their own two feet. I only hoped that wherever they ended up, they wouldn't be able to cause such harm.

"Tell Officer Thorn about them, and maybe have her put out a report. Tell Trent to look out for them. Tell Gloria about all this, somehow, and then break into her safe. And talk about the real estate thing: maybe that was just the fairies messing with her, too. Track down Dansforth to make sure." I looked around as I rattled off my mental to-do list aloud. I didn't speak the last item, though.

Somehow figure out where the other half of Jade is and what it's been doing all this time.

* * *

That afternoon, with half my tasks still undone, I sat listlessly behind my sales counter. The shop was full, and each customer was full of gossip. I hadn't been able to find Dansforth—apparently he was known to be out most afternoons, possibly checking out properties—and I hadn't gotten an interview with Gloria, but I *had* made amends with Officer Thorn. Thorn, unsurprisingly, felt that more information made the merrier, and already everyone in town seemed to know about Ari and Stella. From the sound of it, Gloria had already been sent three gift baskets, four bouquets of flowers, and about two dozen get-well cards. I wondered how she'd take to her newfound popularity.

But what I really wondered—what made it hard to focus—was how to get further in the castle case. Many loose ends were tied up by the fairies' exposure, but just as many were left free, and I had no idea how to find anything out about Jade's alter ego when I couldn't talk to the person in question about it. When I'd fumbled my third sale in a row and William finally got tired of me, relegating me to my lab, I had an idea.

I locked myself in the back room—something I often did when working, just to make sure no one accidentally interrupted an experiment—but left the window to the shop open in case a custom order came through. And then, breathing deeply in my sanctuary, I pulled out Luca's fifth

229

book.

For a moment I sat and observed it closely, deciding what to do first. Part of me still doubted I'd find anything of real use, but I needed to do *something*. Something, I reminded myself, that didn't involve destroying the book.

Luca had been right about the paper: clearly, his expertise in that area outranked mine. I laid the book flat and maneuvered it carefully under my microscope, figuring I'd start by examining the wood fibers. As I took a close look at the grains, counting up rings and any other marks I saw, what drew my attention was the *ink*. It lay in valleys and gorges scored into the paper, a dry pool filling each depression, like rivers and puddles locked in time. I shifted the microscope to give it a closer look.

Intuition was an alchemists' best tool. I trusted my interest in the ink, ready to see where it would lead me. But the ink trails were hard to follow. Unlike the roughly processed wood fibers, the ink lines were precisely and sparingly drawn, and the handwriting was so squiggly it slipped right out from under my lens every time I got it into focus.

I sighed and lifted my head from the instrument. Maybe there was another way to get at the ink. It seemed, from what I *could* see, to be a viscous material that had been applied thickly to the paper and stayed on the surface, rather than sinking in. Therefore, I reasoned, I should be able to scrape a little off and do some tests to see what it was made of. Maybe that information would lead me somewhere—maybe it would turn out that the ink was made of some special sap that had only been available two hundred years ago, or with some mineral that had only *become* available in the region at a certain time, or was also used by some specific people elsewhere and maybe those people would have insights about the Drus, including a very detailed legend about a strange, cursed amulet and creatures of ice and mist.

And maybe, said that voice in my head, which sounded very much like William, *the cover of the book will leap up and do a tap dance.*

"Whatever," I muttered aloud, frowning. "Maybe this won't miraculously solve the case, but I have to try."

Resolved, I shifted away from the microscope, taking the book with me. I'd need magnification to scrape tiny bits of ink from the pages, of course, but my goggles could handle that. I gathered clean white ceramic dishes to hold the ink scrapings. Against the yellowed pages of the book, the ink looked very dark brown, but I'd know its true color soon enough.

I flipped through the book, page by page, looking for especially ink-heavy drawings. I needed something with a nice puddle of ink, something that wouldn't get in the way of Luca's analysis later.

Not that there's much to analyze, observed that same sardonic internal-William voice.

There's the symbols, I thought back defensively.

"The *symbol.*" I turned to the back of the book. Luca hadn't been able to read the symbol because it was smudged. If I was careful, maybe I could get my ink sample from the smudges themselves, thus doing myself *and* Luca a good turn at the same time. Two birds, one extremely sharp scraper.

Looking over the messy image, I decided the risk was worth it. I sincerely doubted that "snowman" was the final image, not when the series so far had been sapling, pages, trees, axes, choir. I didn't get the feeling that this story was going to end with holiday cheer. So, I set my free arm down on the table to stabilize myself, lowered my glasses, and got to work.

Scraping, by definition, was slow and tedious. Each little piece of ink fought before it left the page. I pried at the fuzzy lines around the top of the image, the upper circle—although, I soon discovered, it wasn't truly round. As I tried to trace out the original lines, I mused that it really *did* look like the head of something. Something with a flattened crown and pointed ears that jutted out from absurdly high on the head, above the eyes.

Remember, I had my goggles set to magnification. I was literally looking too closely at the image. It wasn't until I sat up to move some ink scrapings into a bowl and turned back to my work that it hit me.

The image was a stylized *owl.*

28

Handsome Brute

I wasn't exactly sneaking out of town. William probably knew the moment I left the shop. And plenty of people saw me in the streets. Of course, I ignored all their questions about Gloria and the fairies, but I often made a point not to stand around and gossip.

Okay, okay. I *did* sneak. Maybe some of the things Stella said had got to me, a little. I figured it was better this way: I'd get the book and bring it back before anyone missed me. Even *I* could figure out that the owl was a symbol of wisdom and research and, therefore, libraries—which, thanks to Jade, I knew the castle had.

I had plenty of lights with me, and even though the afternoon was waning, it was still sunny. As soon as the town was out of sight, I began running. In no time flat I'd be in the castle library. And in even less time after that, I'd be on the way back to Belville with the last clue in hand.

That was the plan, anyway. But my plan was cut short.

"*Ow!*" My own voice rang out across the forest. I'd been sprinting at a pretty good clip, about as fast as I could manage, by the time I hit the bridge just outside the castle. Unfortunately as I crossed the bridge I hit something else, too. I went flying headlong into the bank at the side of the road.

Splayed across the bank, seeing stars, I clutched my head and told myself I ought to be glad I hadn't gone over the bridge and into the stream below. One step earlier, and I might have.

But the narrow miss didn't change the fact that someone unexpected was on the road. I straightened myself up and glared back toward the bridge, half indignant, half suspicious—and maybe a little guilty too.

"Who's there?" I asked. I addressed a lump of dark clothing which, judging by the hemlines and textures, would be a nice suit if it stood upright.

"Urgh." The person wearing the suit weaved and wobbled as they struggled into a sitting position. They were small, I realized—smaller than me, but still adult human-sized. Judging by the lack of baggage or transportation nearby, they must be from Belville, but I didn't recognize the tan skin or furtive green eyes.

I kept my distance and pursed my lips. "Who are you?"

"Red the alchemist! I might have known. Surely you don't mean to say you don't recognize me," said my victim in a masculine, harried voice. He began to brush dirt from his suit, giving me a better view. But even though he knew me, he only seemed vaguely familiar . . .

"Oh, no!" The man reached up to his throat and choked. I leapt forward, fearing the worst. But then he groped on the ground behind him with one hand and came up with a scarlet cravat balled tightly in his fist. It must have fallen off in our collision. Quickly the man whipped the fabric around his neck and tied it back in place.

234

"Whoa." I fell back a pace. Suddenly, instead of looking at a slender and rather pointy-looking, wiry individual, I was face to face with the large, heroic type. The kind who looks like they might be half giant, and who works out diligently to maintain that appearance. He was paler, and now a full crop of black hair fell over his shoulders and his chin looked like it'd been chiseled from a large and particularly uncooperative rock.

Now I recognized him. "The real estate agent! *This* is where you go every afternoon?"

"Gustav Dansforth," he corrected me, pulling himself up to his full, *glamoured* height. No wonder I hadn't recognized him before: the cravat must have had a powerful spell on it. "And I don't come here *every* afternoon, though I don't see what business it is of yours. I happen to have a standing appointment."

A standing appointment to meet on the bridge by a cursed castle? My skepticism was overcome by new understanding. *Gloria.* "Uh, you know she can't come today, right?"

"Of course I know that." Gustav Dansforth fidgeted with the scarlet silk at his neck, tightening the knot. "She didn't, ah, I don't suppose she told you to come, did she?"

"No," I said slowly, watching him. I hadn't dealt with him much after buying my shop, but he'd always struck me as slick, even arrogant. Now he sounded like he was fourteen years old and about to ask someone to dance.

"Of course not," he repeated, and then cleared his throat.

I paused. My feet itched to continue on to the castle, but there were a lot of loose ends standing in front of me right here. The question was which to pull on to make Dansforth talk. I picked the most obvious first. "You use a glamour?"

235

"It isn't illegal! It's more common than you might think, among those who have money. *You* saw—you can't blame me. No one wants to buy anything from a goblin."

I raised my eyebrow. "You didn't look like a goblin to me."

"Part. My father's grandmother," he said, as though his father had failed him. That made sense: goblins tended to be thin, almost stick-like, and only four feet tall at most. And they *did* have a lot of prejudice against them. *None of that means he had to go to the opposite extreme,* I thought, craning my neck to look up at his fantasy-hero nose. My internal mother chastised me for being so judgmental.

"Don't tell Gloria," Dansforth resumed without preamble. "Swear you won't. I'll tell her myself. One of these days . . ."

The scared schoolboy had come back into his voice. I made a leap of faith. "Have you told her you're in love with her?"

"She knows. Of course she knows." At this, Gustav sagged into the bridge rail behind him and pressed one burly hand over his eyes. The other still clutched at his cravat.

This time it was my turn to clear my throat. I'd already meddled quite a bit in Gloria's affairs, more than enough for one day. But I wondered if it might be charitable to tell him—

"Don't feel sorry for me," he said, interrupting my thought. "I know what you're going to say. I *know* she doesn't love me back. Don't you think I spent enough time trying to convince her that it doesn't matter already?"

"Hmm." As I picked through this rather incoherent, desperate sentiment, I had another realization. "Is that what took up all day, what was it—five days ago? The day Owl was found murdered?"

Gustav heaved the sigh of a tragic actress. "Yes. But it wasn't just that! We meet often. She came to me moons ago with questions about Owl, if he could do the things he threatened to do. He couldn't, of course! But did that stop him? Never. So I'd give her advice. There was always some new scheme he'd come up with. Then finally, he was in jail, and I told her that it was all over, that she should give evidence against him and make sure he never came back. But she wouldn't. Fine, I told her, then we can go away. Together. I've been saving up some properties for myself. I showed them all to her, here, right on this bridge."

"But she doesn't want to go?" I guessed.

"I'll convince her," Gustav said, dropping his hand into a fist.

I sincerely doubted that, but I held my tongue for the moment. "So were you on the road that night, like *late* that night?"

Gustav looked confused about why I'd care for such trivial details. Then he shrugged. "We talked all day. When I got back to town, I heard about Owl's escape. I came right back out here to tell her. But she'd gone up to the castle, and it took me a while to find her. And then she—she didn't want to talk any more. She accused me of following her around." He scoffed.

"Mmhm." The more people told me about Gloria, the more I found myself warming to her. *Although I suppose he was trying to help, in his way. In any case, that takes care of William's mysterious sighting on the road,* I thought. On a whim, I asked, "Did either of you see anyone else in the forest or at the castle?"

"You mean, did we see Owl?" Gustav sneered at me, as though saying *I may be distraught, but I'm not dense.* "No. But everyone knows elves have plant magic. He probably walked right through the woods, right past us. And we never noticed because he used some kind of plant magic to keep quiet."

"Not *all* elves have that," I felt compelled to point out. My patience for listening to the man complain about his rather limited worldview had run out. "That's just an old wives' tale. Plenty of them get by without it. Neither Owl nor Luca ever did anything remotely magical at the bookshop."

Gustav's response was to scoff again, and I rolled my eyes. "Okay, well, thanks anyway for your help."

"Wait—the bookstore." He started up off the rail, as though remembering something. I waited, holding my breath. "That's where Gloria is now, right?"

I sighed. "Yep." *Hopefully Trent can handle this guy . . .*

"I came out here to think," he said unnecessarily, "but I've made my decision. I'm going to go see her."

"Okay, well, tell her hi . . ." he was already striding away, back to town.

I stared after him for a long, quiet moment. Then I smiled. *Now I have several excuses to talk to Gloria when this is done. And she has lots of stuff to* actually *be mad at me about.* The thought was heartening, after the fairies' manipulation.

But in the meantime, there's the question of the castle to answer. I turned away and raced into the shadow of the trees.

29

A Light in the Dark

". . . Hm."

Moments later, after breezing into the castle grounds and leaping through the side door and whisking myself up the stairs and down the halls until I found the old library, I stood. I turned slowly in a circle.

I was stumped.

In my excitement to tie up all the loose ends, I'd forgotten something. It had taken *four* of us to search the music room in any reasonable amount of time. And the library around me was much bigger.

Plus, it was already full of books. What if the one I wanted was hidden in a false cover and stowed somewhere on the shelves?

The library I'd discovered was one of those classic, two-story, circular rooms with wraparound bookcases built into the wall. It took up the entirety of one of the castle towers. Standing there on the wooden floor looking up at bark-covered books and ornately carved banisters, I felt like a squirrel who'd forgotten all the good hiding places.

I spun around again, my gaze searching the room. If I took an extra moment to figure out a plan of attack, it would save me time aimlessly searching later. There was very little furniture in the room aside from the odd table and uncomfortable-looking chair. And nothing on the shelves themselves gave me an indication of where to start a search.

I decided to close my eyes and try some other senses. The castle was quiet—maybe even more so than when I'd visited before. Of course, this time I was alone, so there wasn't the usual noise of companions. A shiver went down my spine as I thought again of Jade's comment about sensing living beings in the castle, and what that insinuated: nonliving beings. Non-breathing, non-noisemaking beings. Would a dark unicorn count as one of those?

Stop being ridiculous, I told myself. *Time to focus.* My mother had always told me that making a plan was like taking a breath. You take everything in, hold it for a second while you consider, and then make your step. And I had a lot to consider. Like had it really been wise to come alone? And was that a step on the wooden floorboards behind my back?

"Rrred."

"Jade!" My eyes snapped open and I turned, smiling. "I was in such a rush, I didn't even think to call out to you."

"I noticed. By the time I sensed you open the door, you were already upstairs." The room was too light for me to see him, but his voice was amused. "I wasn't sure what to do, but I thought it best to let you know I am here. If I can help at all, I would like to. And I am glad to see you again."

"Same, and listen close, because I've got a lot to tell you," I said, proceeding to fill him in on Gloria's situation and Thorn's plans and what I'd found out about the last book. "I'm pretty

240

sure it's in here somewhere. And I thought if I could just come and get it really quick—"

"You would further ease everyone's suffering." Jade's tone was sympathetic.

"Right. Something like that." I blushed. "I would ask you to help me look, but I'm still not sure—does talking about the books, or dealing with them, put you in any danger?"

Jade hesitated. I told him firmly, "Be honest."

"I do have a sense of something," he admitted. "Something dangerous, as if I were holding my hand too close to a flame. But that is all." When I failed to look mollified, he added, "It is only the—the curse I cannot talk about, Rred. The Drus I can speak of."

"Okay, here's what we're going to do," I decided. "You're going to stand right here in the middle of the room and not go near any books or possible book hiding places. And if you start to feel any worse, you let me know immediately. Okay? And I'll start my search. While I look, maybe you can fill me in one some clues about the Drus."

"Of course, Red." Jade's voice was faint and earnest. Not wanting to dwell on that nor on why I felt warm all over, I stalked toward the one door in the room. As the biggest landmark amongst the books, it would serve as my starting point.

Behind me, Jade cleared his throat. "What would you like to know?"

"Um. Let's start with the symbol I'm looking for. I figured it's an owl perched on a branch—I told you that already. What would the Drus think about an owl?"

"An owl," Jade repeated as he thought. I pulled my goggles down over my eyes and examined the door frame, listening intently. "You were right to come to this room. The Drus were aware of the owl as a symbol for learning and perspicacity. Because the Drus lived in the trees, they thought of the owl—of all birds—living on the same level as them. Is this useful?"

"Keep going," I told him as I moved on to the bookcase itself. I examined the carvings first. "Tell me literally everything you know about owls and Drus. You don't think," I added abruptly, my eyes glued to the etched oak under my fingers, "it had anything to do with *Owl*, did it?"

Jade took my confused question and made sense of it. "The books were written before Owl came to Belville, and I doubt Owl ever found them."

"Right. Why find them and then hide them way out here again," I agreed. "Okay, back to owls, the animal, then."

"The Drus did have a belief about their eyes," Jade said, as though just remembering. "Not the eyes in particular, that is, but—you have seen how owls' eyes seem to give off light at night? Such animals were considered to have been blessed by the sun or the moon and were often drawn surrounded by rays of light. By contrast, unblessed animals were thought to emit shadow, and were rarely drawn because no one wished to invite that into their life."

I paused. My throat went dry. "Like the—the dark unicorn," I managed. "Is that something you can talk about, Jade?"

Jade paused until I finally looked back over my shoulder. All I could see was a shimmer standing in the golden light from the windows above. But Jade noticed my look and coughed apologetically.

"I can . . . a little. It is . . . they were considered the worst kind of luck. An equal counterpart to the unicorn most of the world knows. They are real, those creatures, but . . . very rarely seen."

"But," I said carefully, "they aren't the same as the creatures here on the grounds, right?"

"No. I looked for the creatures, Rrred, as I'd promised you. And . . . I do not think they are alive. At first I thought they might be, because I can sense them, but I do not think . . . I do not think they are any more."

"Like, in between the time we discovered Owl's body and today, they've died? Or like they were always dead?"

"Not always. But they did not die recently, either." Jade shivered audibly.

Well, there's a typical Jade-ism, I thought. I regretted it immediately as not very kind; obviously Jade was upset by something, either the creatures or the dark unicorn talk. And I was certain he had good reason to be upset.

But they aren't mist creatures, I reminded myself. *The mist was Jade's, because he wanted to reflect the moonlight. Wait—*

"Jade," I said, straightening and brightening at once. "I've had an idea. The owl thing. There were lines all over the symbol, too. Maybe it was a halo of light! What if the owl *is* a light?"

"You mean the book is hidden near a light in here?" Jade's voice sounded normal again, excited even.

"Exactly." My gaze swept the room. In previous visits to the castle, I'd noticed that the Drus didn't rely on many light fixtures—they appeared to have been big believers in natural light. But *every* library had to have lights of some kind, and this one was no different. With a triumphant "aha!" I noticed one on my left and strode toward it.

The light was a sconce, set into the bookcase as though part of one huge furnishing, which, knowing Drus carpentry, it probably was. From the back of the shelf, a branch-like arm extended, ending in a shallow bowl that probably once held oil (or whatever the Drus used to produce light; I was curious, but I pushed my professional interest aside). The space around on either side was free of books for a good six inches, filled in with carvings. I ran my hand over each wooden flower and twisting vine, searching for the telltale edges of a secret compartment.

"Okay, no luck here," I admitted after a moment. "How many more are there in the room?"

"Three more on this level," said Jade promptly. I was glad to hear his voice still came from the center of the room.

Each one for a cardinal direction, I realized, as I sought out the next light. *Naturally. Because when doesn't a symbol need extra layers of symbolism?* I spent time looking over the next light, the northern one, but found nothing. I moved to the third light a little less excited. It was getting late, and no amount of speed was making searching light-fixtures go by any faster.

"Jade," I called, thinking maybe we could speed things up. "Pick a direction."

"Pardon?"

"Not to go to," I clarified, my head halfway in the sconce as I balanced the tip of my boot on one of the lower shelves. "Which direction do you think the Drus would have chosen to hide the book in?"

"Ah. The west," Jade said after a moment.

"Are you sure? I was there first."

"But it would have been the west. For the ending of the story, and of the Drus. Look again, Rred. Please?"

"Oh, all right. Maybe I was too excited and missed something," I admitted, smiling toward the center of the room as I extracted myself from the eastern sconce and hurried back to the western one.

This time I was more careful. I levered myself up on the shelf for a closer look. From inside my breast pocket I fished a tiny lightstick, activated it, and shone it over the carvings.

"Hm, hm, hm, where would I hide a small flat rectangle in here," I mumbled, thinking aloud. The metal-lined oil-bowl poked me in the cheek. "Maybe it was wrong of me to look for edges. A really good carpenter could obscure those in a mess like this. Let's see what else can I look for? How about . . . grains in the wood?"

As I said the words, I noticed a portion of the carving where the grain switched direction. Without my goggles and my light, I'd never have seen it. Grinning, I tugged at the mismatched flower—first one way, then another. Finally I pulled it straight up, like a cork stopper on a bottle. With a little screech and a small cloud of dust, it relented. I dropped to the ground with the sixth book in my hands.

"So now," said Jade, still far away and sounding more amused than ever, "are you done climbing on the bookshelves?"

"That was nothing. You should have seen Luca in the music room," I retorted, beaming. "Jade, this is it. We got it!"

We'd already taken a long time searching the library; the light outside was growing dim. But I decided to skim through the book quickly here, on my own, before making the run back to town. It wouldn't change whether or not I turned the book in, but it would help me prepare.

With a deep breath I flipped through the pages. It was just an end to the story: that was it. No hidden artifacts or secrets or time travel or wells of unstoppable power.

And no oaths of vengeance, either.

I breathed again, this time a sigh of relief. The book was exactly what Luca had suspected it would be, and therefore we were yet another step closer to clearing him.

"Rred? Are you all right?"

"I'm fine, Jade. Thank you very much for your help." I smiled in his direction. "I just need to run this over to the others." I tucked the book in a pocket and, when Jade was quiet, asked, "You don't mind, do you? Would you like to come with me?"

"I will follow in a little while, when it is fully dark. Sometimes, traveling in the daylight, I feel . . ."

Jade didn't elaborate, but I got the point. Thoughts of what his physical form might be struck me once again, making my stomach queasy—but I pushed them aside. *One thing at a time.* It would only take a moment to run back to town. Gathering my energy once more, I bid Jade farewell.

I didn't actually make it to Belville, though, because as I closed the castle door and rounded the corner, I heard someone calling my name.

30

Folly

"Red! Red, help!!" The voice was distinct, but too strained to be recognizable. I made my decision without thinking about it.

I raced around the side of the castle. There at the back, near the greenhouse door, a person knocked on the glass. I still had my goggles on and unthinkingly, I zoomed in on the movement. It was someone in a forest green cape surrounded by menacing figures.

And that someone was Cairn.

I was within speaking distance in an instant. The creatures wouldn't let me get near her, though; they formed a semicircle which, as soon as I arrived, turned ominously towards me.

"What are you doing here?" Even as I asked the question, I looked for my own answers. Cairn was upright, with no trace of a limp or stiffness in her legs. *Maybe the effect wore off of her too, like it did Gloria.*

"I was looking for you, Red!" Cairn cried. Her voice was breathless and hoarse. Not too surprising, I thought, for someone who'd ventured a league out of town after days of bed rest only to be chased around by snarling creatures. "I was so worried—"

"It's going to be fine," I told her. Whether or not I believed that, I willed it to be true. I grabbed two lightsticks from my tool belt and lit them both, one clasped in each hand. Cairn herself was holding a lit crystal protectively in one fist, but apparently in the waning sunlight it hadn't been enough to scare off the creatures. "We're going to figure something out."

Cairn's reply was anguished. "*Why* won't they leave me alone? Why don't the lights get rid of them?"

"I don't know. Jade did say they'd become more desperate—"

A twig snapped as the rightmost creature stepped forward, its eerie gaze on me. They crept through the dappled darkness created by the trees overhead, inch by inch. They weren't within lunging distance yet, but they would be soon.

"And they're after *you,* too," Cairn wailed. "What can they want? Is it—it must be that book!"

"Book?" I gritted my teeth as I stared down the creatures. I still couldn't get a fix on what they were. Somehow they seemed larger than they'd been before. The center one was almost as tall as me.

"You came here to get the last book for Owl's assistant, didn't you? That must be what they want!"

"You mean Luca? Yeah, I did. But who told you I was coming here?"

Cairn wrung her hands as she watched the creatures, which were now fixed solely on me. Perhaps they figured Cairn would stay put while they dealt with me, as a new threat. *Are they so smart?* I wondered, along with about a million other things. Cairn's reply hardly registered at first. "That nice boy Gustav came by to see Gloria, and he said he'd met you on the bridge. I *knew* you'd be coming here. You're such a sweet girl, Red. But volunteering to find those books has put you in danger! It's drawing the creatures to you!"

I couldn't help but think that Cairn's suspicions sounded a lot like Thorn's. "I don't know—it's possible."

The leftmost creature growled.

"Red, dear, we need to do something. *Now.*"

"If they want the book, then maybe we can distract them," I said. I hated the thought of sacrificing Luca's book, but it wasn't just my life at stake. It was Cairn's, too, and I wasn't about to let anything else happen to her.

"Or maybe," Cairn said quickly, "maybe you can get into the greenhouse, and let me in from the inside. Can you jump in through the hole in the glass, Red?"

Something *ping*ed in the back of my mind. I hesitated.

"If you get in, you can let me in," Cairn repeated. "We'll be safe in there. We must be!"

"I don't want to leave you out here," I said, stepping back involuntarily as the creatures stepped closer.

"We'll make a distraction," said Cairn desperately. "Here, take my cape. I think that was how they saw me in the first place. I'll throw it to you."

"Really?" *A costume change literally right in front of the monsters?* I trusted Cairn and her experience, but still. Her plan seemed to assume a lot of stupidity on the creatures' part. "You think it'll work?"

"I think they're attracted to the darkness of it. Like moths to a flame," Cairn said. Her words came out more easily now, but I could hear her shudder.

I caught the bundle of fabric as she lobbed it over the creatures' heads, watching carefully to see how they reacted.

Something fell from the cape—maybe a brooch or pin. The creatures didn't notice, though, and it didn't matter; when I waved the dark green fabric, they did seem to focus on it rather than me.

Moving as one, the creatures stepped closer.

"Okay, I'll distract them and then make a run for it. You just lay low and get to the greenhouse door," I said, focusing on the creatures in front of me. "If anything goes wrong, just yell. Here goes!"

With a deep breath, I backed up several paces, still waving the cloak next to me like an extra person. Then with all my might I tossed it sideways and raced right for the creatures. Whatever powers they had, prescience wasn't one of them. They scattered in surprise as I passed.

My own short cloak billowed behind me as I ran, an unwieldy sail. I prayed it would fit through the glass with me. Cairn didn't say anything, but I could hear her gasp.

I couldn't hear the creatures, though. Again Jade's voice played in my mind. *I do not think they are alive . . .*

Time to think about that later, I told myself. I focused on the missing glass. William was big for a dog, but he was still smaller than me. I'd have to aim carefully to get in through the hole he'd left. I'd dive in, pivot to the right, and let Cairn in through the door.

Good thing the Officer never came back to patch things up properly. The glass patch Trent had made leaned against the wall a few feet away.

My foot faltered as it hit the patio leading up to the greenhouse. *Officer Thorn hasn't had time to come back out here with Trent. So how did Cairn get here alone?*

With one last exhale, I launched myself through the broken

glass.

I tucked and rolled and hit the flagstone floor still moving. The folly came up fast, but I managed to miss it. When you have super speed, you get used to the occasional crash landing. Particularly if your mothers force you to take gymnastics classes all through childhood. Gods above, I'd hated those.

"Red!"

Mechanically I stopped, turning back toward the hole in the glass. But even as I did so, I knew that I'd made a mistake.

The greenhouse was filled with stained green light, and outside the sky was purple as the sun set. In an unsettling turn of events, the creatures had actually followed me inside. And outside, Cairn's face loomed large as she looked in between the shards of broken glass.

But it wasn't the Cairn I knew. Without her cape, she was so much more slender than I'd always thought. I'd seen her as a comfortably plump older woman, human, harmless. Had it just been the cape that made her seem that way? Or had it been something else—maybe a glamour in the brooch that fell? I had no way of knowing for sure. But as I locked eyes with her in that moment, I didn't recognize this new Cairn, so much thinner and smoother, pointy ears framing dark braided hair. I didn't recognize the hardness in her face.

Not the hardness—nor the triumph.

"Nicely done, Red," she told me.

I swallowed. And asked the question I should have asked at the beginning. "Cairn . . . why do you know about the books? We never talked about them with you."

"They're dangerous, Red. Owl always thought so too. You shouldn't go messing with the past. Especially when it wasn't yours in the first place."

"And why," I said, my voice rising as the creatures advanced around the folly, "are you really here?"

"I wanted to warn you, Red. You know I've always looked after you. I never meant for you to get mixed up in this. If it hadn't been for Gloria and that boy, everything would have been perfectly fine. But it's too late now. I'm sorry, Red . . . but it's time for the past to die."

The last thing I saw was the swish of her wrist as the overgrown vines all around me latched on to my torso and threw me over the bricks and into the folly.

31

Beastly

My first thought was of the vines at the crime scene. Vines strong enough to lift a person . . . or to deliver a blow to the head and then close the heavy castle doors.

But of course after that came a complete jumble of thoughts, colored by outrage over what Cairn had done. And, admittedly, chagrin that I hadn't realized any of this sooner.

"Not that 'this' amounts to much," I muttered to myself, since I appeared to be alone. My lightsticks had fallen with me and now illuminated the folly; maybe it was too much light for the creatures to brave. Maybe they were biding their time. Either way, they knew full well where I was. I could get up and sing the Beyond anthem and it wouldn't be putting me in any more danger.

But because I didn't follow that particular line of pursuit, I distinctly heard the clicking of glass on glass as Trent's patch was set into place on the greenhouse wall above me. Cairn—whoever she was—was barricading me in the greenhouse. Covering up her tracks.

"William is going to kill me. I go out on my own, refusing to trust my friends, and promptly get bamboozled by someone I never thought to doubt," I continued muttering. I couldn't help it: I actually laughed aloud at my own idiocy.

Once that bit of shock was over, I turned to more practical matters. Moving carefully, I ascertained that no parts of me or my equipment were broken. I'd have some nasty bruises in the morning and my entire left leg was already sore, but my boots and gloves had saved me from the worst of the scrapes. I gathered up all the things that had fallen out of my pockets, including the sixth book.

I stood up and considered my options for escape. I could yell for Jade, but the wound of Cairn's betrayal was still raw. Why hadn't Jade noticed her on the grounds and said anything to me before I left? Why hadn't he ever told me about her and Owl? Surely he'd known they were connected. Jade may have been distracted by all the talk of books, of course, but the alternative was too much to think about. I couldn't handle discovering that another of my friends was—less than friendly.

No, I could get myself out. Of that, I was certain. The only question was how. I had some fey rope tucked along my belt, but climbing out with a rope could be ill-advised, if the creatures were still up there. What if they broke the line while I was halfway up? I shook my head. *Stop questioning everything and focus.*

My hand moved to my hip pocket for a flask of acid. It was destructive, but also the most self-reliant way of escape I could think of. I'd use the acid to weaken the bricks in a line up the wall. I didn't have enough to actually melt through them, but I could weaken their structure. And with my gloves and their hardened, pointed fingertips, I'd be safe from a similar fate. In the uneven brick surface created by the acid, it should be easy enough to make handholds for myself. If I moved fast, I'd be able to climb out.

But before I could grab the acid, my fingers brushed over the top of something clipped onto the band around my thigh. I'd forgotten all about it. Ever since the night we'd found Owl, I'd taken to carrying flares.

Without thinking I grabbed one and set it alight, tossing it in the greenhouse above me. Again, destructive, but at this point I wasn't worried about maintaining the historical integrity of the castle. Luca could lecture me later if he liked. In the meantime, if I was lucky, the explosion of light would daze or even scare off the creatures above.

Also, okay, maybe it was satisfying to my sense of betrayal and mortification to strike back at the world with an explosion. Very satisfying.

As bits of ash and bright red embers rained down around me, I began my ascent. I had to make the best of my opportunity. Most of all, I had to get out there and warn everyone about Cairn. I had to, finally, get to the bottom of—

"Rred? Red! What are you doing in the folly?"

I went suddenly still and, in absence of upward motion, I slid down the brick wall a little. "Curse it, Jade! Don't distract me. I'm almost out."

"Why didn't you wait for me to come?" asked Jade as I focused on the bricks before me. One step, then two, then with a quick lunge I was out.

I steadied myself against the fake well, looking around warily as I replied, "I didn't think of the flare catching your attention, actually. I was just trying to scare off any creatures. Looks like . . . it worked." *Better than I expected, actually,* I thought. We seemed to be alone. *Did the explosion somehow make them dissipate, like real mist?*

"Why didn't you want to catch my attention?"

"It's not that I didn't want to, it's—" I paused, and finally caught my breath. I couldn't see Jade, but he sounded wounded. Just as I had been. "Jade, I'm sorry, I didn't mean to hurt your feelings. But—well, I didn't think of it because—have you sensed anything that's gone on since I left?"

"A quarter of an hour ago?" Jade sounded bewildered. "No. I didn't even think you were still herre, until I heard the flare. Why—how? How did you end up here? How could I not have known?"

"I don't know." My voice was calm at last. I had the book; the creatures were gone, Cairn was absent, for the moment; and Jade was here. *But would Cairn really have left?* a part of me wondered. Thinking, worried, I asked Jade, "Did you ever . . . have you ever met Cairn?"

"No. Is she connected to the castle somehow?"

"Yes, she was friends with Owl, and she was attacked by—gods and goddesses," I murmured quietly. Cairn's symptoms had never matched Gloria's because *neither* of them had really been affected by the creatures. *Cairn must have faked it somehow. That's how she's suddenly fine now.* "No. Oh no. I mean, yes, Jade—yes, she's involved. But not in the way I've been thinking. I think she's still here. We need to find her."

"But I can't sense her," Jade repeated.

"That's ridiculous," I said, frustrated not at Jade but at the lack of information. "She's alive. You could see and hear and feel her if she were here. Why wouldn't—"

A crash outside the greenhouse cut me off. I went as still as a doe.

256

"Did you hear that?" I whispered to Jade.

"Yes," he said, still clearly consternated. "Rred, what is happening?"

"A lot. I can't explain it all right now. But I think we're in danger," I whispered as another crash sounded, nearer now. Something big was coming our way. "Listen. If anything happens to me, you need to get Thorn. In fact, it might be best if you go now—"

"I'm not leaving you—"

Crash.

"Get William too, while you're at it—"

"But you could be hurt—"

CRASH.

"Yes I know but we really don't—"

"CINNABAR SUNSET," William roared. "DON'T YOU DARE DO ANYTHING SO *RECKLESS* EVER AGAIN!"

* * *

The shards of glass and dust—most of it emotional dust of shock and guilt—settled slowly. There in the greenhouse, Jade shimmered, I cringed, and William glowed up a veritable thunderstorm. The air around the tip of his furry tail literally crackled with blue energy.

"Do you have *any* idea what it's like to be in the middle of ringing up the most tedious purchase in *history* and suddenly every single hair on your back stands up because your *business partner* has somehow snuck off and *gotten herself into mortal peril?* You are going to tell me *exactly* what I've gotten in the middle of," William commanded from his perch. He balanced his front two paws atop the wall of the folly, bringing his black gaze up to my shoulder height. "But don't think I'm not going to yell at you. As soon as this is all over, I'm going to be yelling at you for *hours,* and nothing you say right now can change that."

"I recognize that, and I'm sorry, William," I said, and hurried on, "See, I figured out where the sixth book was, and I thought it'd be a simple in-and-out job. And it was, with Jade's help. But there's something else going on. Cairn showed up and—and the creatures were after her, at least that's what it seemed like, but now I'm thinking maybe she controls them somehow. She convinced me to jump in here in order to open the door for her, before I realized how suspicious it was, her being at the castle at all. Then she started yelling about the past and left me in here with the creatures and closed up the . . ." *Oops.* Looking over William's shoulder, I saw that he'd created a new hole, a perfect match to the old one, right next to Trent's patch. "Cairn controlled vines to knock me in the folly so I lit a flare to scare the creatures and Jade showed up and I got out of the stupid folly and then you burst in," I finished in a rush.

William whined. "Cairn *controlled vines?* That's elf magic."

"Believe me, I was just as surprised, but when you get a look at her you'll get it. She must have been using a glamour. I think it broke when she gave me her cape, trying to confuse the creatures."

"That'd have to be a ridiculously strong glamour. But if she's been using it for years . . ." William shook his ears.

"Not the time to geek out over magic," I told him. "We have to get Cairn before she leaves!"

"But you have no idea where she is," William guessed. His eyes darted to the corner behind me, the deepest shadow of the greenhouse, where Jade had retreated in an effort to make himself visible.

"I can't account for it," Jade admitted. His arms were crossed over his body and he seemed to sway from foot to foot.

"I can." William's anger subsided into grim self-satisfaction. "It makes sense now."

When he didn't elaborate immediately, I prompted, "Is Cairn not alive somehow? Is she one of those creatures too?"

"No. In fact, I'll bet that she is what they've been after this entire time," William mused. "There's another reason Jade wouldn't be able to sense her, Red. It's the same reason I can be fooled by the work of a sorcerer, just like Gloria said. A sorcerer created me, and on an even playing field, that sorcerer would have the upper hand against me."

"But Jade wasn't created," I protested. "Jade's a . . ."

A person, I was going to say. But it wasn't totally true. He was part of a person, as he'd put it once. Part of a cursed person.

"No," I whispered as it hit me.

Behind me, Jade rustled in his ivy shadow. "She rreturrned, then."

"Don't the Seers have a saying, Red? 'All your evil deeds will come back to you'?" William's tail wagged, a gesture not of friendliness but of the beginning of a hunt. "Cairn is the elf in the story who cursed the Drus prince. The 'past' she was yelling about, what she doesn't want you or Luca or anyone else to know, is the truth of what she did."

32

Hunter and Hunted

Strangely enough, my first thought wasn't *why* or *how* or even *this is all very well, but she's still out there and we need to catch her.* I stood there covered in bits of brick and glass and ash, and I thought, *She put some beastly dark-unicorn curse on Jade and we still haven't seen hide nor hair of a creature with a horn. What if she came back to finish off Jade and whatever else of him is out there? What if it's out there with her now?*

Fortunately, William had taken over the hunt for me. This was why William was, truthfully, the better detective between us two.

Not that I would ever admit as much aloud.

"Come on," William growled, crackling again. "She won't have left without being sure Red was stuck. And even if she did, I doubt your 'creatures' let her off the grounds."

"That's a good point. Jade can't sense her, but you did say . . . gods," I murmured as another realization hit me. I looked back at Jade's corner but couldn't see his eyes. "Oh, Jade, I'm so sorry. Do you think the creatures are . . ."

"I think they are rremnants of the Drus, yes," said Jade, very quietly. "The few who stayed."

"Time for revelations is over," William announced. "Now's the time for catching criminals. Come on!"

Without so much as a backward glance, he leapt out of the greenhouse the way he'd come in. I looked back at Jade once more.

"By the gazebo," he whispered. Then, stronger, he added, "William is right. I think they are by the gazebo. I'm afraid the door to the garden has been overgrown from the outside. Can you get out through the new hole in the glass, Red?"

"I guess I'd better." With one last smile bereft of happiness but full of sympathy for Jade, I lined up with the back of the greenhouse and vaulted after William.

* * *

The scene in the garden was not so much a showdown as a siege. Jade had been right—it centered on the decrepit gazebo. Cairn stood in its center, holding up the same glowing charm she'd had earlier and clearly praying with all her might. All along the outer rails, just barely more than an arm's reach from her, creatures shifted restlessly. Now that I viewed them from the back—and with eyes unclouded by adrenaline—I realized sadly that Jade was right. They were bipedal. They were gnarled and shadowy and scary, but underneath that, you could tell that they'd once been elf-like creatures.

With her free hand Cairn gestured wildly, and in response the nearby fruit trees waved menacingly at the Drus. *Plant magic, just like Dansforth said.* There were more Drus now than before, however, and they weren't intimidated by moving trees. Cairn's effort only tired herself out.

The sun had set fully now, and the night was cloudy. William blended into the darkened landscape perfectly. He sat just behind the ring of Drus, his eyes fixed on Cairn.

"Red!" she cried as I ran up. "Don't tell me that an alchemist could side with these monsters!"

"By 'monsters,' I suppose you mean the Drus you dragged into an internal war and then cursed?" I asked grimly. A crackling of dry leaves to my right indicated that Jade had joined us, too. "You should know better than to think that you can kill the past."

"*He* is with you," hissed Cairn. From a good three yards' distance, even in the twilight, I saw her eyes flash as she noticed Jade. Her eyes went straight to him. I suppose no amount of darkness could conceal her own work from her. "I should never have trusted you. You've been too close to them all along."

"'Them' who, Cairn?" I asked. "Tell us your side of the story."

"My *side!*" She laughed sharply and for a moment her concentration on her charm broke. The trees stilled. The light wavered. The ring of sepulchral Drus thickened. "It is not my 'side' of a bedtime tale. It's the truth. I should have framed *you* from the very beginning. I should have used one of your little potions to break into the police station. But it was so much easier to plant the pendant on the gnome."

"Why come back to Belville at all?" I coaxed. Jade had said that the elf *returned,* and the Cairn I'd known had only been in Belville a few years longer than me. So I took a leap. "Why make a life here, when you could have stayed away?"

Cairn stepped back, as though the question—or perhaps the movements of the Drus—frightened her. "You think this has been any kind of life? I only did what I had to. I came back because I couldn't stay away. The curse—it's mine. The fate of the Drus is *mine*. I made it. Do you hear me?"

That last question she shouted viciously at the ring of shadows. It only served to aggravate them.

Beside me, William muttered, "Not exactly a criminal mastermind, is she?"

"She is unraveling," Jade murmured from my other side. He said it like someone watching a star, their northern star, implode.

"I had to come back," Cairn continued, now looking at me once more. "But I couldn't find it."

"The books?"

"The castle," she retorted, as though I was the one acting bizarrely. "The Drus hid it away. Before they died. Owl, that pitiful excuse for a scholar, had the maps and the greed to find it. But I had to show him the pendant so he'd believe me. I had to give it to him so he could make the gates appear."

Well, that's a different story about Owl and the pendant than she told Thorn, I thought.

"If only I'd never given it to him," Cairn moaned. Her arm trembled. The light spell and the constant threat clearly wore on her. "If he'd never got hold of the pendant, everything would have been fine."

"Where did *you* get the pendant?" I asked, just to keep her talking.

"From Kalos, of course," snapped Cairn. "Some trinket his mother had given him. I had to get it off him before I could take my revenge. Imagine, thinking a necklace could protect anyone!"

She laughed again, painfully. The circle of Drus was darker now and taller.

"And then Owl kept it?" I frowned as I tried to link the dots together. I could see Owl being selfish and callous enough to keep his prize to himself, but I didn't yet see why this had been the fatal step Cairn thought it was.

"I let him keep him," Cairn said nonsensically. "I thought it would do me some good, watching that horrid man order Kalos around."

Jade moved sharply next to me, and I turned, my eyes wide. "Jade! That was why you were tied to Owl? He used the pendant to control you?"

"No longer," said Jade firmly, his eyes glinting as he stared at Cairn. "He began to weaken, just as she does now."

At this point Cairn's laughter was an uncomfortable shriek. "Yes! Yes, that's it. He *weakened*. I—even I! Living here, in this town. Seeing it every day. It was impossible. And then *you* showed up, and made friends with him, and I knew you'd figure it out eventually. I never should have let that cursed scholar talk me into it. Always talking! Even in jail. I only wanted the pendant. But he was determined to go to the castle again! He broke away from me. But I knew exactly where to find him. He thought he'd find power here. Ha! He found death!"

"That clears that up, then," William remarked. "Red, I don't think we have much time left."

"It was a mistake," Cairn said, addressing me one last time. "I never should have told you about the pendant. But I had to, to get you to destroy it. I kept the Witch busy so the officer would take it away and destroy it once and for all. But she didn't! And you—you would not stay put! You wouldn't stay away from them. You wouldn't stay out of the forest!"

With this final remark, she stamped her foot and brought

down her hand in a fist, like a toddler in the throes of a tantrum. But that hand had been maintaining her light. The instant the light came down and flickered out, the shadows of the Drus converged.

"Wait, don't let them—" I leapt forward, arm outstretched, but no amount of speed could have undone that moment. Cairn was already surrounded. Already dead.

"Looks like revenge has been had all 'round," William observed dryly.

Like a fog, the Drus were dissipating. I watched them, my eyes on the body prone on the gazebo floor. Then a thought occurred to me. I wheeled.

"Jade—Jade, how are you?"

My gaze sought him desperately, finally caught on the glimmer of his eyes in the shadow of the trees. He looked and sounded exactly as ever as he said, "I'm not sure, Rred."

"Not all curses die with the caster," William told me. His voice wasn't without a gruff touch of pity as he added, "It's just like the book said. Elf curses are known to last forever."

33

Rose and Thorn

William and I walked slowly back into town, Jade drifting behind us. Night was fully upon us and he looked solid enough in the dark, but he seemed more ghostly than ever somehow. I suspect he followed us because he didn't want to be alone. I didn't want him to be, either.

We'd made it about halfway when Thorn came thundering up the road and met us. Like William, she was full of indignation and commands. Turning a deaf ear to any protests, she marched us straight to the station, where we spent what felt like an eternity. Jade lingered there, too, pacing the darkened edges of the room.

"Of course, I knew something was afoot," the Officer announced, sitting back in her office chair. It was past dinner time by then, but she gnawed on a toothpick like it contained all the nutrition she'd ever need. My stomach grumbled. Impervious, she explained, "Trent finally came to the station to look at the pendant this evening. Took him about two shakes to realize it wasn't anything like what Cairn had said. We rushed back to the bookstore, but by that time, she'd already crept out right under Luca's nose. We've been searching all over town ever since."

"Funny," grumped William. "Turns out booksellers don't make good jailers."

"He had no idea who she really was, and as I keep trying to explain to you, Officer, some of us have stores to run," I grumped right back. "Why didn't you come right to the castle? Didn't Dansforth tell you he saw me out there?"

Thorn glowered at the paperweight on her desk, as though considering picking it up and throwing it. "Dansforth, that rat, told me that you ought to be back in town already."

I paused, and then laughed. Suddenly, viewing myself from the real estate agent's eyes, my antics seemed even more unfathomable than ever. "Well, I *was* going pretty fast when I hit him."

"He was still making assumptions," William growled. "Trust a goblin not to think beyond his own nose."

"*William,* that's incredibly rude. Wait," I said, "you knew about his glamour?"

"His, yes," William answered, smug. "It's not as good as he thinks it is."

"That brooch of Cairn's seems like a doozy, though," Thorn said. We'd brought it and the cape to Thorn, who'd locked them away in a safe. "But not enough to fool the Drus completely, it seems. No wonder she wanted Owl to look like a grandma—like herself—her *glamour,* that is. Hoping to fool them into thinking she was gone, no doubt. The real question is, how d'you think she got the necklace on Dusty?" Thorn stared at the ceiling as though she could see the pendant hovering there in front of her. In reality, she'd assured us that the artifact was secured in the same locker as the other accessories. "Think she had help?"

I bristled. "If you're suggesting Jade had something to do with it, why don't you just ask him?"

"Because I can't see or hear him, Red. And I still think it's creepy that you can," said the Officer affably.

"I have had nothing to do with Cairn," said Jade from somewhere at the back of the room. "Only Owl. She fooled me—*they* fooled me."

"Cairn wouldn't have given Jade the pendant," William agreed. "Her whole game was keeping it from him and watching from afar. I know the type."

I shook my head. Cairn's vehemence at the end had been repulsive. To Officer Thorn I clarified, "Jade says he didn't do it. But the pendant went to Gloria first, remember? The fairies found it after the murder and gave it to her in order to frame her—they pretty much admitted to that. Then she gave it to me, and—honestly," I realized, "Cairn probably picked my pocket after the fake attack. And right after that, Dusty went up to the apartment to fix something, so he was right there. Speaking of, are you going to let him go now?"

Thorn stared at me for a moment, sucking on her toothpick. Then she grinned. "All right, Mother," she said, reaching for her keys. "I'll go down and get him right now."

In the ensuing cacophony of reproach and explanation and finally good-natured ribbing, I realized how tired I was. *How is it,* I wondered, *that solving real-life mysteries is so much harder than solving esoteric alchemical ones?*

* * *

When we finally spilled out of the police station and into the early morning, I was grateful for the silence. Even if it came with a lot of neighbors' watchful eyes. Everyone within a two-block radius, it seemed, had their noses pressed up to their windows. *Doesn't anyone in this town need to sleep?* I wondered irritably. Ignoring them took all my concentration as we headed back to the shop.

It wasn't until I'd finally arrived at my back porch that I remembered we hadn't tied up all the loose ends. "Hey—Jade?" I scanned the shadows, trying to remember if he'd left the station with us.

At my side, William harrumphed. "Don't you think you've caused him enough trouble for one day?"

"I didn't cause any of this trouble," I protested. "I just wanted to see if he wanted that pendant back. Maybe we should have got Thorn to give it to him."

"What's a shadow going to do with jewelry?"

"Be nice," I insisted, swatting at William's tail. He disappeared into the shop. I lingered just a moment, but it seemed like Jade wasn't going to appear.

"You can fix it all up tomorrow," William called out to me. "What's an extra night going to hurt?"

"Fine," I said, turning in. "But that means you're going to have to spend another morning tending the shop."

"Wait!"

The voice wasn't William—it came from the side yard—but it also wasn't Jade. I hesitated, my hand on the back door as I squinted into the shadows.

"It's just me," said Gloria, stepping onto the porch. She walked stiffly, only half-visible in her customary blacks and grays; even her red plume of feathers seemed to droop. "Jeez, Red, bit jumpy?"

"Oh! Sorry." I stepped out to meet her. "It's been a long day. And night. And, to be fair . . . I don't think you've ever come over here before." *Usually you just wait out in front of your shop to bite my head off as I pass by,* I thought, and wondered. Would Gloria without the fairies' influence be different?

"Yeah, well." Gloria paused at the edge of the patio, shrugging uncomfortable shoulders. Even a bit ragged and awkward, she was still impossibly beautiful.

When a long moment passed, I guessed, "Trent let you out, huh? Or did you sneak out as well?"

"As well as who? Cairn? So that rumor is true?" Gloria looked thoughtfully at me, then shrugged again, just one shoulder, almost nonchalant. "I made him let me go. I took a bunch of that goop with me and promised to use it. It's not half bad. If everything you make works like that, then maybe you should consider making some stuff for the salon."

"Really?" The smile grew on my face regardless of the fact that what she'd actually said was only half a compliment. "You want me to make products for you?"

Gloria looked away. "Only if you have nothing better to do."

"I'd love to," I told her. "You know . . . I did kind of take over business at your shop there for a minute today, Gloria. I'm sorry. I acted out of turn."

"Whatever." Gloria stared long and hard at the ground before looking back up at me. "I probably should have done it ages ago. Too lazy, I guess."

"You aren't lazy. They were taking advantage of you and twisting things around. They even did it to me when I was there. It's hard to see through that kind of thing when that's all you have to go on."

"But it wasn't all I had, was it?" Gloria's statement surprised me. "You were never as bad as they made it sound like you were. You really *were* innocent. I should have seen that."

"Gloria . . . was that . . . an apology?"

She shrugged once more. "Take it how you will. I don't care." Then, clearing her throat, she said, "Remember what you asked me? Back at Lavender's?"

"You mean, why you stay here? Yeah." Hoping for answers, I made myself comfortable by settling on the edge of a nearby planter. *Maybe now I'll finally meet the* real *Gloria.*

Gloria didn't sit, but she let her weight settle into one hip as she sighed. "For the record, I never wanted any of this. I was just—I was just trying to help out my dad." She looked up, ostensibly to blow smoke rings. But for a moment I swore I saw the starlight glint off of tears. "He and the guy you know as 'Owl' got into a bad business deal a long time ago. Dad couldn't pay anything back, but I had just got out of school, so Owl arranged this whole thing." She waved her hand around the patio, probably meaning her own shop rather than mine. "At first I thought he was just being nice and it was my good luck, getting a chance to pay him back. More fool me, huh?"

"More like more fault on him," I corrected, scrunching my nose. "Sounds like Owl had a real talent for manipulation."

"Yeah. It's too bad about Luca." Gloria glanced at me, then looked up again. "Maybe I should've done something. But between them, the fairies and Owl, it just didn't seem like anything could ever change. Or that anyone would ever care."

"I get that," I said softly. "But why didn't you want me to go to the castle?"

"I thought . . . I knew there was some kind of elf-curse on it. Every time I was there I could feel it. And—gods, I know this sounds stupid. But everything was so twisted. I thought

271

if you figured out about the curse, you'd know an elf had to have done it, and you'd blame me. I didn't know about Cairn," Gloria added, an afterthought.

I shuddered. "No one did. Except Owl."

"I should've, though," she went on as though I hadn't spoken. "Sometimes her stuff would get delivered to my shop by mistake, and some of it was really weird elven stuff. I should have known they wouldn't be sending that to someone who wasn't one of them. But instead of wondering, all I did was complain about all the plant fibers getting all over the shop."

"Plant fibers?" I straightened up. *Flax.*

"Packing material," Gloria said dismissively. "Listen. I know I haven't been the nicest to you. I just—I've been staying here out of my own sense of duty. I guess that answers your question. But this, everything with the fairies, and you—it's made me realize how much people can twist that around on you. So I've decided . . . If I stay now, it'll be because I want to."

"I'm glad," I told her honestly. I stood, because I could tell she wanted to leave. "And even if you don't stay, Gloria, you can always count on William and me."

Gloria didn't say anything at first. But as she turned to go, she looked back over her shoulder. "Red? Take care, okay?"

"Sure thing." I beamed at her through the darkness. "You, too."

34

Restoration

Like clockwork the next morning Officer Thorn showed up, bright and early. Over earl gray and danishes, she informed us that she'd already been out to the castle for a look around—and to collect Cairn's body.

"Quiet as a dormouse out there," she proclaimed. "Oh, Red, here's that pendant for you. You can take care of delivering to your ghost friend or whoever else, right?"

"Not a ghost," I muttered out of reflex as I reached across the kitchen table and grabbed the pendant from her. "But yeah, I will. I'm headed over to Luca's first to give him the last book. Do you want to be there for that?"

"Eh." Thorn shrugged and finished off half a pastry in one bite. "Give me the spark notes later. As far as I'm concerned, this case is wrapped up. I've got a speech for the Guild to write in Vic's honor, and it's due this afternoon."

William was strangely quiet about the whole thing. I took my chance and headed out quickly before he found his voice and began to berate me for leaving him alone behind the cash register again.

The castle may have been 'quiet as a dormouse,' but the streets of Belville certainly weren't. What should have been a ten-minute walk cost me nearly half an hour. It wasn't just the other folks walking between the shops, either: shopkeepers poked their heads out their front doors, people in carriages stopped in the street, and I swore someone even popped out from a bush. Everyone wanted to know what had happened to Cairn and if the 'beast' at the castle had finally been locked away.

"Everything's fine," I kept repeating. Visions of dark unicorns played uneasily in my mind, though.

Fortunately, when I got to the bookstore, Luca hadn't opened up yet. Remembering his invitation, I went around to the back door and was quickly let in.

"I can't do it, Red," he confessed in an undertone, ushering me into the darkened shop. "I can't open. All those questions and the incessant talking and people staring! How does Officer Thorn do it?"

"Officer Thorn is being particularly evasive this morning," I told him. "She should've come with me and apologized to you, if you ask me. But she said she's busy."

"I don't need her to do that," Luca said, wavering. "I mean, what would I say to her if she did?"

"Don't worry about that yet," I said, chuckling and settling on the desk. As Luca perched on his stool next to me, I poked at his wringing hands to get him to stop. "I have some things for you to look at before you open. Are you sure you don't want to turn on at least one light?"

"I can see just fine in the dark," Luca insisted.

I shrugged and turned to business, giving him a quick rundown of the day before.

"So Cairn was the one who let Owl out, and then the one who killed him," Luca surmised. "And all that getup really was to make him look like her. That's so—it's so—"

"I really don't think she was stable after killing Owl," I admitted to him. "She said herself that she felt like she was 'weakening.'"

"There's actually a lot of research out there on curses and how they affect the curser as much as the cursed," Luca informed me, slipping into scholar-mode. "I never really got to know Cairn myself, but a lot of those symptoms sound like the classic egomania associated with wreaking dark magic. Owl told me once that the thing about people who are cursed is—" Luca faltered, then pressed on. "People who are cursed are easy to confuse. But the literature suggests that people who curse others are often confused to begin with."

"Speaking of literature." I drew the last book out of my pocket with a small smile. "Here—I found this in the castle library yesterday. It's yours."

Luca took the book, but he hesitated.

"Hey," I said more gently. "It's okay. Whatever Owl didn't want you to know, it's not like you have to bear it alone. I'm right here. Why don't we read it together?"

This time, Luca smiled faintly. He shifted so I could see the book too, and we began to read:

There was no hope for Prince Kalos, and so there was no hope for the Ring of the Moon. Seeing this, the Queen in her wisdom declared that she would lead the remaining Drus to a place of sanctuary, somewhere far away. Though she wept to leave her son behind, she knew that if she did not lead her people, they would flee wildly

and never be seen nor heard from again. Already the
Drus were afraid of the castle they once had loved, and
terrified of the cursed Prince they once had nurtured.
They could not stand to meet the eyes of the hideous
creature he had become, horned and patterned all over
with the marks of decay. And so it was that the Drus
abandoned their home and their future. What became of
the elves, it is not known. But nowhere in the forest does
a sweet-cherry, that symbol of abiding love and courage,
remain.

"That's not true," I murmured as I finished reading the passage for the second time. Something I hadn't noticed when I skimmed it in the castle library stuck out to me. Luca, a faster reader than I, looked at me in surprise. I hastened to explain, "About the sweet-cherry, I mean. See, that pendant Cairn was talking about—the one Owl told you was a scholar's necklace—I'd bet anything it's sweet-cherry wood. I know it's not a living tree, but it must mean something. Here, I actually have it with me . . ."

My voice trailed off. As I rummaged in my pockets, I happened to glance up, and I caught sight of something at the window—a glint out in the street.

"Hold on, just a minute," I said to Luca. With no further explanation, I vaulted over the desk and unlocked the front door and slipped outside.

And bumped right into Jade, who in the morning light I could not see very well but could certainly feel.

"There you are," I said reasonably. "I was looking for you last night. You should come in. We were just talking about—"

"No," Jade interrupted in his soft manner. "Rred, my friend,

276

I can't go in there."

"What do you mean, you can't? It's not warded."

"I can't," Jade said again, more firmly and yet more quietly than before. "Not . . . yet."

"Don't you *dare* disappear on me now that we're so close to tying everything up," I insisted, grabbing hold of his shoulder. "Is it the pendant that's making you this way? Or is it—"

Something about the bookshop?

Something about Luca.

Luca, who wouldn't hurt a fly, but would surely try to give it a lecture. Luca, whom I'd never seen without a hood and floor-length robe. Luca, who had suffered more than anyone at Owl's hands.

Luca, who had wanted nothing more than to learn about the cursed castle, though he never quite understood why.

Jade's hand found mine, clutched around the wooden pendant. He whispered, "Owl and Cairn knew that you would figure it out in time. And I knew it too. You are a good friend, and you see very clearly. You look very closely. Whether you learned that skill from your heritage or your science, it is valuable.

"Give the pendant to him. He does not remember, but it is his."

35

A Magical Life

Two days later, as the sun set, I stood wiping my brow in front of my shop. Business boomed at Red's Alchemy and Potions—a business mostly of gossip, but folks who came in for one thing often bought a few more, so I didn't mind.

I'd just closed up the shop for the day and William had scampered off on some errand of his own. I stood alone on the sidewalk, enjoying the last bits of warm sunlight before winter set in. And, at the same time, considering the subscript on my sign.

And object finding services.

Did I really want to keep that up there, after the way my first official "case" had gone? Sure, all the long-lost books had been found, and the surrounding crimes solved. But there had been so many close calls, and so much pain uncovered; and in the end—

"You know, I never did pay you," Luca said.

A dark hooded form stood on the sidewalk just behind my shoulder. I turned with a scowl.

"If you try to slip coins into my pockets or leave promise

notes with William one more time, I swear by all that's holy I'll turn every scrap of gold you own into nickel," I threatened.

"All right, all right, I give," said Luca with a grin, his hands outspread. "For now."

How could I explain to him that it was payment enough just to have been able to help? Somehow, I couldn't find the words.

When I'd gone back into the bookstore and given that pendant to Luca, his first reaction had been fear. I think, were the tables turned, my reaction would have been the same. How could it not be, realizing so suddenly that you'd only lived half your life, and that everything was about to change? So when he asked me to stay, I agreed at once. And when he asked me later to promise not to tell anyone exactly what had happened when he put the necklace on, and not to give away the secret of what he truly looked like under his hood, I agreed to that too.

Personally, I didn't really like that Luca felt he had to hide behind his scholars' robes. It turned out that ever since I'd known him—ever since he'd come to town, suspiciously shortly after Owl had discovered the old castle—a glamour in the hood had hidden the dark, twisted horn protruding from his forehead, just the way the sleeves hid the deep green tattoos along his arms. A glamour much like Cairn had used to hide her elfish nature. I didn't like that symmetry.

But then, I was hiding a few marks of my own, so who was I to judge?

Everything that had happened was deeply a part of Luca, just as Jade was a part of him once more. There was no way I could charge him for helping him take back what had always been rightfully his.

"So," said Luca, standing next to me. "Have you found your next project yet?"

"I don't know if I want another one."

"Oh, come on. Are you saying you didn't have any fun at all?"

"Luca, any 'fun' that involves putting peoples' lives at risk is just downright irresponsible," I protested vaguely. I had the most annoying feeling that my cheeks were hot. Luca and Jade were the same person now, and essentially, they always had been; Owl and Cairn had simply forced them apart for a while, Owl exercising control over Luca through a pendant of his own. That was the real reason Luca couldn't remember his life before the bookshop. But once he had switched Owl's "filtering" necklace for the real Drus one, all that awful work had been undone. Sometimes—okay, often—I wondered how much Luca now remembered of Jade's experiences.

"I guess I wouldn't know much about responsibility," Luca said cheerfully. "Still being cursed forever and all. Did I tell you I can fade into shadows now? I'm thinking of leaving the bookstore and joining the spy school and everything."

"You are not," I retorted incredulously. When Luca was silent, I stepped back to really look at him. "Are you? I guess I can understand if the bookstore has bad feelings for you now, but—"

"Oh, it isn't that," Luca assured me. "I'll always love books. And actually, the past year or so . . ." He paused, then said more seriously, "he kind of—started to crack after a while, you know. What you said about Cairn weakening, and Owl . . . that had been going on for a while. I could feel it even when I didn't know what was going on."

"Sure. They took you from that castle full of bad intentions, but I imagine watching you wander around town being a literal ray of sunshine despite everything they'd done undermined even *their* evilness," I observed. I had to remind myself to take a deep breath and unclench my fist. Neither Cairn nor Owl was around anymore for me to be angry at. And honestly, that was for the best all round.

"You think I'm a ray of sunshine?" Luca's eyes twinkled as he laughed at me. "Didn't you hear what I just said about shadows?"

"Please. You're as bad as William sometimes."

"Admit it," Luca insisted. "You like helping people. You're really good at it. You should keep the sign up and find someone new to help."

"Luca, things could have been so much worse," I said suddenly. "Cairn and Owl might never have weakened at all. Those creatures might have scared someone off or even killed them for good. We might never have gone through with finding the books and Cairn might have got Dusty or any one of us stuck in jail, or worse—"

"But she didn't," Luca interrupted calmly. "It didn't happen that way, Red. If you want to think about it that way, Cairn also could have just killed me. If she really did want the whole thing to end after Owl got himself stuck in jail, it would have been simpler to go after me. But she didn't, probably because she couldn't bring herself to. The curse was her greatest work. If she'd have killed me or Jade, she wouldn't have had anything left to spite.

"Listen, I'll admit, I don't really know why Cairn or Owl did any of the things they did. But I know why I was able to take back control of my own story. And a lot of that is because of you."

When I was silent, Luca looked up the street and smiled. "And William and Officer Thorn and Trent and everyone else, too. Speaking of . . ."

I followed his gaze, but I grimaced rather than grinned. Officer Thorn was trotting down the street toward us, with William tagging along at her heels. Every few steps he'd surge forward, and then with a large bound she'd retake the lead. In fact, it looked a bit like they were having a race without wanting to admit to the fact and just flat-out run.

In the last few feet William shimmered and then zoomed to my side in a blur of blue magic. "Red!"

Thorn pulled up right after him. "Cheater!"

Luca laughed.

"What is it with you two?" I asked, looking from one to the other.

William glowed. "I found something on the hillside outside of town—"

But Thorn was louder. "We've had reports of a missing set of pearls and—"

"How can you even understand them?" Luca asked me quietly, as the two continued to shout over each other.

"Think if I can't, I can plead innocent and not answer any of their questions?" I mused.

"Not a chance," said Luca, his face alight. He clapped my shoulder sympathetically. "My friend, it looks like your next case just found you."

Acknowledgments

It took a community of friends to solve the mystery in *Beauty and the Alchemist,* and likewise it took the support of so many people to bring this book to life!

Somewhat chronologically, I'd like to thank my parents for encouraging my interest in reading (we have to begin at the beginning, right?) and my wonderful partner for listening to me read early chapters aloud (despite the fact that he'd rather be poring over dusty old tomes). I owe so much to Richelle at Richelle Braswell Comprehensive Editing, too—writers, definitely check her out! And thank you so much to the members of my writing club, who were unfailingly supportive even when my writing made no sense at all. Finally, a *huge* thank you to the other authors who encouraged me, the amazingly supportive book community on Instagram, the Cozy Mystery Book Club, the Cozy Mystery Tribe, and my incredibly brave ARC readers.

And of course, I'm very thankful to you. Yes, you, reading this. I hope your time in Belville has been worthwhile!

THE ALCHEMICAL TALES

About the Author

Elle adores cozy mysteries, fairy tales, and above all, learning new things. As a historian and educator, she believes in the value of stories as a mirror for complicated realities. She currently lives in New Jersey with a grumpy tortoise and a three-legged cat.

Find more stories of Red and her friends at ellehartford.com. And while you're there, sign up for Elle's newsletter to get bonus material, behind-the-scenes sneak peeks, and terrible jokes!

And P.S.: I'm already hard at work on the next book in the series, *Cold As Snow.* It's coming in September 2022! Check out my website for more.

You can connect with me on:

🌐 https://ellehartford.com

🐦 https://twitter.com/HartfordElle

📘 https://www.facebook.com/ElleHartfordAuthor

🖉 https://www.instagram.com/ellehartford

🖉 https://www.goodreads.com/author/show/21951829.Elle_
Hartford

Subscribe to my newsletter:

✉ https://beyondwriting.eo.page/beauty

Also by Elle Hartford

The Carousel Capers

Prequel to Beauty and the Alchemist—discover the tales of Owl's misdeeds . . .

Life is no fairy tale in the magical small town of Belville. When Red buys her dream storefront in the quaint Market Square, she knows she'll be putting in hard work to make it a success.

But what Red *doesn't* expect is a tiny antique carousel horse statue turning up in her mail. And she isn't at all prepared for the slew of criminals and friends, greed and mystery that follow in its wake! It turns out that the carousel horse has a deep, dark secret. If she wants to head off doom, Red will have to brave ghostly forests, watery depths, wild mine cart rides, and even a fancy party or two.

In this series of short stories, each chapter focuses on a new carousel statuette–and a new mythical horse. Join Red and her friends as they try to take the reins of this galloping mystery before they find themselves left in the dust!

Lightning Source UK Ltd.
Milton Keynes UK
UKHW020736250822
407828UK00012B/1880